WARRIORS

TIGERSTAR & SASHA

#1: INTO THE WOODS

WARRIORS
TIGERSTAR & SASHA
#1: INTO THE WOODS

CREATED BY
ERIN HUNTER

WRITTEN BY
DAN JOLLEY

ART BY
DON HUDSON

HAMBURG // LONDON // LOS ANGELES // TOKYO

HarperCollinsPublishers

Warriors: Tigerstar and Sasha Vol. 1:
Into the Woods
Created by Erin Hunter
Written by Dan Jolley
Art by Don Hudson

Cover Colorist - Jason Van Winkle
Digital Tones - Lincy Chan
Lettering - Lucas Rivera
Cover Design - Tina Corrales

Editor - Lillian Diaz-Przybyl
Digital Imaging Manager - Chris Buford
Pre-Production Supervisor - Lucas Rivera
Managing Editor - Vy Nguyen
Creative Director - Anne Marie Horne
Editor-in-Chief - Rob Tokar
Publisher - Mike Kiley
President and C.O.O. - John Parker
C.E.O. and Chief Creative Officer - Stu Levy

A  Manga

TOKYOPOP and  are trademarks or registered trademarks of TOKYOPOP Inc.

TOKYOPOP Inc.
5900 Wilshire Blvd. Suite 2000
Los Angeles, CA 90036

E-mail: info@TOKYOPOP.com
Come visit us online at www.TOKYOPOP.com

For information address HarperCollins Children's Books, a division of HarperCollins Publishers,
195 Broadway, New York, NY 10007.
www.harpercollinschildrens.com

ISBN 978-0-06-154792-8
Library of Congress catalog card number: 2007909574

16   PC/ BV 20 19 18 17 16 15 14 13
❖
First Edition

Dear readers,

I was always fascinated by the idea of Tigerstar befriending a loner like Sasha. After all, he declared himself the sworn enemy of any cat who lived outside the Clans. When we met Sasha, she revealed herself to be a proud, independent cat who had enough respect for Clan values to want her kits to be raised as warriors. What did she see in Tigerstar? He may have been a great warrior—fearless, strong, and farsighted in planning his march to leadership—but he was hardly a romantic hero. And to make things even more mysterious, Sasha obviously knew the horror that Tigerstar had brought to the forest because she made her kits promise not to tell their new Clanmates who their father was; she didn't want her children to grow up with their father's reputation hanging over their heads.

But Sasha also raised Hawkfrost and Mothwing to have respect for Tigerstar's strengths—his courage, his sense of pride and ambition, and his willingness to fight for what he believed in. So Sasha must have genuinely loved the cat who murdered and lied his way to leadership, and who nearly destroyed all the Clans when he tried to manipulate Scourge into allying with him. What happened when she met him? How long was it before she saw his true colors? What made her leave her beloved kits in RiverClan?

It's time for Sasha to tell her story. . . .

Best wishes always,
Erin Hunter

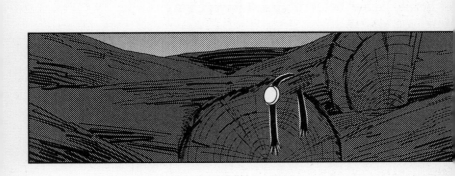

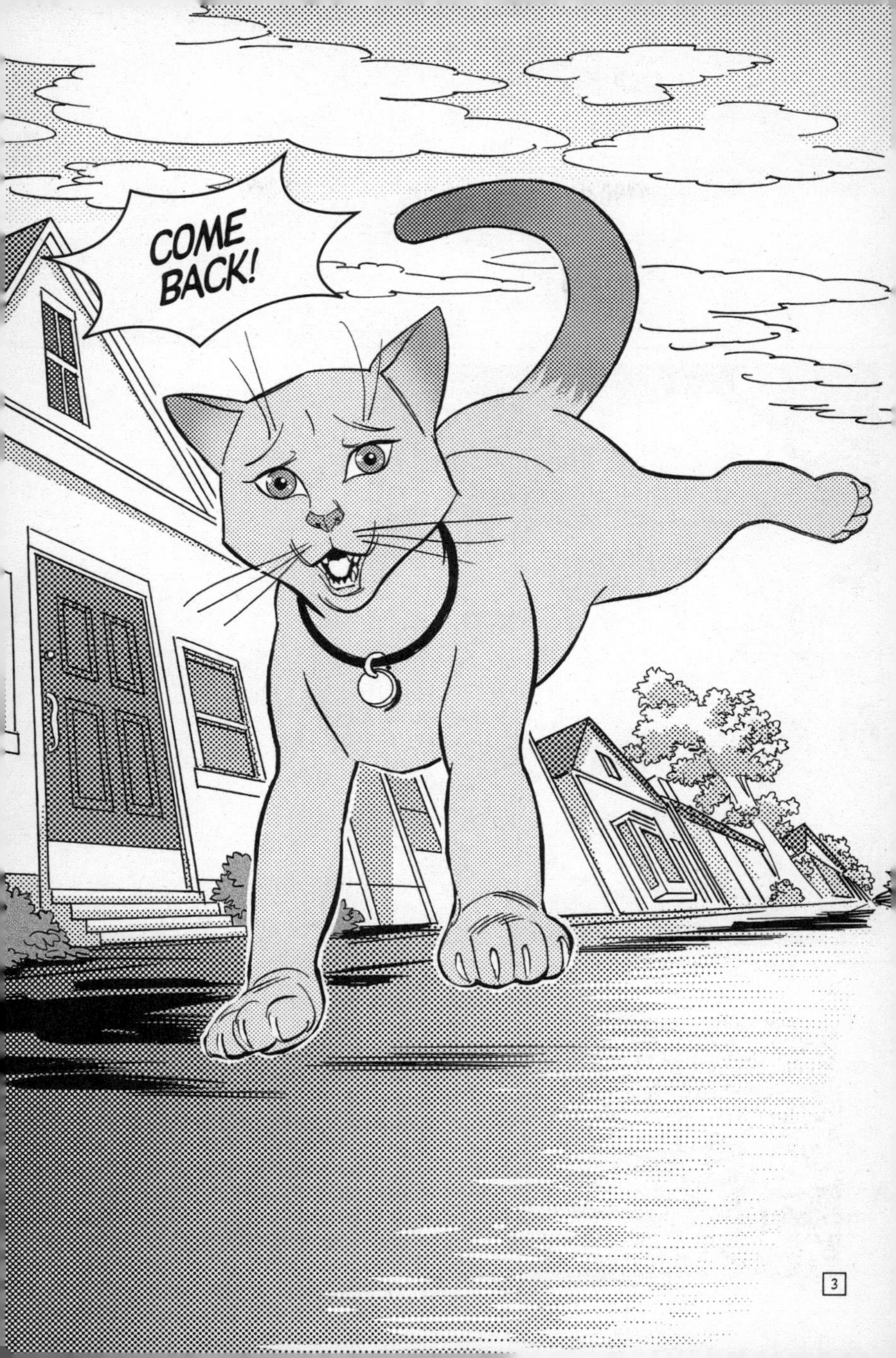
COME BACK!

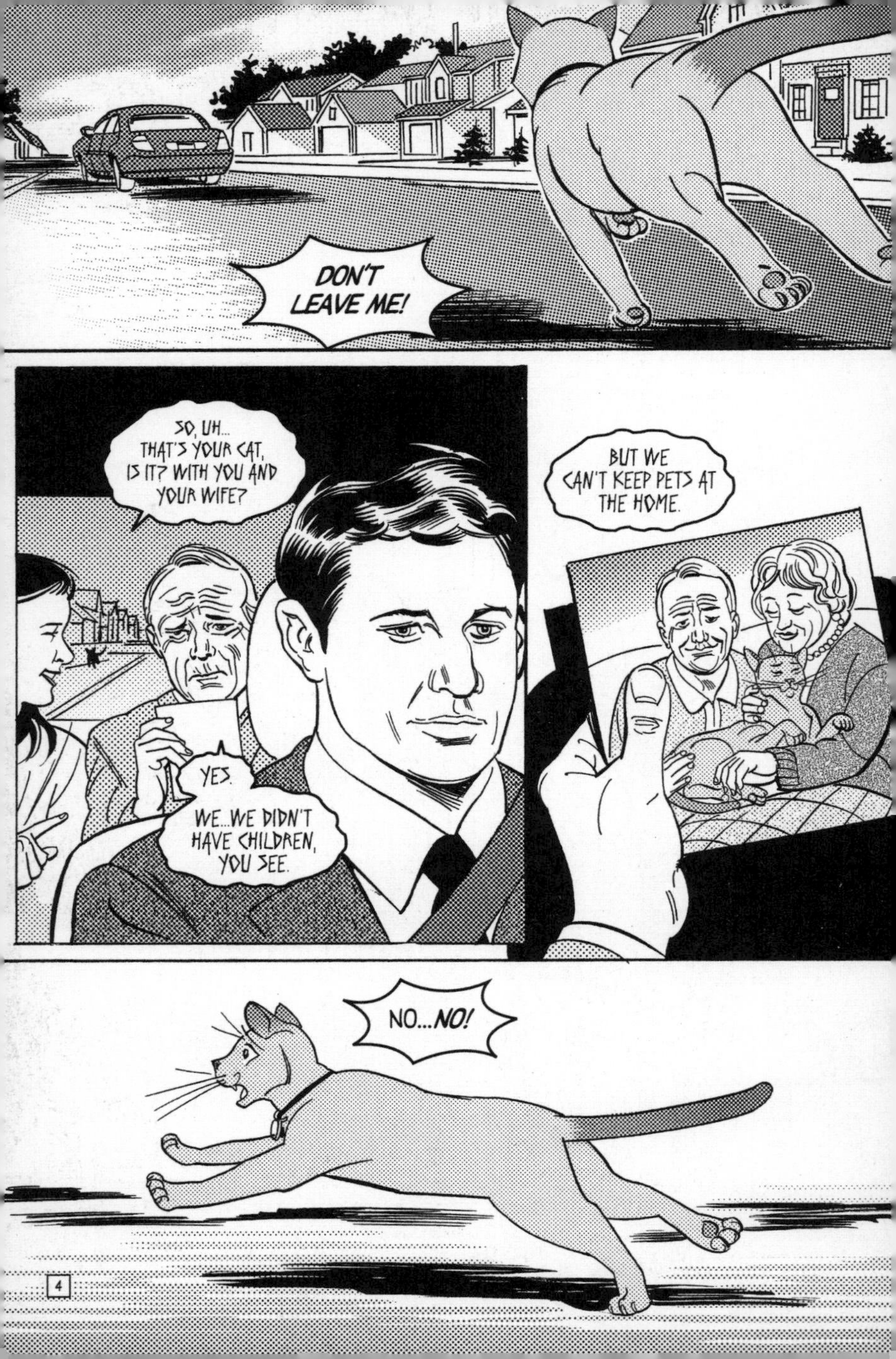
DON'T LEAVE ME!
SO, UH... THAT'S YOUR CAT, IS IT? WITH YOU AND YOUR WIFE?
YES.
WE...WE DIDN'T HAVE CHILDREN, YOU SEE.
BUT WE CAN'T KEEP PETS AT THE HOME.
NO...NO!

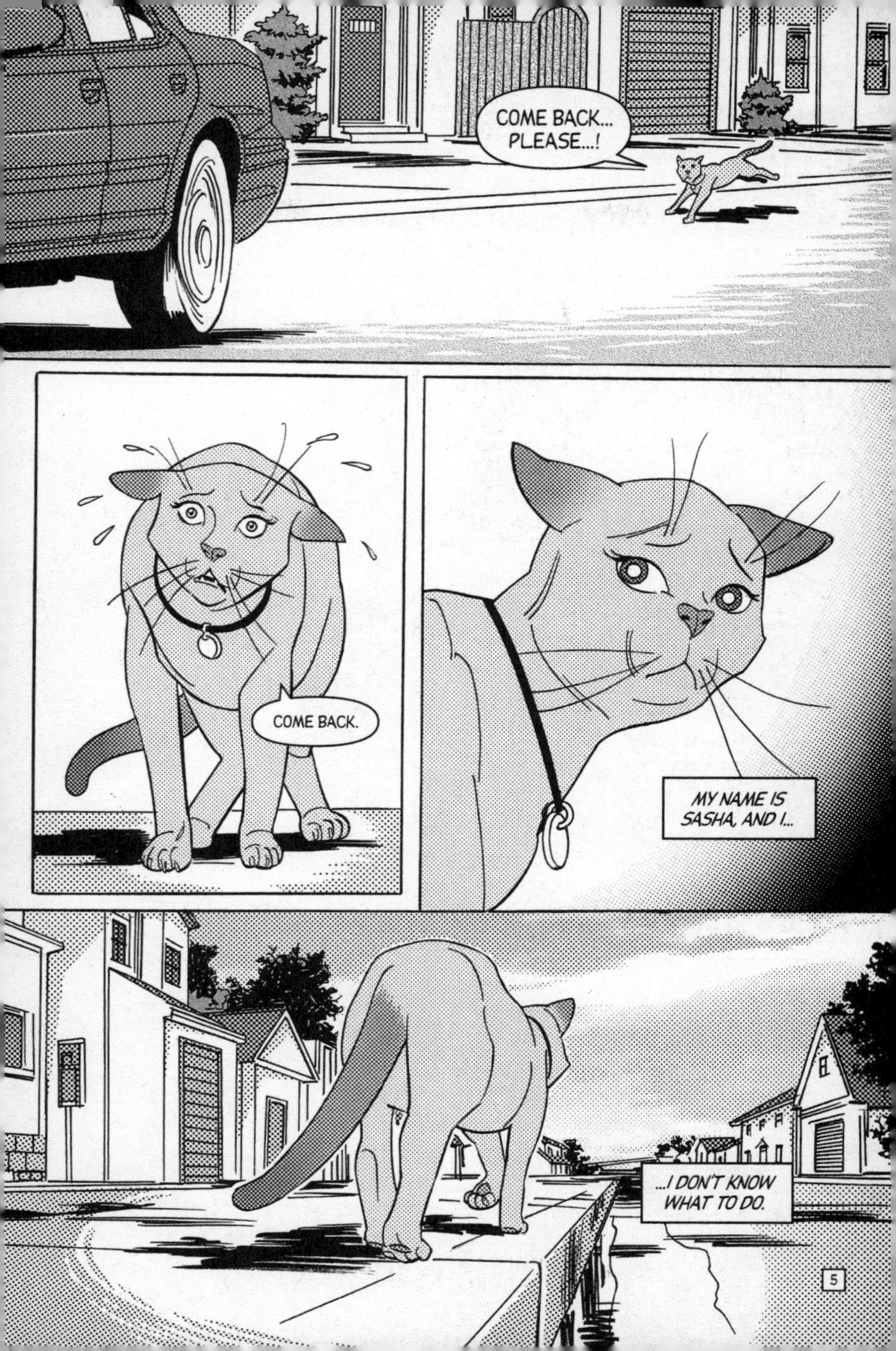
COME BACK... PLEASE...!
COME BACK.
MY NAME IS SASHA, AND I...
...I DON'T KNOW WHAT TO DO.

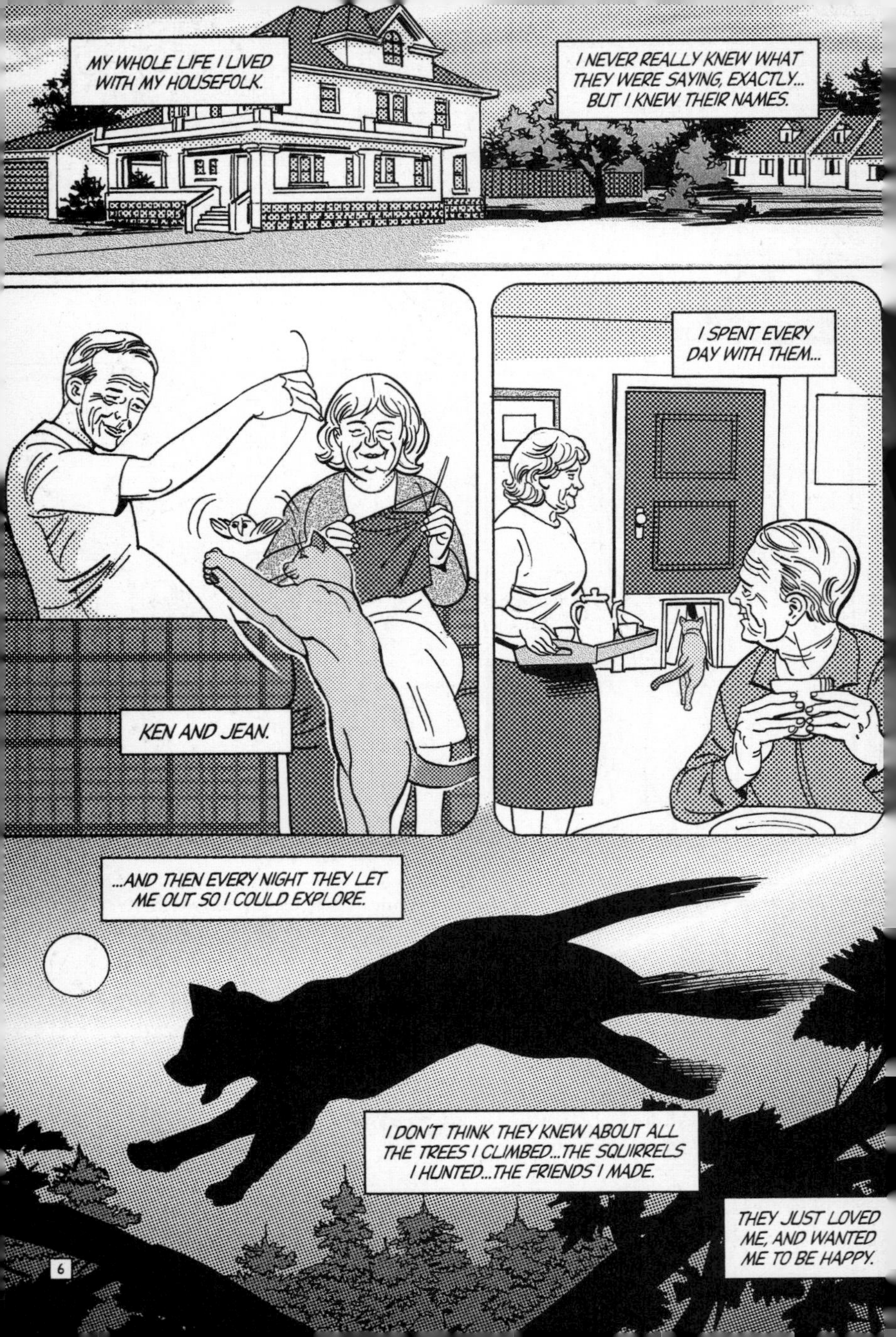
MY WHOLE LIFE I LIVED WITH MY HOUSEFOLK.
I NEVER REALLY KNEW WHAT THEY WERE SAYING, EXACTLY... BUT I KNEW THEIR NAMES.
KEN AND JEAN.
I SPENT EVERY DAY WITH THEM...
...AND THEN EVERY NIGHT THEY LET ME OUT SO I COULD EXPLORE.
I DON'T THINK THEY KNEW ABOUT ALL THE TREES I CLIMBED...THE SQUIRRELS I HUNTED...THE FRIENDS I MADE.
THEY JUST LOVED ME, AND WANTED ME TO BE HAPPY.

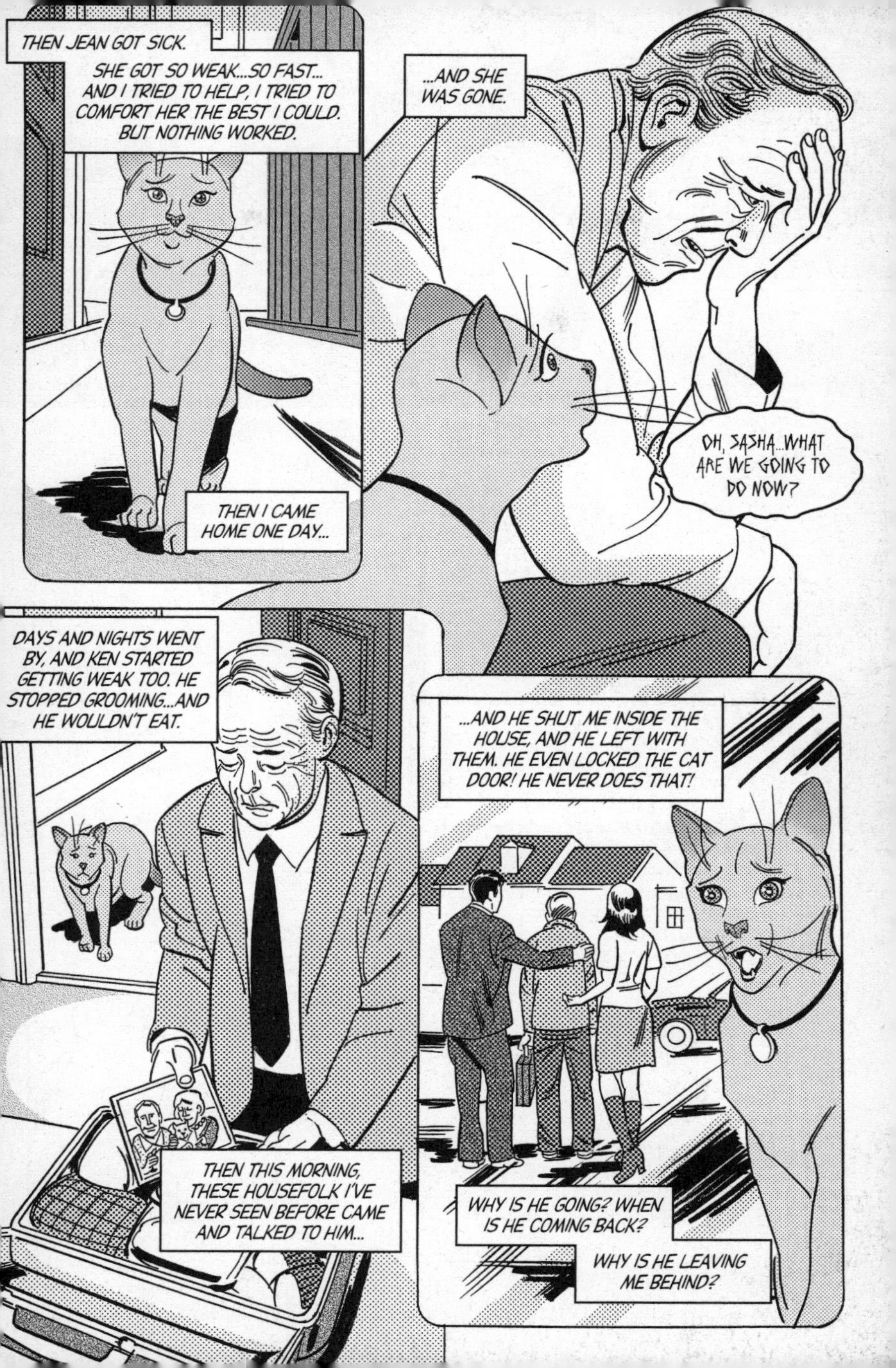
THEN JEAN GOT SICK.
SHE GOT SO WEAK...SO FAST... AND I TRIED TO HELP, I TRIED TO COMFORT HER THE BEST I COULD. BUT NOTHING WORKED.
THEN I CAME HOME ONE DAY...
...AND SHE WAS GONE.
OH, SASHA...WHAT ARE WE GOING TO DO NOW?
DAYS AND NIGHTS WENT BY, AND KEN STARTED GETTING WEAK TOO. HE STOPPED GROOMING...AND HE WOULDN'T EAT.
THEN THIS MORNING, THESE HOUSEFOLK I'VE NEVER SEEN BEFORE CAME AND TALKED TO HIM...
...AND HE SHUT ME INSIDE THE HOUSE, AND HE LEFT WITH THEM. HE EVEN LOCKED THE CAT DOOR! HE NEVER DOES THAT!
WHY IS HE GOING? WHEN IS HE COMING BACK?
WHY IS HE LEAVING ME BEHIND?

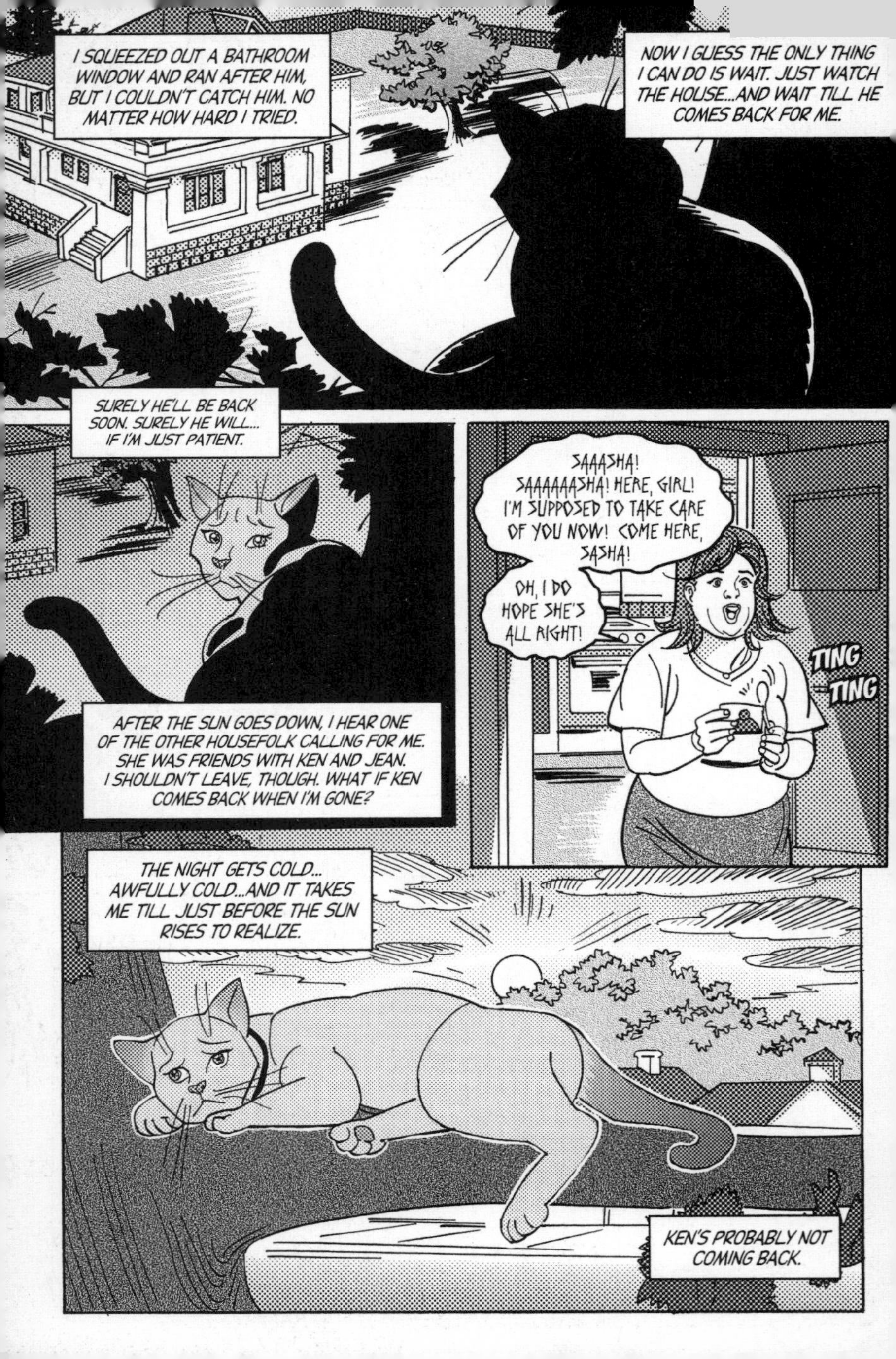
I SQUEEZED OUT A BATHROOM WINDOW AND RAN AFTER HIM, BUT I COULDN'T CATCH HIM. NO MATTER HOW HARD I TRIED.
NOW I GUESS THE ONLY THING I CAN DO IS WAIT. JUST WATCH THE HOUSE...AND WAIT TILL HE COMES BACK FOR ME.
SURELY HE'LL BE BACK SOON. SURELY HE WILL... IF I'M JUST PATIENT.
AFTER THE SUN GOES DOWN, I HEAR ONE OF THE OTHER HOUSEFOLK CALLING FOR ME. SHE WAS FRIENDS WITH KEN AND JEAN. I SHOULDN'T LEAVE, THOUGH. WHAT IF KEN COMES BACK WHEN I'M GONE?
SAAASHA! SAAAAAASHA! HERE, GIRL! I'M SUPPOSED TO TAKE CARE OF YOU NOW! COME HERE, SASHA!
OH, I DO HOPE SHE'S ALL RIGHT!
TING TING
THE NIGHT GETS COLD... AWFULLY COLD...AND IT TAKES ME TILL JUST BEFORE THE SUN RISES TO REALIZE.
KEN'S PROBABLY NOT COMING BACK.

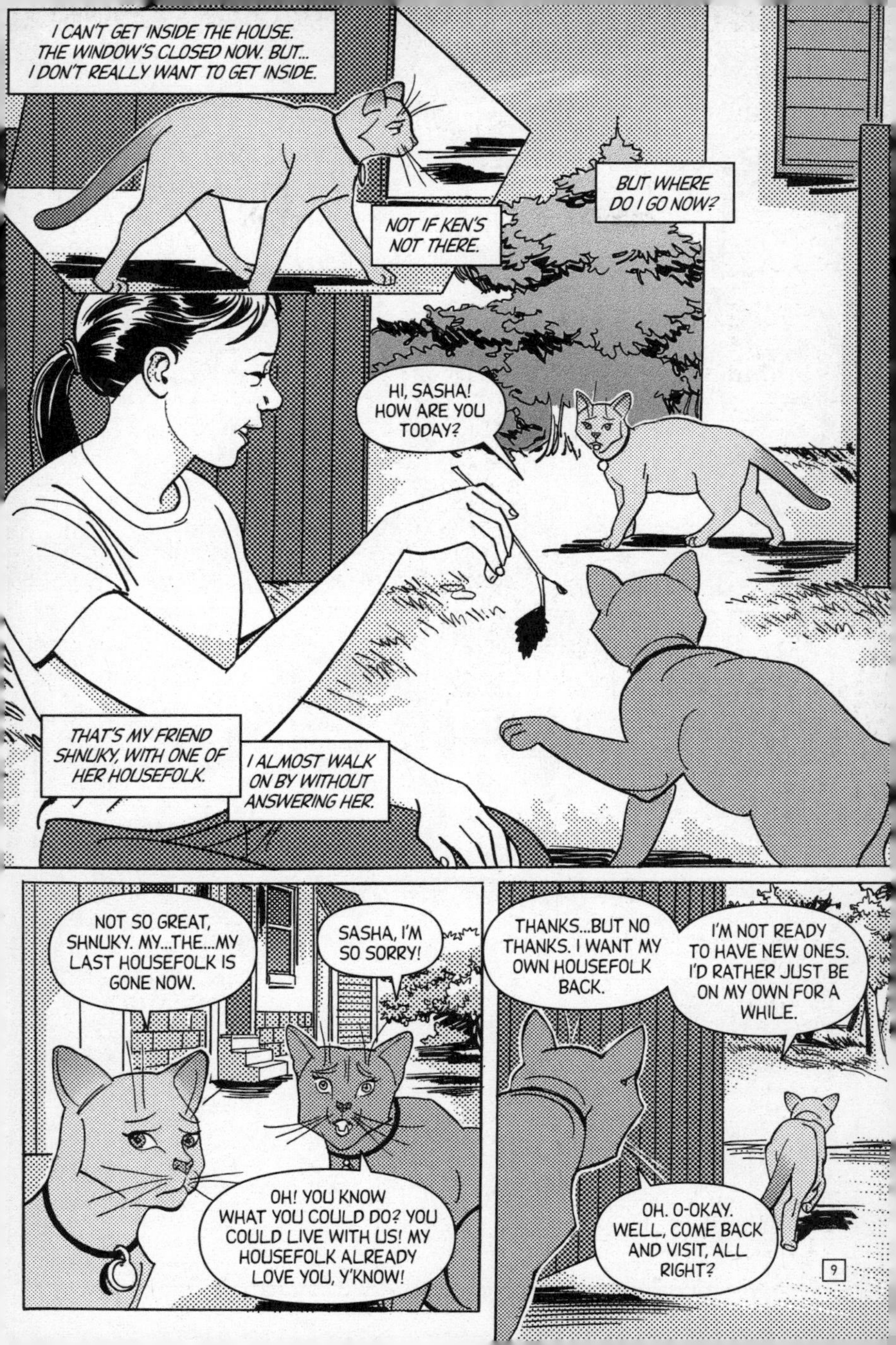
I CAN'T GET INSIDE THE HOUSE. THE WINDOW'S CLOSED NOW. BUT... I DON'T REALLY WANT TO GET INSIDE.
NOT IF KEN'S NOT THERE.
BUT WHERE DO I GO NOW?
HI, SASHA! HOW ARE YOU TODAY?
THAT'S MY FRIEND SHNUKY, WITH ONE OF HER HOUSEFOLK.
I ALMOST WALK ON BY WITHOUT ANSWERING HER.
NOT SO GREAT, SHNUKY. MY...THE...MY LAST HOUSEFOLK IS GONE NOW.
SASHA, I'M SO SORRY!
OH! YOU KNOW WHAT YOU COULD DO? YOU COULD LIVE WITH US! MY HOUSEFOLK ALREADY LOVE YOU, Y'KNOW!
THANKS...BUT NO THANKS. I WANT MY OWN HOUSEFOLK BACK.
I'M NOT READY TO HAVE NEW ONES. I'D RATHER JUST BE ON MY OWN FOR A WHILE.
OH. O-OKAY. WELL, COME BACK AND VISIT, ALL RIGHT?

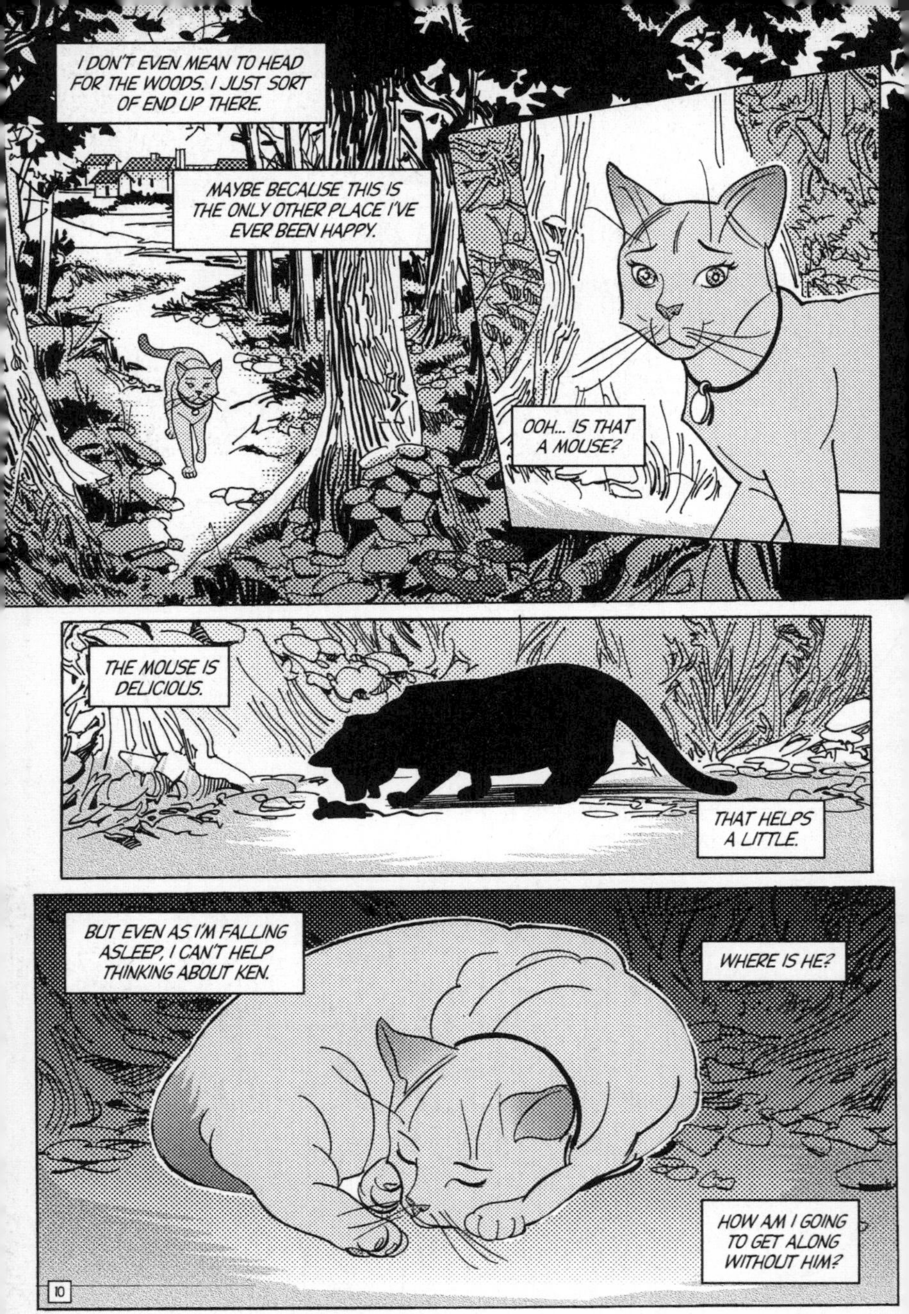
I DON'T EVEN MEAN TO HEAD FOR THE WOODS. I JUST SORT OF END UP THERE.
MAYBE BECAUSE THIS IS THE ONLY OTHER PLACE I'VE EVER BEEN HAPPY.
OOH... IS THAT A MOUSE?
THE MOUSE IS DELICIOUS.
THAT HELPS A LITTLE.
BUT EVEN AS I'M FALLING ASLEEP, I CAN'T HELP THINKING ABOUT KEN.
WHERE IS HE?
HOW AM I GOING TO GET ALONG WITHOUT HIM?

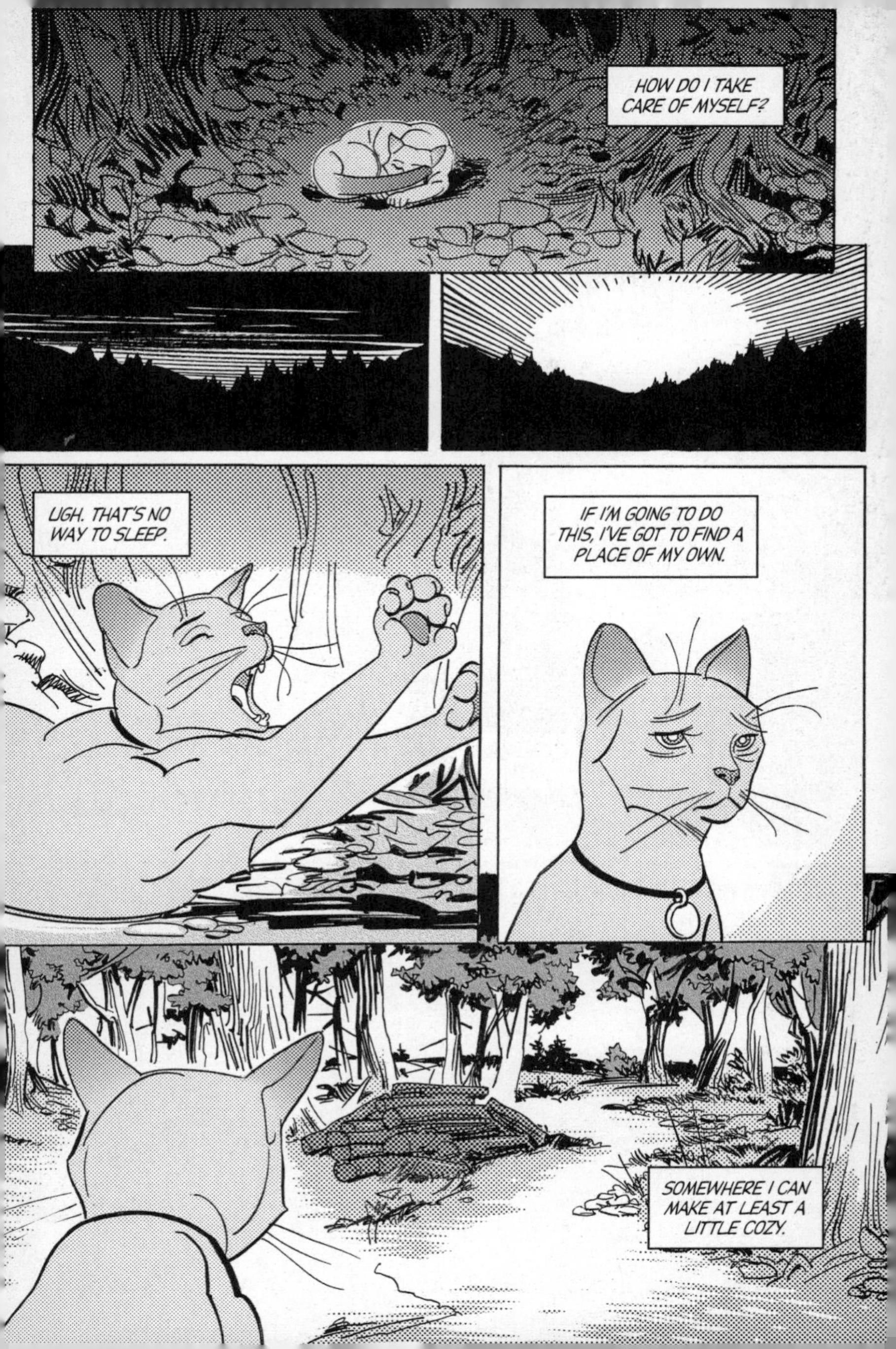
HOW DO I TAKE CARE OF MYSELF?
UGH. THAT'S NO WAY TO SLEEP.
IF I'M GOING TO DO THIS, I'VE GOT TO FIND A PLACE OF MY OWN.
SOMEWHERE I CAN MAKE AT LEAST A LITTLE COZY.

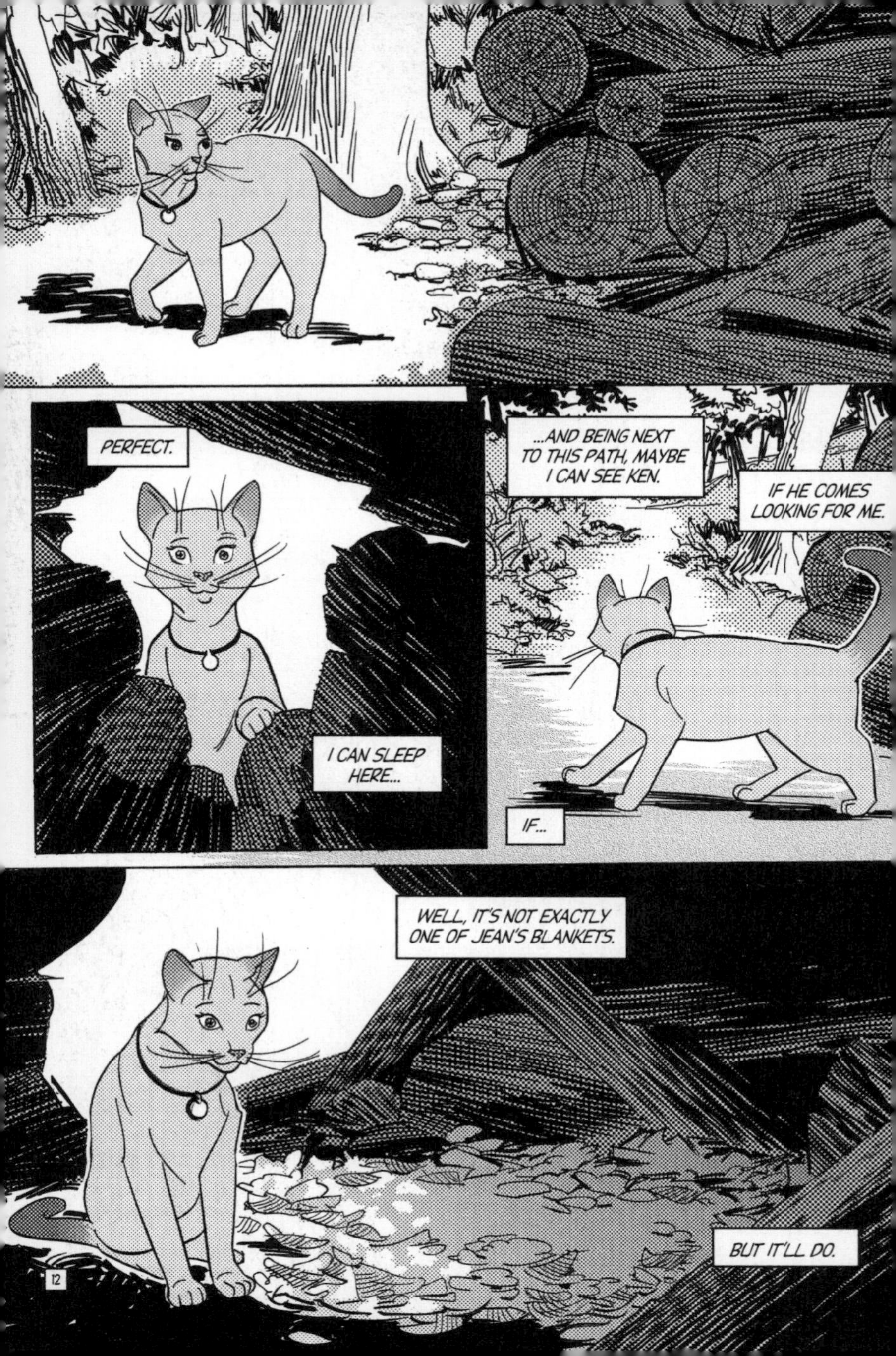
PERFECT.
I CAN SLEEP HERE...
...AND BEING NEXT TO THIS PATH, MAYBE I CAN SEE KEN.
IF HE COMES LOOKING FOR ME.
IF...
WELL, IT'S NOT EXACTLY ONE OF JEAN'S BLANKETS.
BUT IT'LL DO.

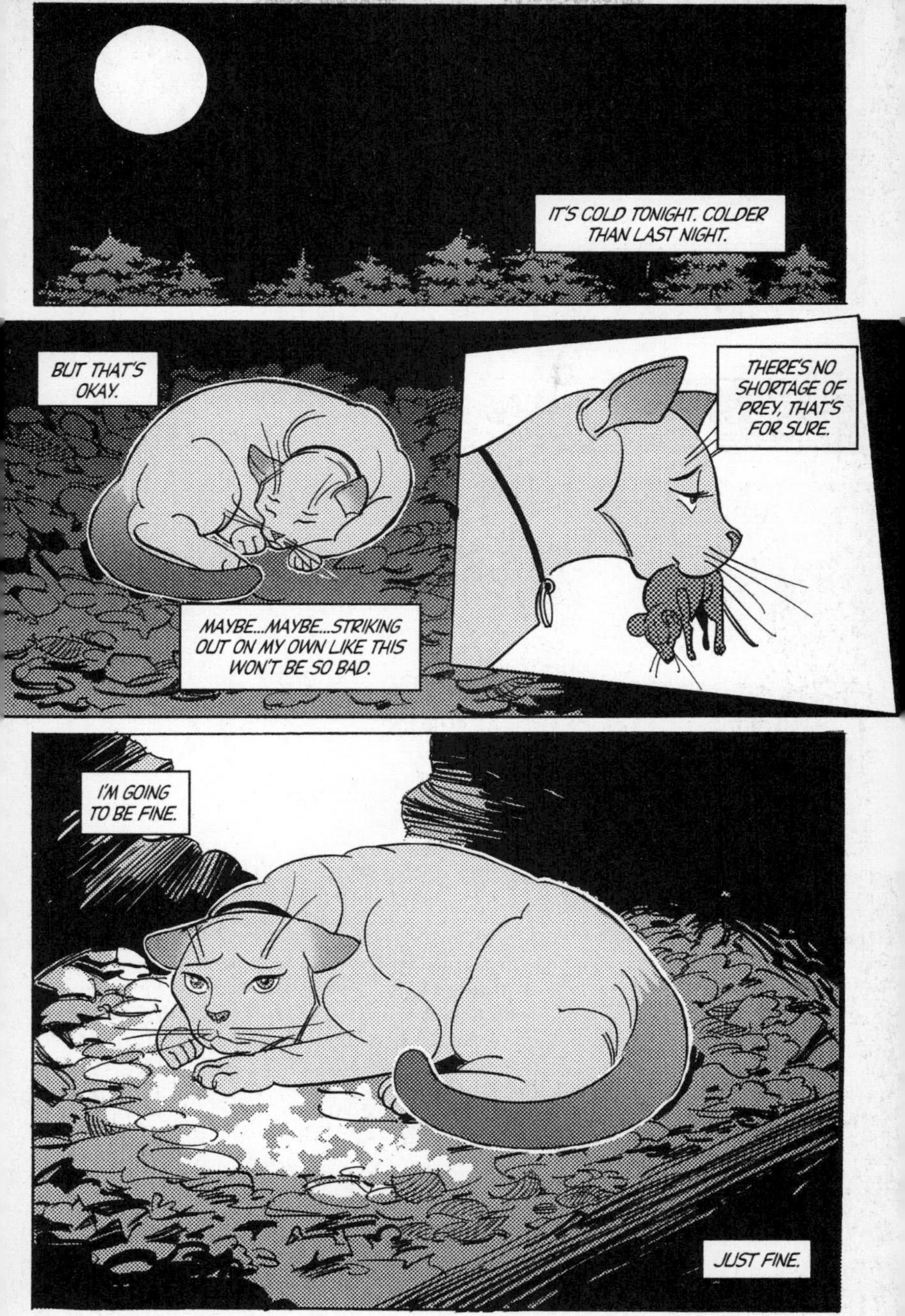
IT'S COLD TONIGHT. COLDER THAN LAST NIGHT.
BUT THAT'S OKAY.
MAYBE...MAYBE...STRIKING OUT ON MY OWN LIKE THIS WON'T BE SO BAD.
THERE'S NO SHORTAGE OF PREY, THAT'S FOR SURE.
I'M GOING TO BE FINE.
JUST FINE.

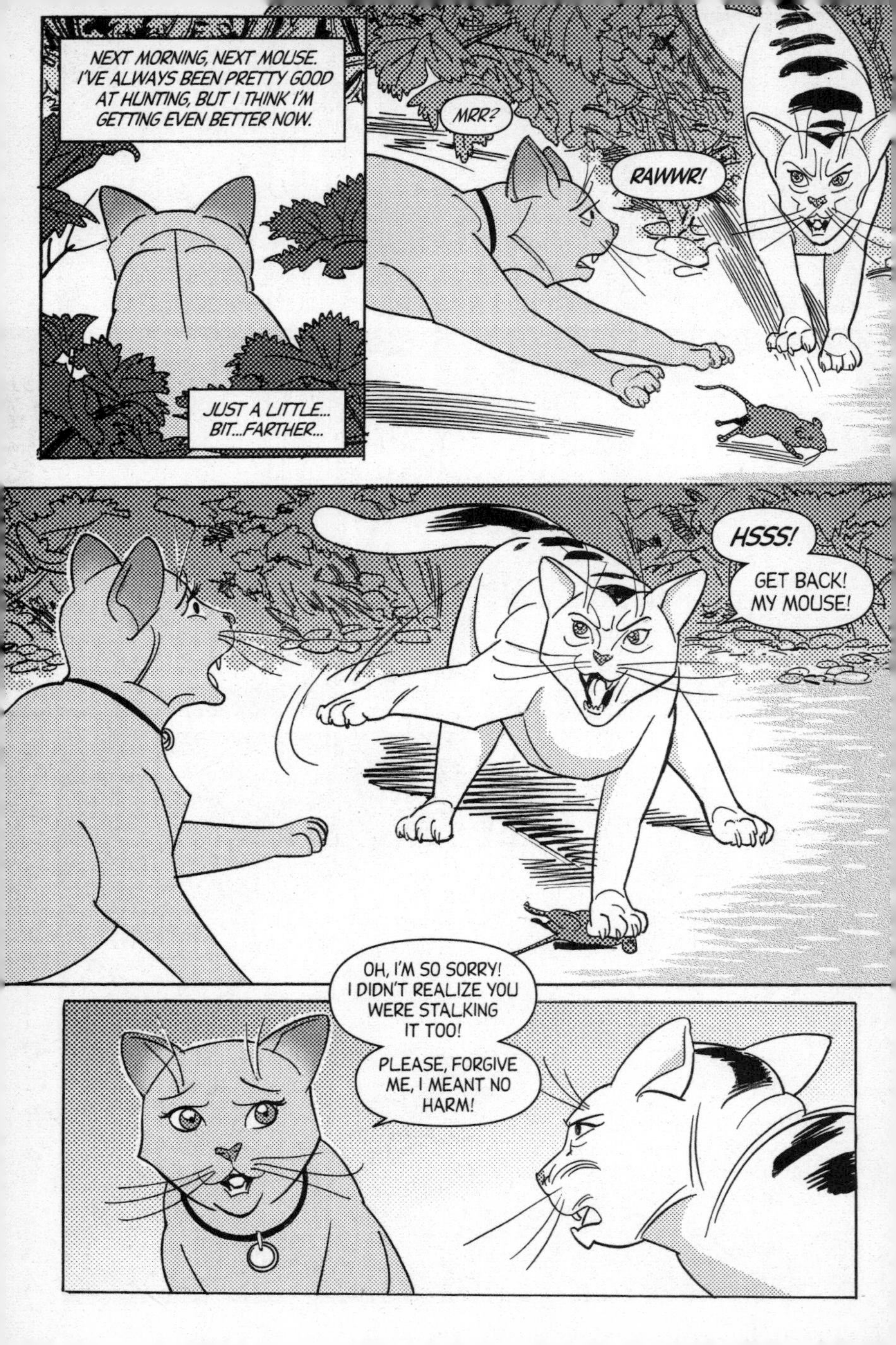
NEXT MORNING, NEXT MOUSE. I'VE ALWAYS BEEN PRETTY GOOD AT HUNTING, BUT I THINK I'M GETTING EVEN BETTER NOW.
JUST A LITTLE... BIT...FARTHER...
MRR?
RAWWR!
HSSS!
GET BACK! MY MOUSE!
OH, I'M SO SORRY! I DIDN'T REALIZE YOU WERE STALKING IT TOO!
PLEASE, FORGIVE ME, I MEANT NO HARM!

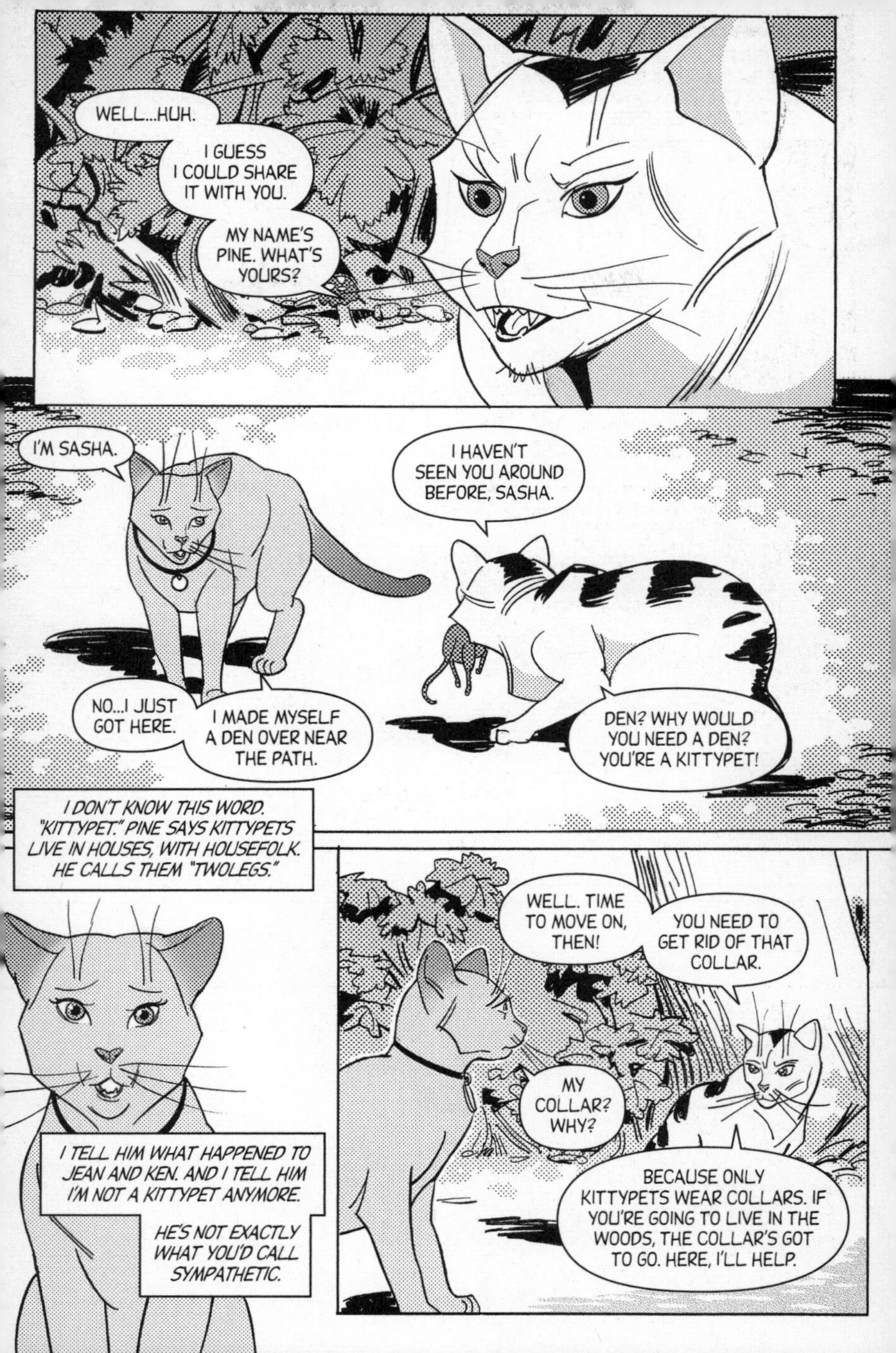
WELL...HUH.
I GUESS I COULD SHARE IT WITH YOU.
MY NAME'S PINE. WHAT'S YOURS?
I'M SASHA.
I HAVEN'T SEEN YOU AROUND BEFORE, SASHA.
NO...I JUST GOT HERE.
I MADE MYSELF A DEN OVER NEAR THE PATH.
DEN? WHY WOULD YOU NEED A DEN? YOU'RE A KITTYPET!
I DON'T KNOW THIS WORD. "KITTYPET." PINE SAYS KITTYPETS LIVE IN HOUSES, WITH HOUSEFOLK. HE CALLS THEM "TWOLEGS."
I TELL HIM WHAT HAPPENED TO JEAN AND KEN. AND I TELL HIM I'M NOT A KITTYPET ANYMORE.
HE'S NOT EXACTLY WHAT YOU'D CALL SYMPATHETIC.
WELL. TIME TO MOVE ON, THEN!
YOU NEED TO GET RID OF THAT COLLAR.
MY COLLAR? WHY?
BECAUSE ONLY KITTYPETS WEAR COLLARS. IF YOU'RE GOING TO LIVE IN THE WOODS, THE COLLAR'S GOT TO GO. HERE, I'LL HELP.

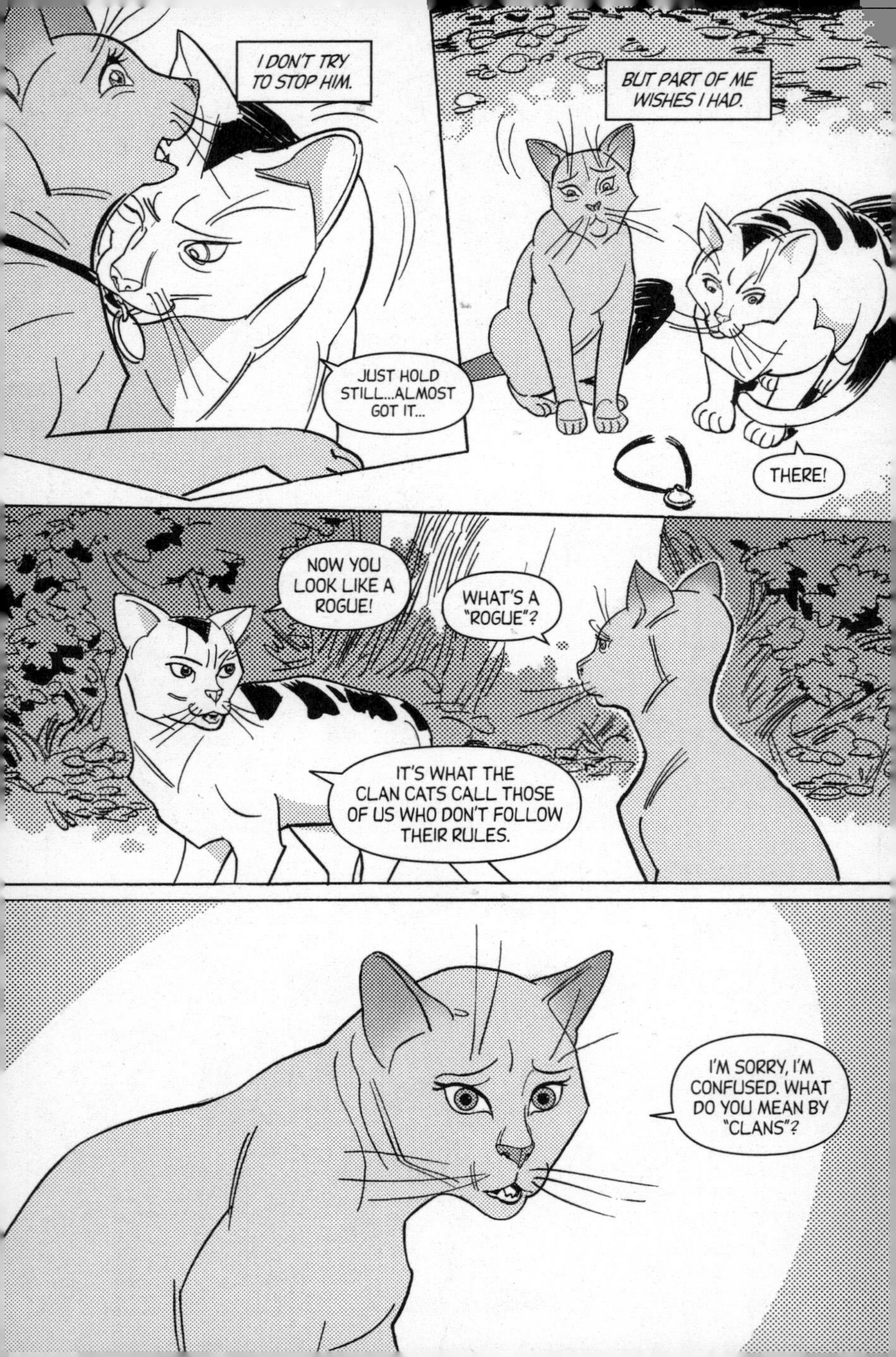
I DON'T TRY TO STOP HIM.
JUST HOLD STILL...ALMOST GOT IT...
BUT PART OF ME WISHES I HAD.
THERE!
NOW YOU LOOK LIKE A ROGUE!
WHAT'S A "ROGUE"?
IT'S WHAT THE CLAN CATS CALL THOSE OF US WHO DON'T FOLLOW THEIR RULES.
I'M SORRY, I'M CONFUSED. WHAT DO YOU MEAN BY "CLANS"?

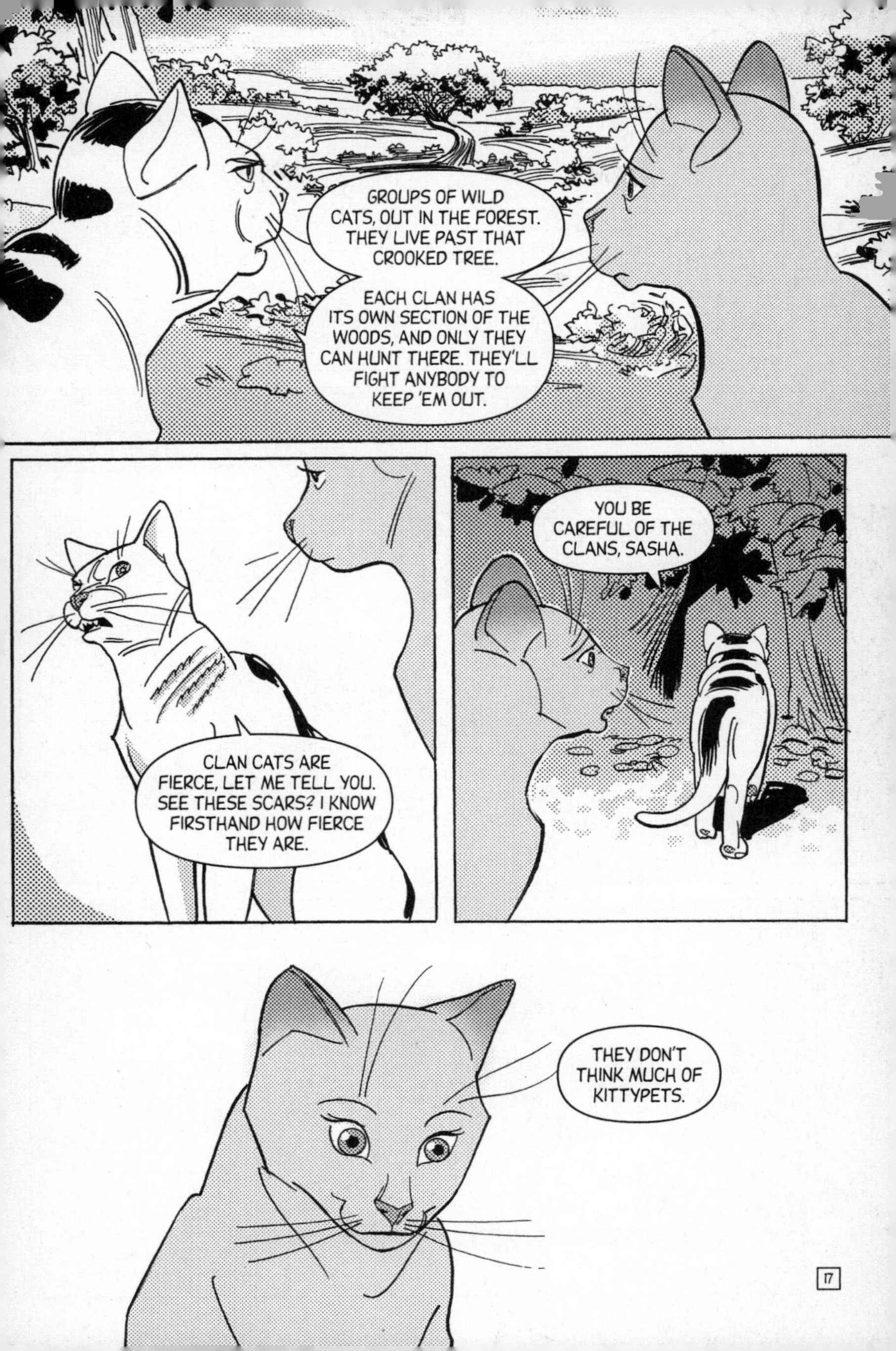
GROUPS OF WILD CATS, OUT IN THE FOREST. THEY LIVE PAST THAT CROOKED TREE.
EACH CLAN HAS ITS OWN SECTION OF THE WOODS, AND ONLY THEY CAN HUNT THERE. THEY'LL FIGHT ANYBODY TO KEEP 'EM OUT.
CLAN CATS ARE FIERCE, LET ME TELL YOU. SEE THESE SCARS? I KNOW FIRSTHAND HOW FIERCE THEY ARE.
YOU BE CAREFUL OF THE CLANS, SASHA.
THEY DON'T THINK MUCH OF KITTYPETS.

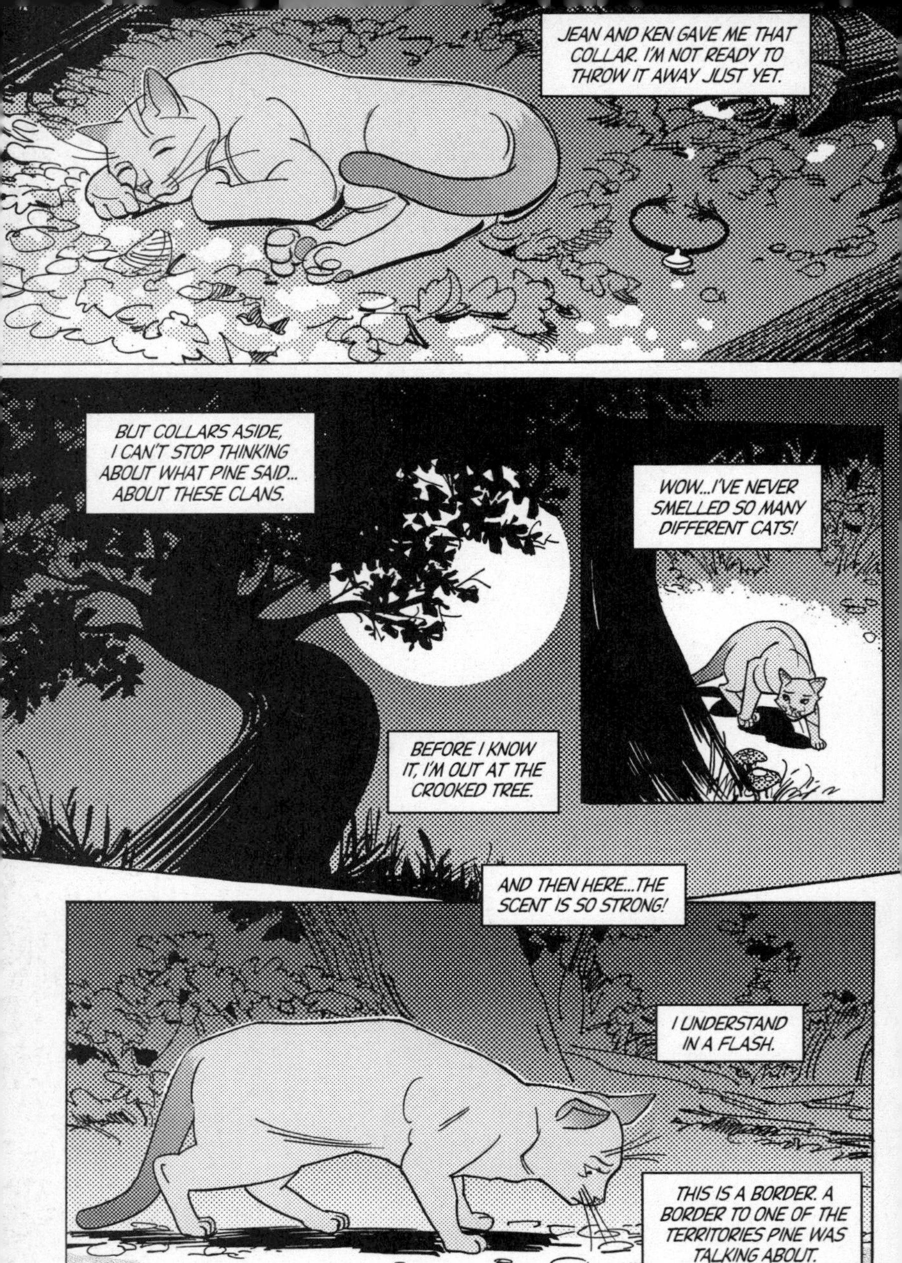
JEAN AND KEN GAVE ME THAT COLLAR. I'M NOT READY TO THROW IT AWAY JUST YET.
BUT COLLARS ASIDE, I CAN'T STOP THINKING ABOUT WHAT PINE SAID... ABOUT THESE CLANS.
BEFORE I KNOW IT, I'M OUT AT THE CROOKED TREE.
WOW...I'VE NEVER SMELLED SO MANY DIFFERENT CATS!
AND THEN HERE...THE SCENT IS SO STRONG!
I UNDERSTAND IN A FLASH.
THIS IS A BORDER. A BORDER TO ONE OF THE TERRITORIES PINE WAS TALKING ABOUT.

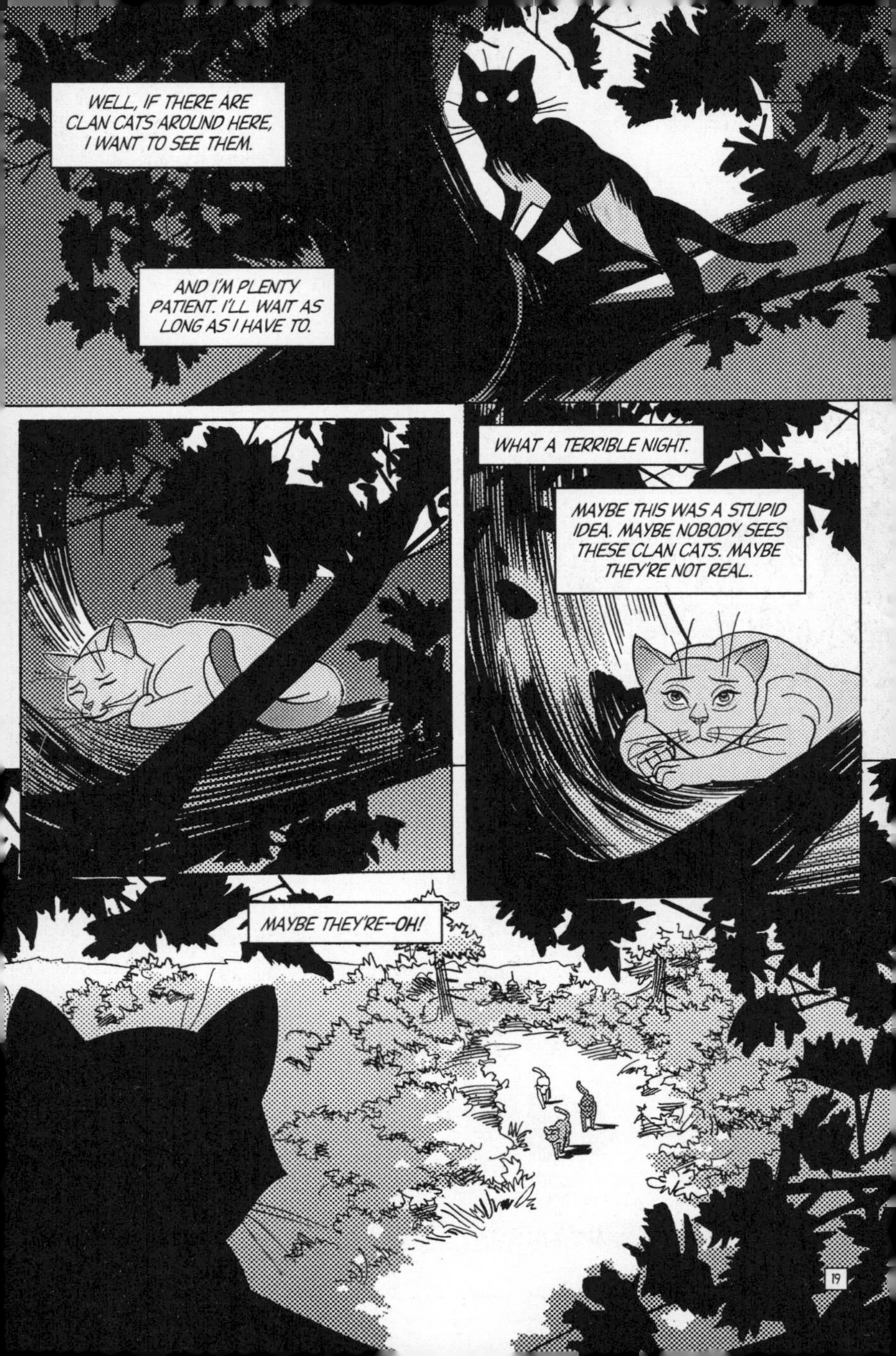
WELL, IF THERE ARE CLAN CATS AROUND HERE, I WANT TO SEE THEM.
AND I'M PLENTY PATIENT. I'LL WAIT AS LONG AS I HAVE TO.
WHAT A TERRIBLE NIGHT.
MAYBE THIS WAS A STUPID IDEA. MAYBE NOBODY SEES THESE CLAN CATS. MAYBE THEY'RE NOT REAL.
MAYBE THEY'RE--OH!

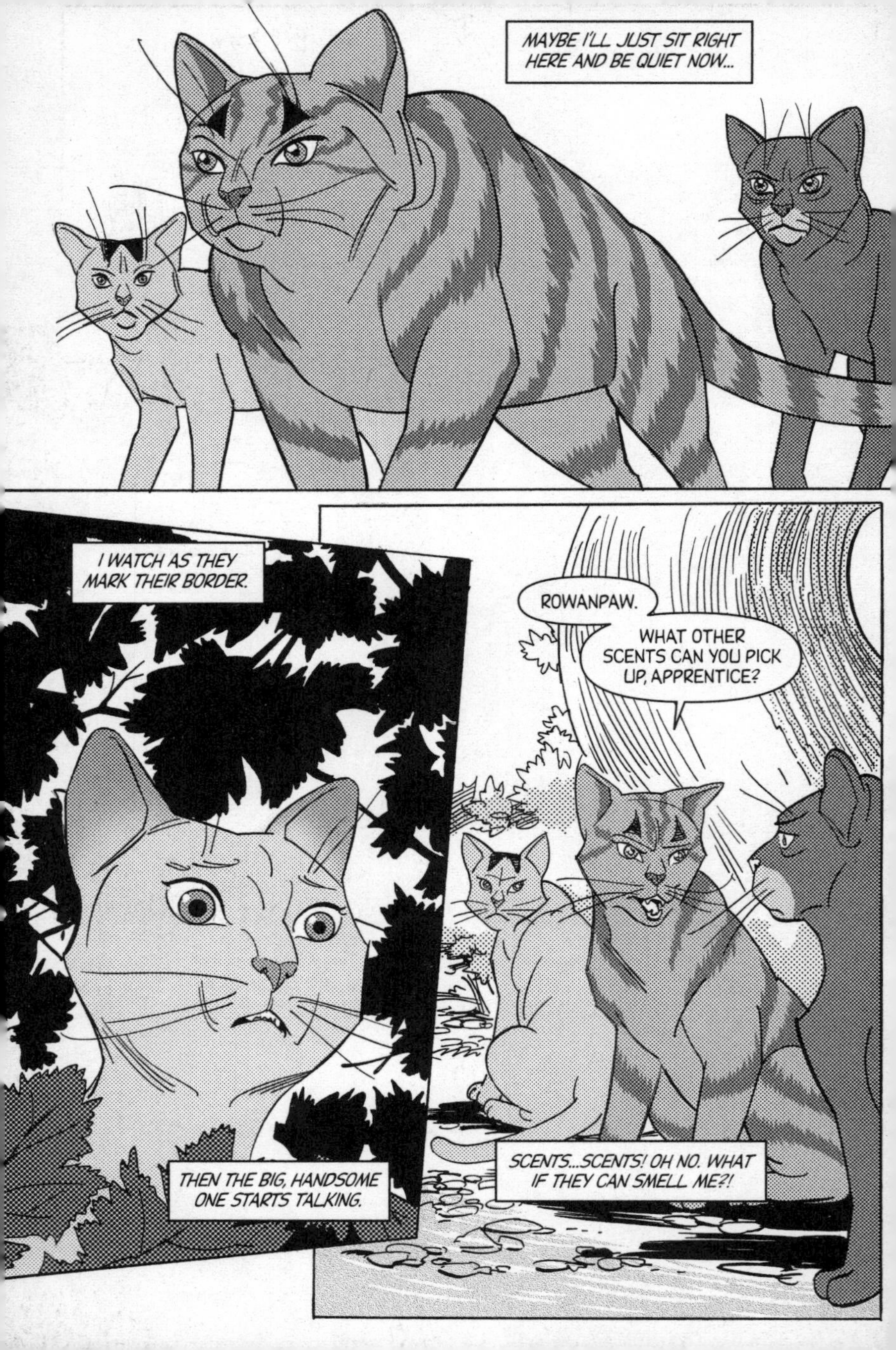
MAYBE I'LL JUST SIT RIGHT HERE AND BE QUIET NOW...
I WATCH AS THEY MARK THEIR BORDER.
THEN THE BIG, HANDSOME ONE STARTS TALKING.
ROWANPAW.
WHAT OTHER SCENTS CAN YOU PICK UP, APPRENTICE?
SCENTS...SCENTS! OH NO. WHAT IF THEY CAN SMELL ME?!

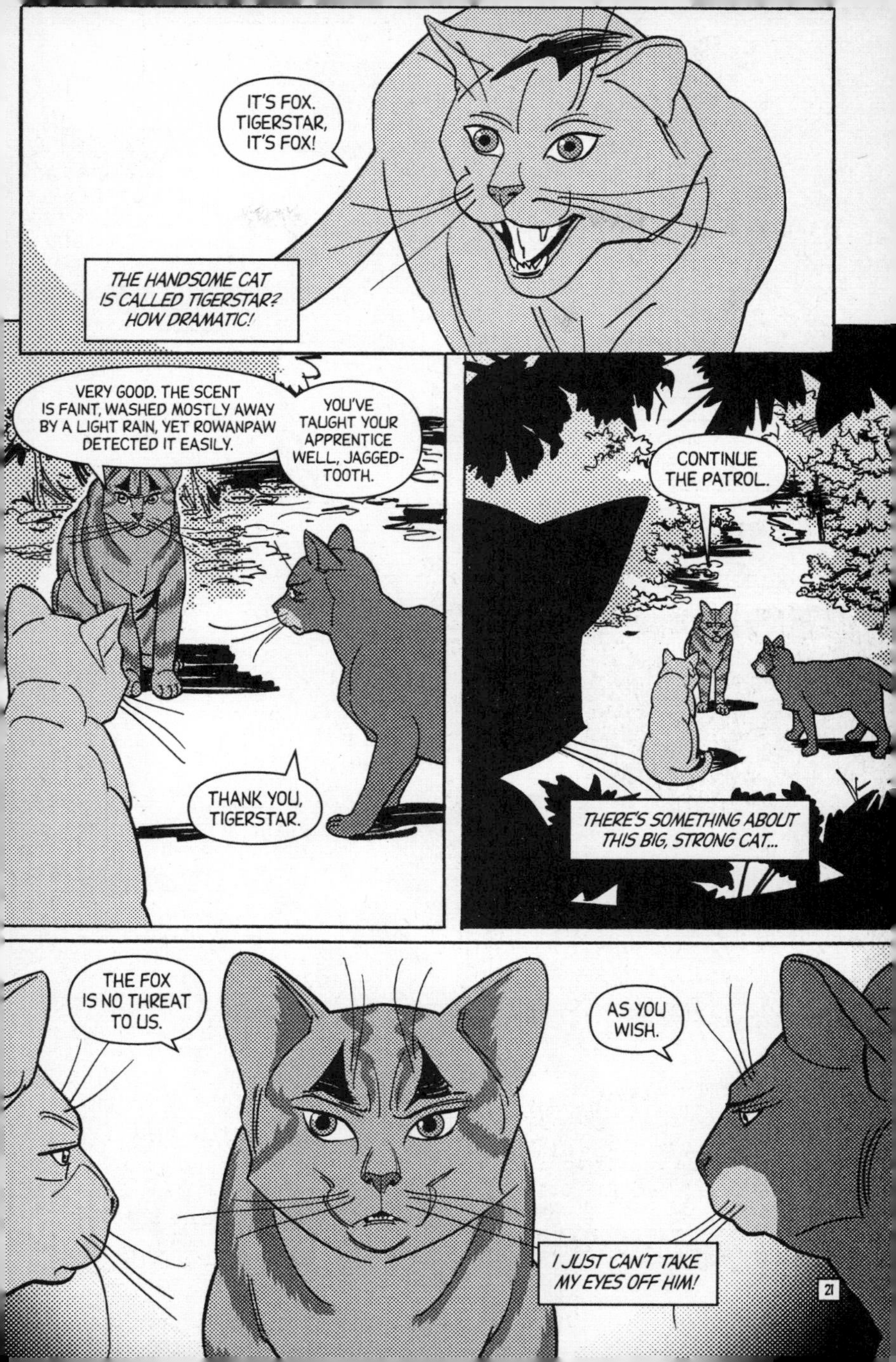
IT'S FOX. TIGERSTAR, IT'S FOX!
THE HANDSOME CAT IS CALLED TIGERSTAR? HOW DRAMATIC!
VERY GOOD. THE SCENT IS FAINT, WASHED MOSTLY AWAY BY A LIGHT RAIN, YET ROWANPAW DETECTED IT EASILY.
YOU'VE TAUGHT YOUR APPRENTICE WELL, JAGGED-TOOTH.
THANK YOU, TIGERSTAR.
CONTINUE THE PATROL.
THERE'S SOMETHING ABOUT THIS BIG, STRONG CAT...
THE FOX IS NO THREAT TO US.
AS YOU WISH.
I JUST CAN'T TAKE MY EYES OFF HIM!
21

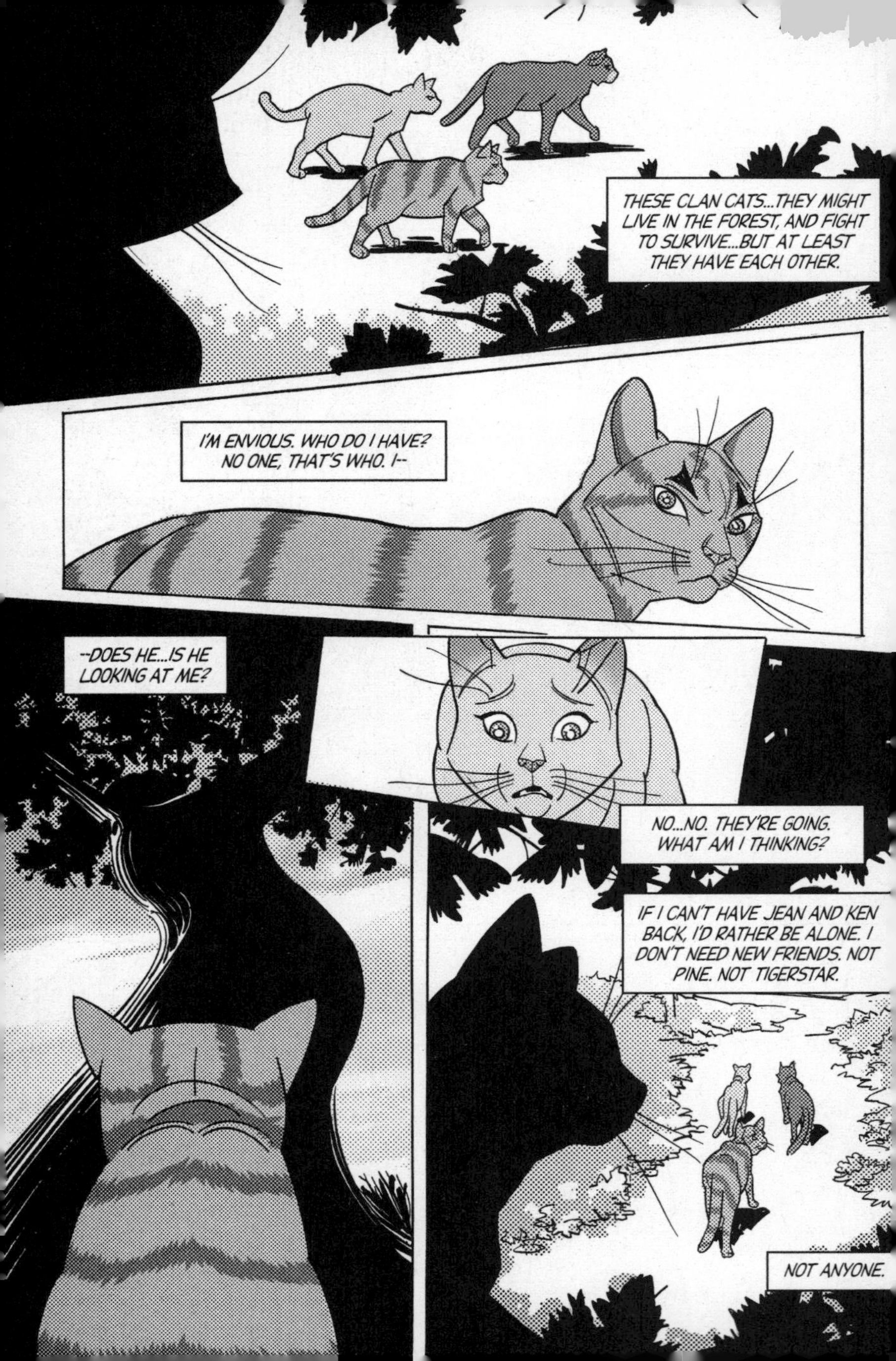
THESE CLAN CATS...THEY MIGHT LIVE IN THE FOREST, AND FIGHT TO SURVIVE...BUT AT LEAST THEY HAVE EACH OTHER.
I'M ENVIOUS. WHO DO I HAVE? NO ONE, THAT'S WHO. I--
--DOES HE...IS HE LOOKING AT ME?
NO...NO. THEY'RE GOING. WHAT AM I THINKING?
IF I CAN'T HAVE JEAN AND KEN BACK, I'D RATHER BE ALONE. I DON'T NEED NEW FRIENDS. NOT PINE. NOT TIGERSTAR.
NOT ANYONE.

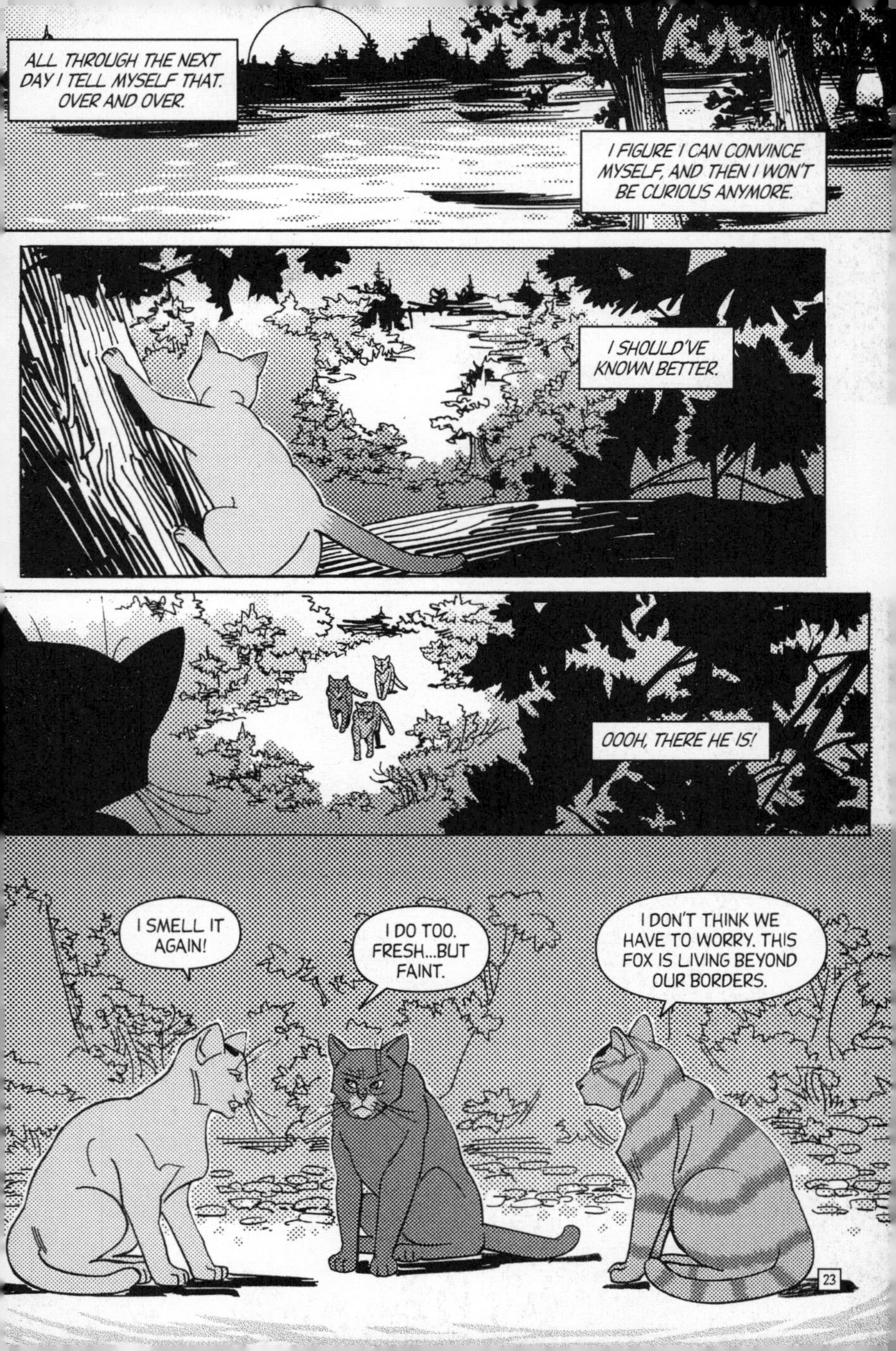
ALL THROUGH THE NEXT DAY I TELL MYSELF THAT. OVER AND OVER.
I FIGURE I CAN CONVINCE MYSELF, AND THEN I WON'T BE CURIOUS ANYMORE.
I SHOULD'VE KNOWN BETTER.
OOOH, THERE HE IS!
I SMELL IT AGAIN!
I DO TOO. FRESH...BUT FAINT.
I DON'T THINK WE HAVE TO WORRY. THIS FOX IS LIVING BEYOND OUR BORDERS.

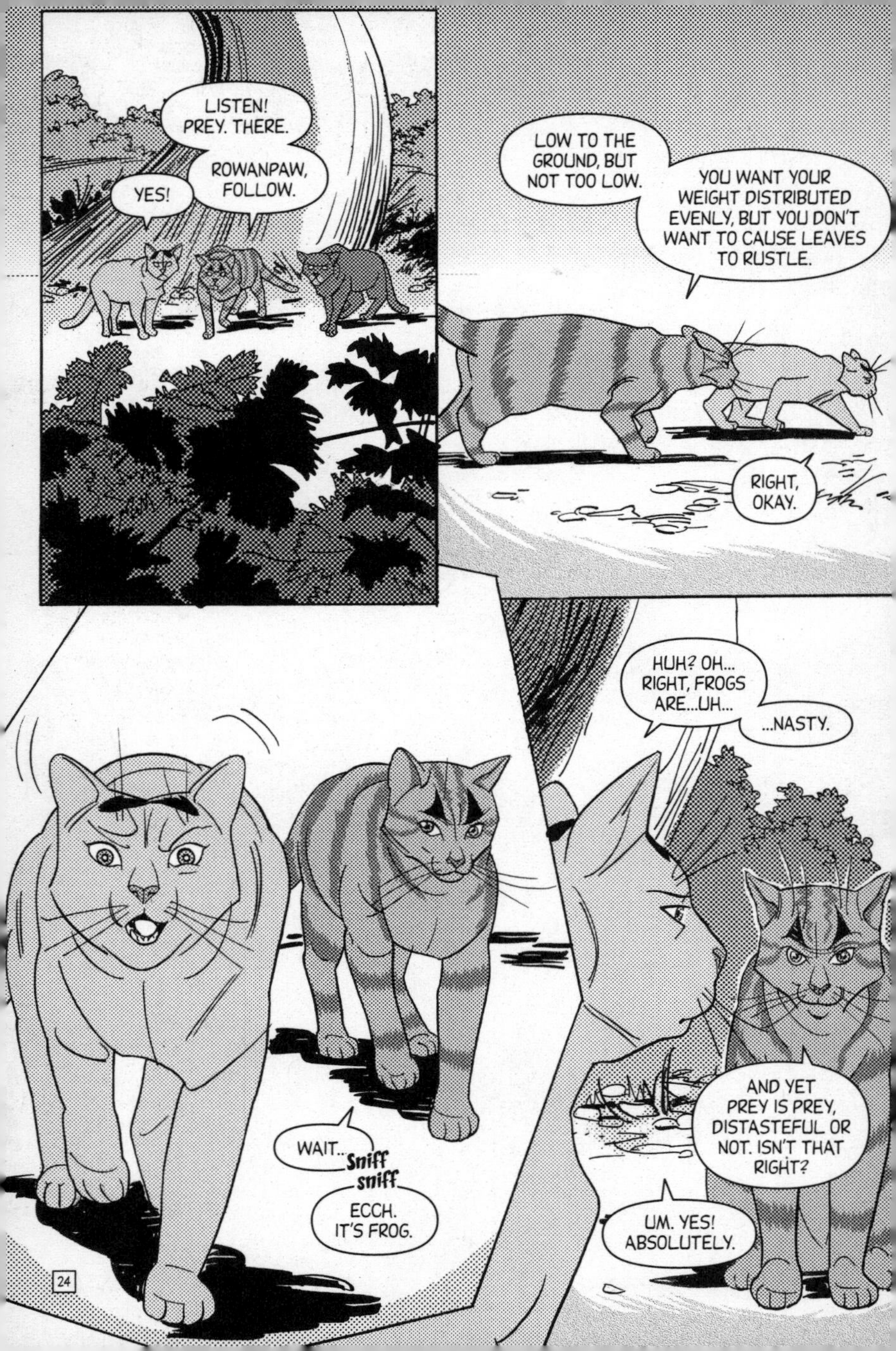
LISTEN! PREY. THERE.
ROWANPAW, FOLLOW.
YES!
LOW TO THE GROUND, BUT NOT TOO LOW.
YOU WANT YOUR WEIGHT DISTRIBUTED EVENLY, BUT YOU DON'T WANT TO CAUSE LEAVES TO RUSTLE.
RIGHT, OKAY.
WAIT...
Sniff sniff
ECCH. IT'S FROG.
HUH? OH... RIGHT, FROGS ARE...UH...
...NASTY.
AND YET PREY IS PREY, DISTASTEFUL OR NOT. ISN'T THAT RIGHT?
UM. YES! ABSOLUTELY.

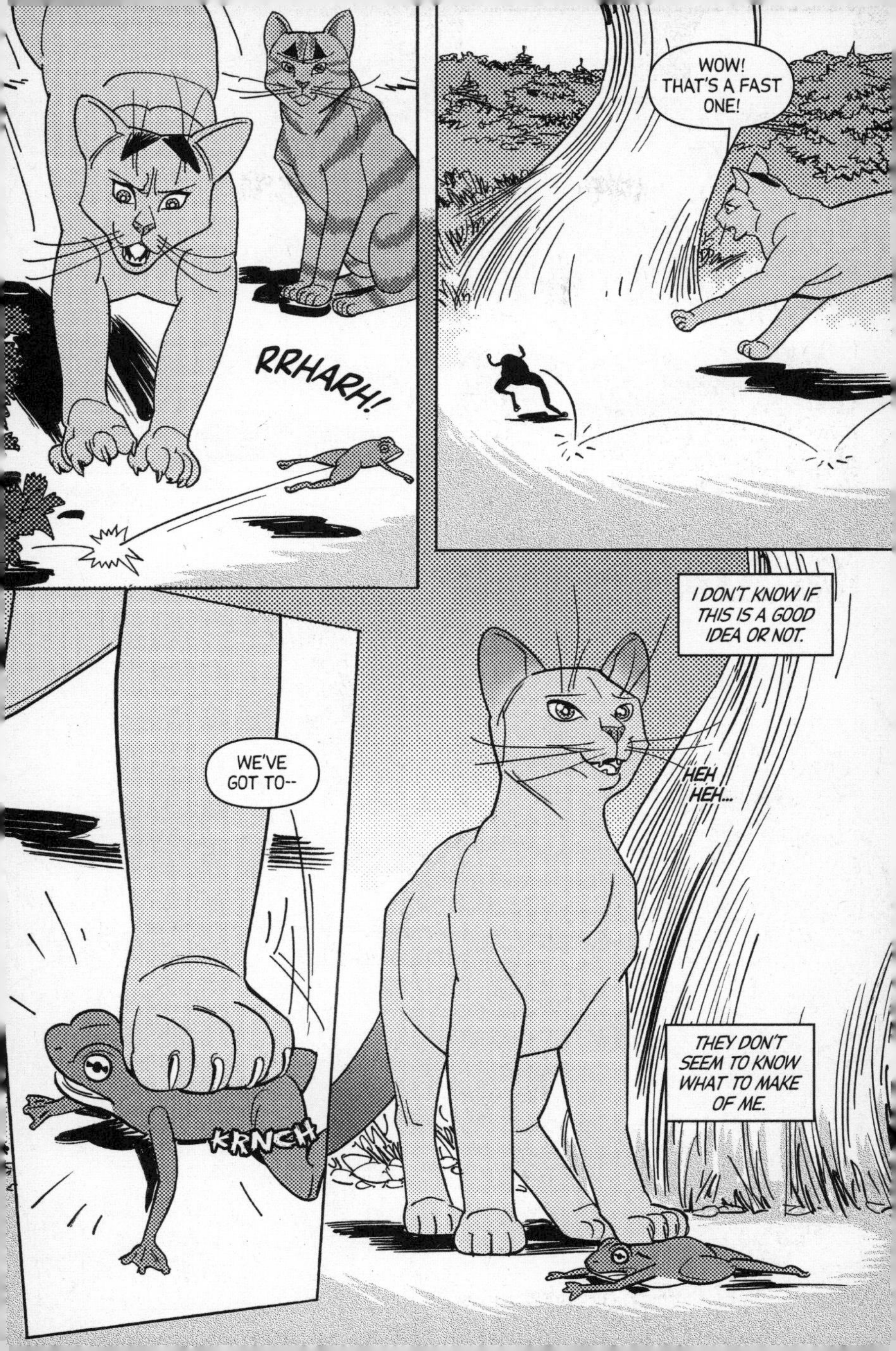
RRHARH!
WOW! THAT'S A FAST ONE!
WE'VE GOT TO--
KRNCH
I DON'T KNOW IF THIS IS A GOOD IDEA OR NOT.
HEH HEH...
THEY DON'T SEEM TO KNOW WHAT TO MAKE OF ME.

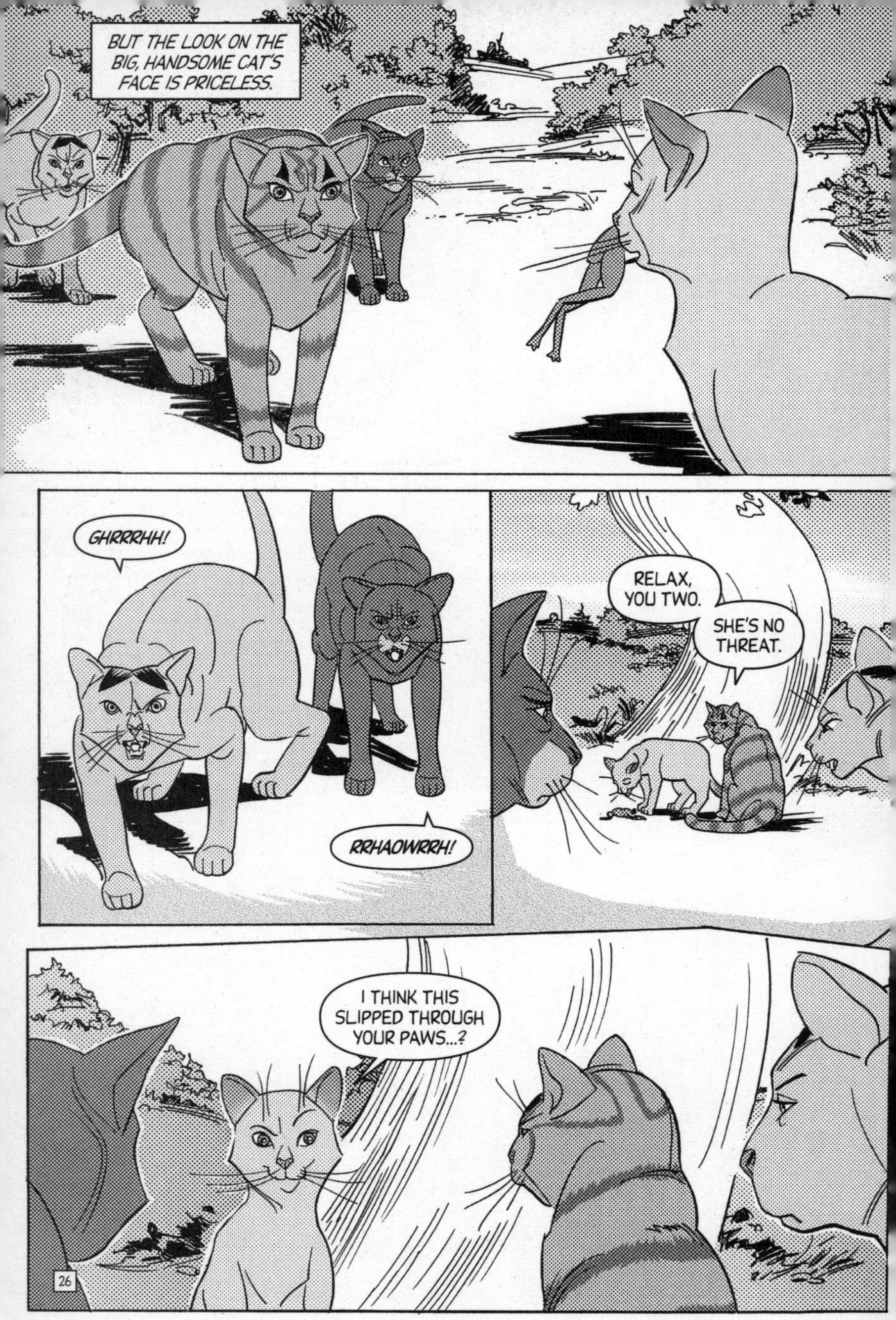
BUT THE LOOK ON THE BIG, HANDSOME CAT'S FACE IS PRICELESS.
GHRRRHH!
RRHAOWRRH!
RELAX, YOU TWO.
SHE'S NO THREAT.
I THINK THIS SLIPPED THROUGH YOUR PAWS...?

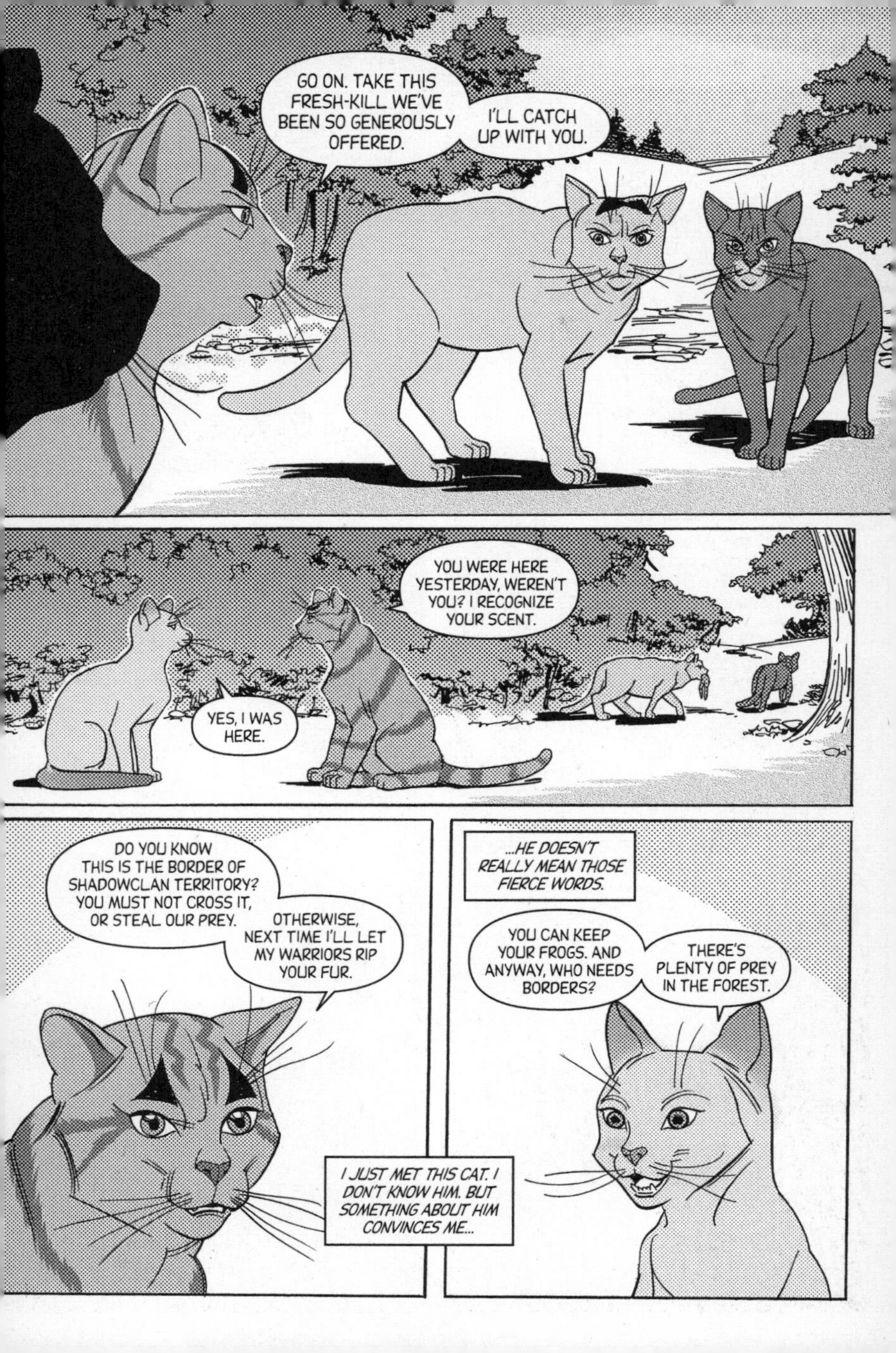
GO ON. TAKE THIS FRESH-KILL WE'VE BEEN SO GENEROUSLY OFFERED.
I'LL CATCH UP WITH YOU.
YOU WERE HERE YESTERDAY, WEREN'T YOU? I RECOGNIZE YOUR SCENT.
YES, I WAS HERE.
DO YOU KNOW THIS IS THE BORDER OF SHADOWCLAN TERRITORY? YOU MUST NOT CROSS IT, OR STEAL OUR PREY.
OTHERWISE, NEXT TIME I'LL LET MY WARRIORS RIP YOUR FUR.
I JUST MET THIS CAT. I DON'T KNOW HIM. BUT SOMETHING ABOUT HIM CONVINCES ME...
...HE DOESN'T REALLY MEAN THOSE FIERCE WORDS.
YOU CAN KEEP YOUR FROGS. AND ANYWAY, WHO NEEDS BORDERS?
THERE'S PLENTY OF PREY IN THE FOREST.

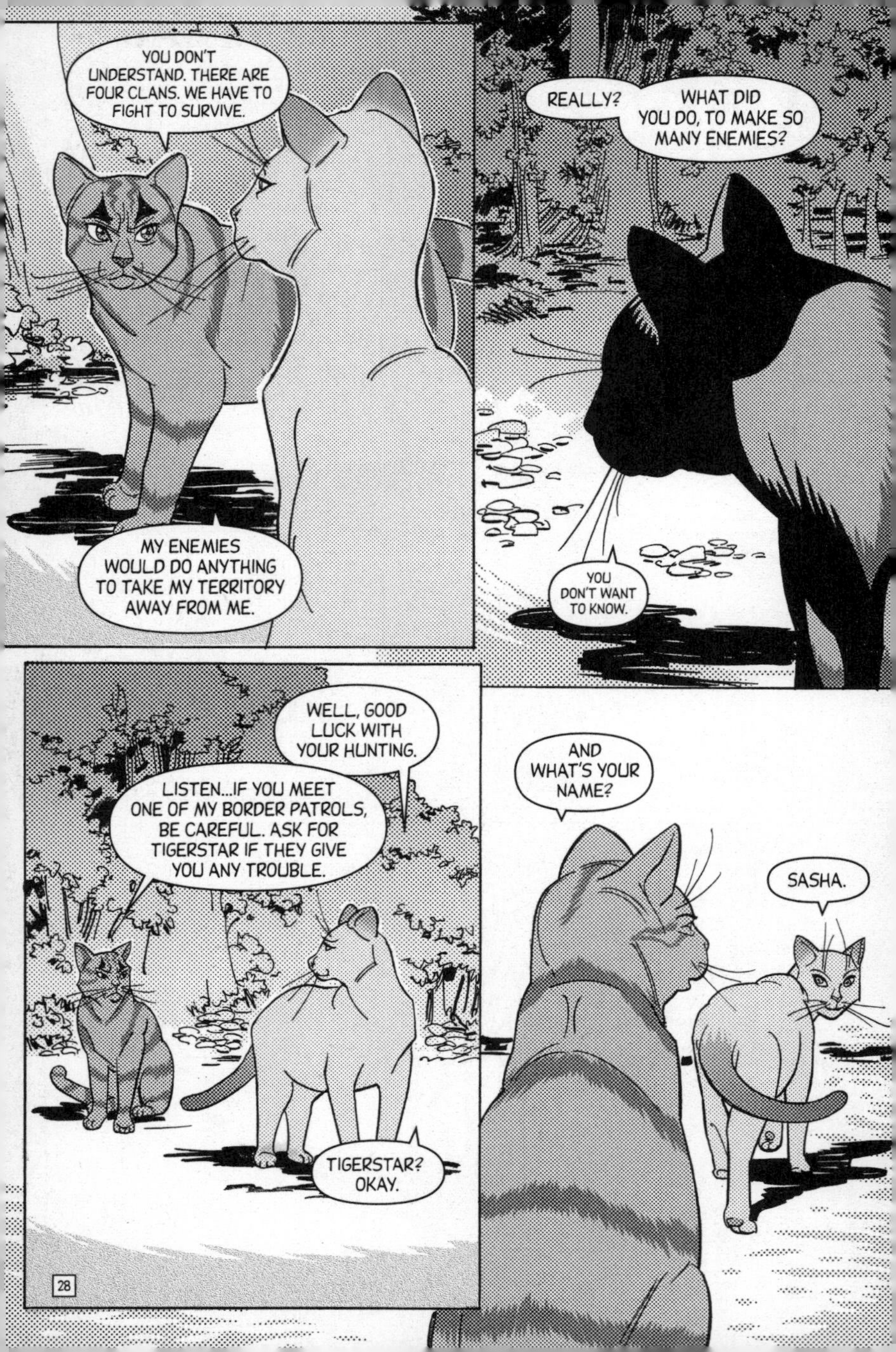
YOU DON'T UNDERSTAND. THERE ARE FOUR CLANS. WE HAVE TO FIGHT TO SURVIVE.
MY ENEMIES WOULD DO ANYTHING TO TAKE MY TERRITORY AWAY FROM ME.
REALLY?
WHAT DID YOU DO, TO MAKE SO MANY ENEMIES?
YOU DON'T WANT TO KNOW.
WELL, GOOD LUCK WITH YOUR HUNTING.
LISTEN...IF YOU MEET ONE OF MY BORDER PATROLS, BE CAREFUL. ASK FOR TIGERSTAR IF THEY GIVE YOU ANY TROUBLE.
TIGERSTAR? OKAY.
AND WHAT'S YOUR NAME?
SASHA.

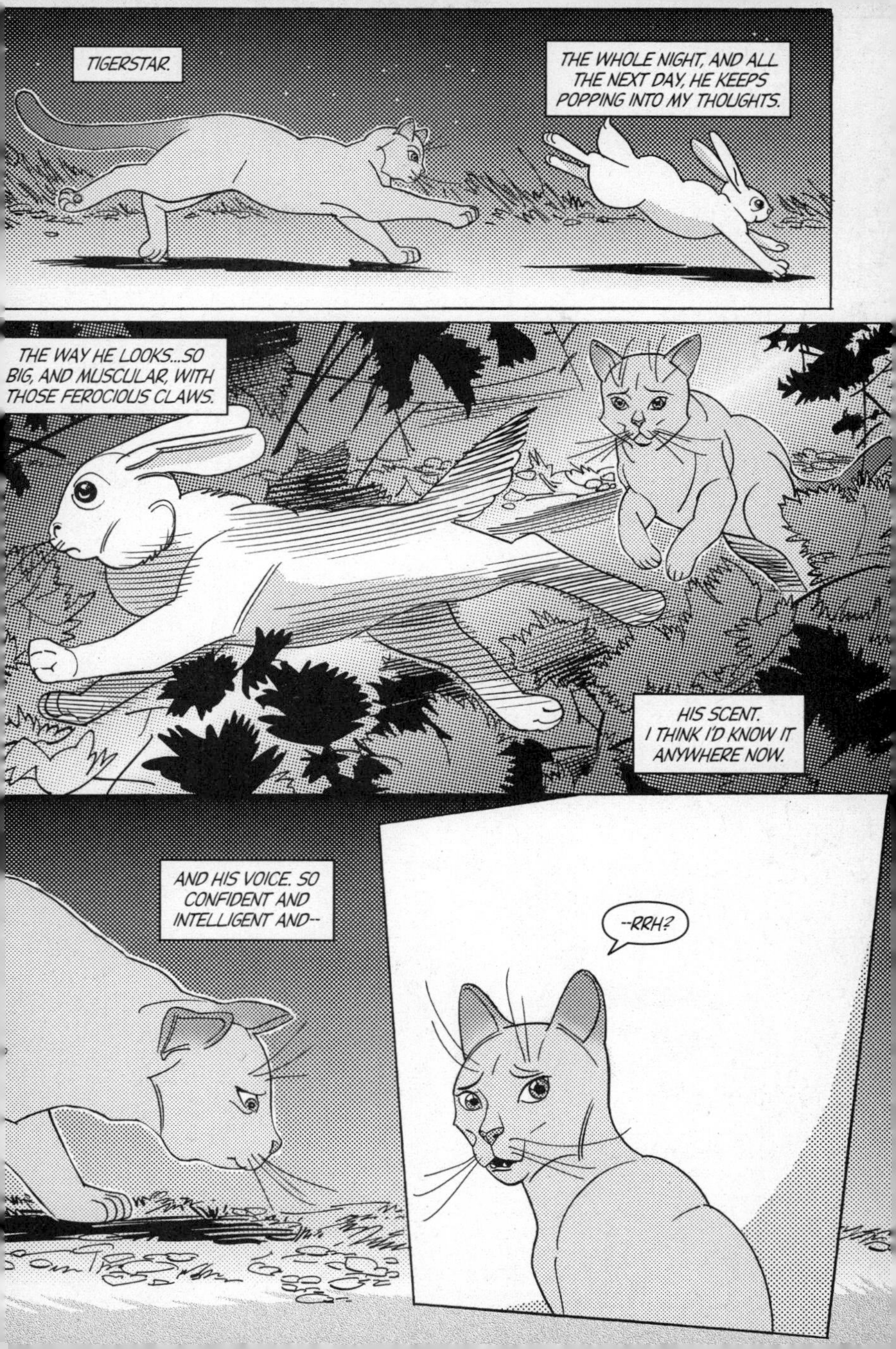
TIGERSTAR.
THE WHOLE NIGHT, AND ALL THE NEXT DAY, HE KEEPS POPPING INTO MY THOUGHTS.
THE WAY HE LOOKS...SO BIG, AND MUSCULAR, WITH THOSE FEROCIOUS CLAWS.
HIS SCENT. I THINK I'D KNOW IT ANYWHERE NOW.
AND HIS VOICE. SO CONFIDENT AND INTELLIGENT AND--
--RRH?

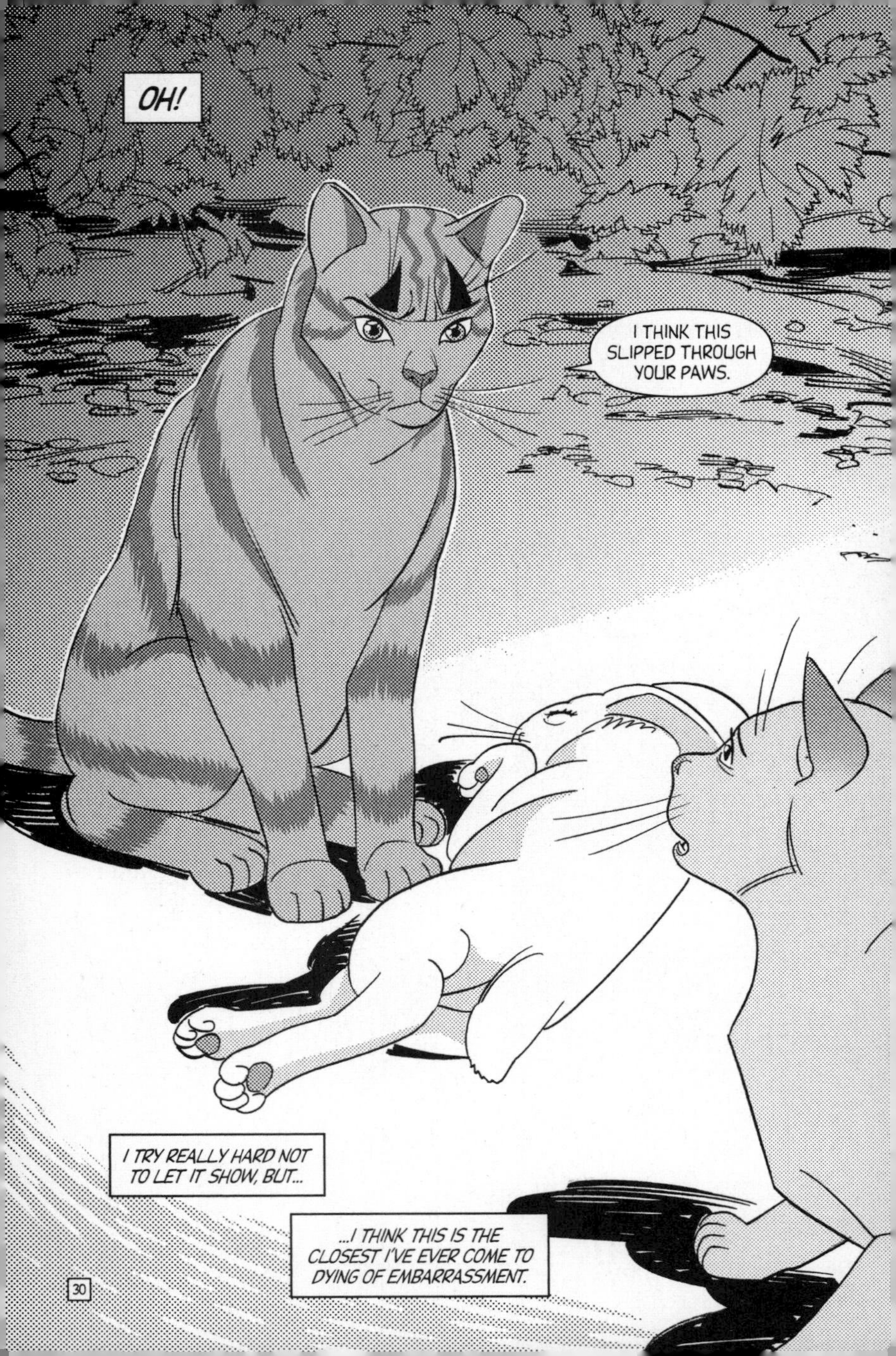
OH!
I THINK THIS SLIPPED THROUGH YOUR PAWS.
I TRY REALLY HARD NOT TO LET IT SHOW, BUT...
...I THINK THIS IS THE CLOSEST I'VE EVER COME TO DYING OF EMBARRASSMENT.

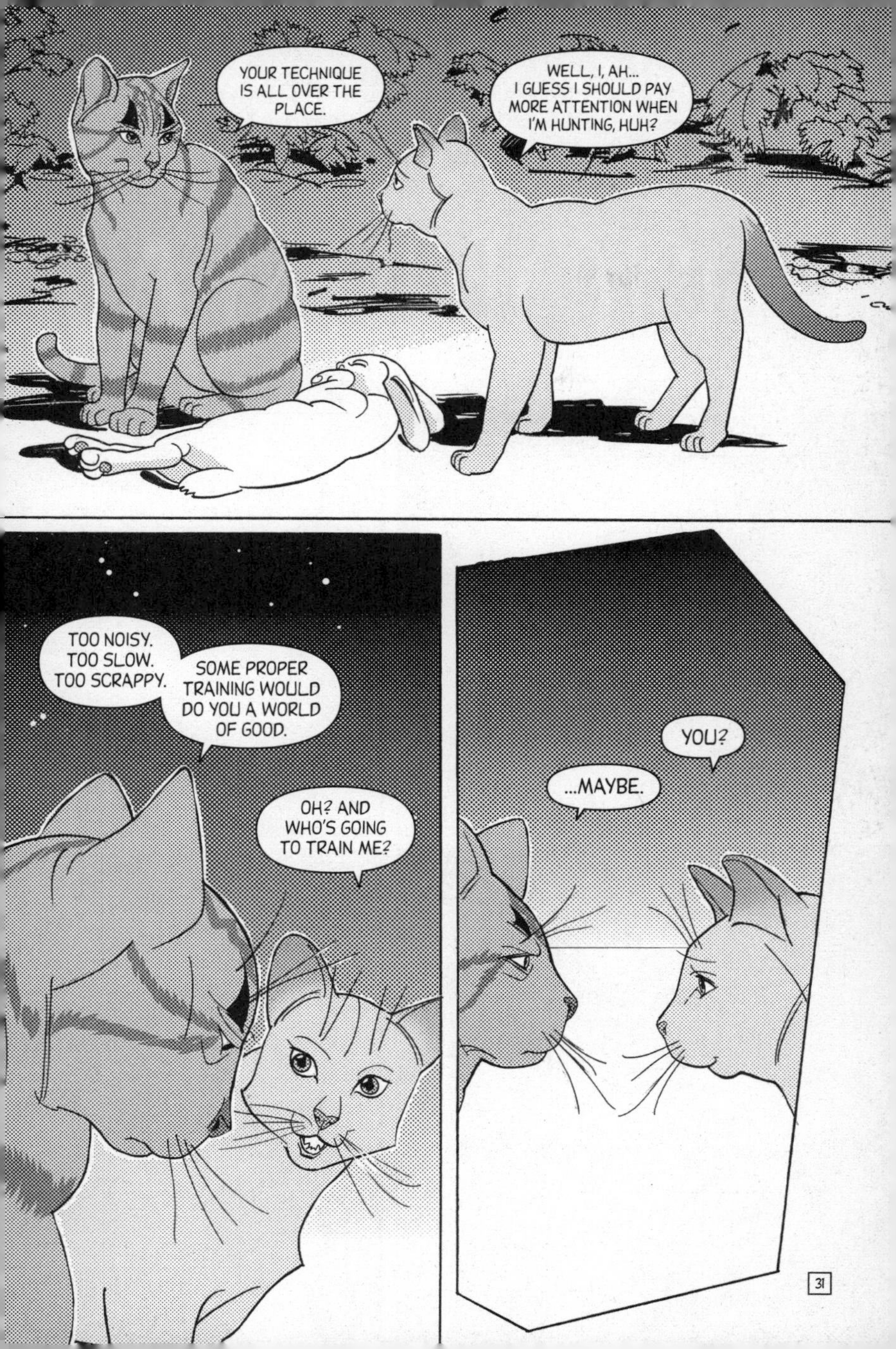
YOUR TECHNIQUE IS ALL OVER THE PLACE.
WELL, I, AH... I GUESS I SHOULD PAY MORE ATTENTION WHEN I'M HUNTING, HUH?
TOO NOISY. TOO SLOW. TOO SCRAPPY.
SOME PROPER TRAINING WOULD DO YOU A WORLD OF GOOD.
OH? AND WHO'S GOING TO TRAIN ME?
YOU?
...MAYBE.

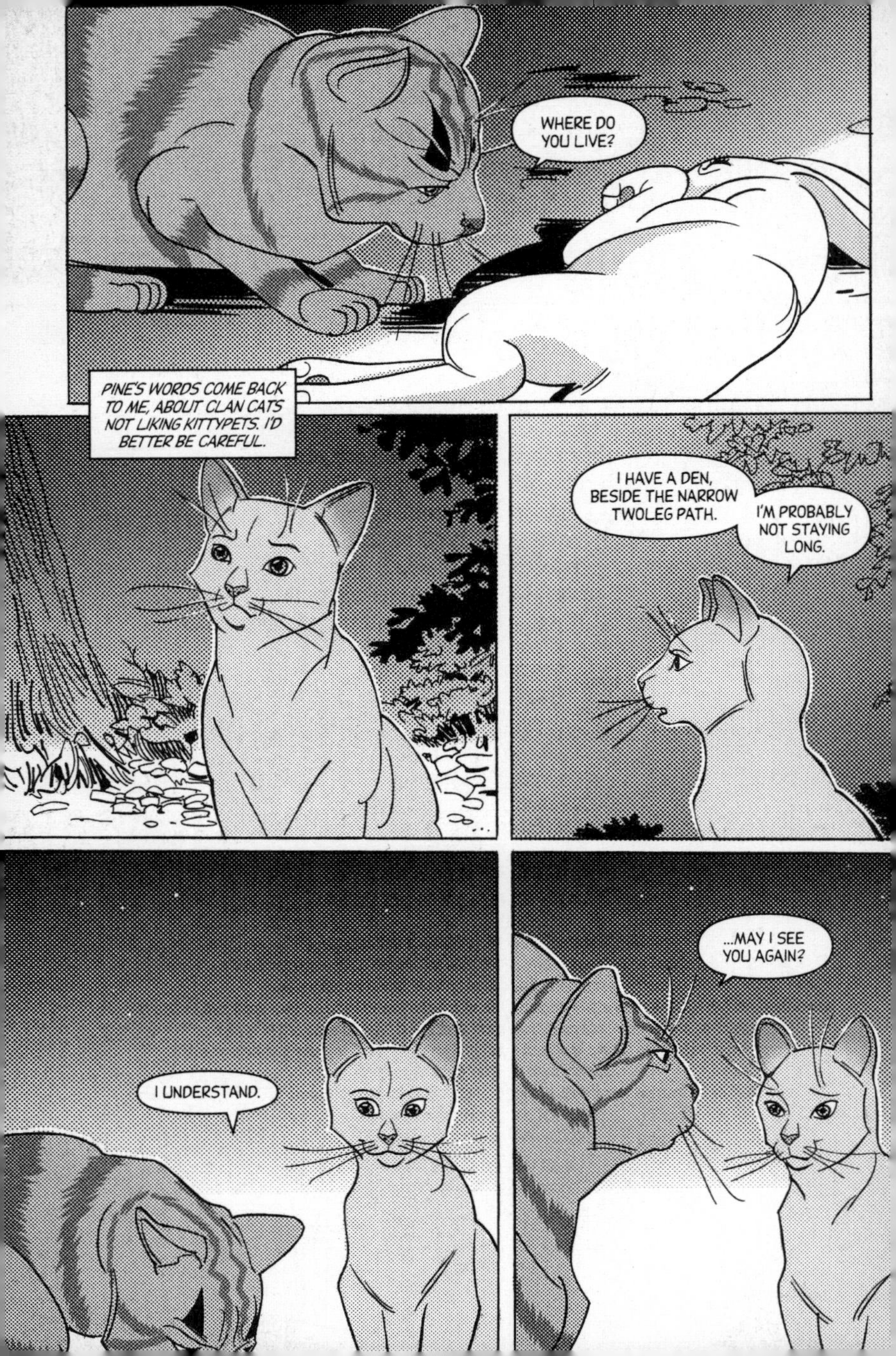
WHERE DO YOU LIVE?
PINE'S WORDS COME BACK TO ME, ABOUT CLAN CATS NOT LIKING KITTYPETS. I'D BETTER BE CAREFUL.
I HAVE A DEN, BESIDE THE NARROW TWOLEG PATH.
I'M PROBABLY NOT STAYING LONG.
I UNDERSTAND.
...MAY I SEE YOU AGAIN?

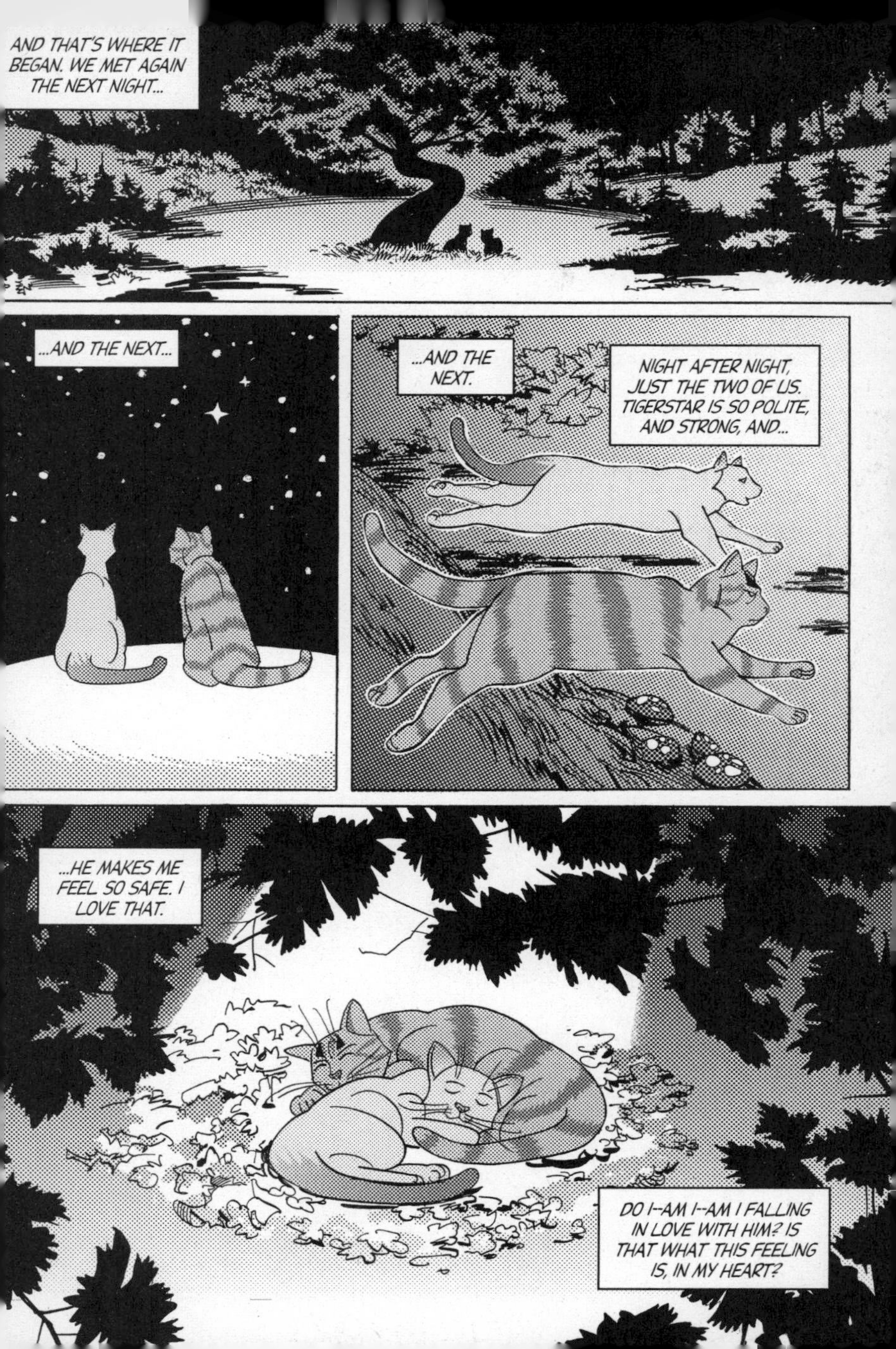
AND THAT'S WHERE IT BEGAN. WE MET AGAIN THE NEXT NIGHT...
...AND THE NEXT...
...AND THE NEXT.
NIGHT AFTER NIGHT, JUST THE TWO OF US. TIGERSTAR IS SO POLITE, AND STRONG, AND...
...HE MAKES ME FEEL SO SAFE. I LOVE THAT.
DO I--AM I--AM I FALLING IN LOVE WITH HIM? IS THAT WHAT THIS FEELING IS, IN MY HEART?

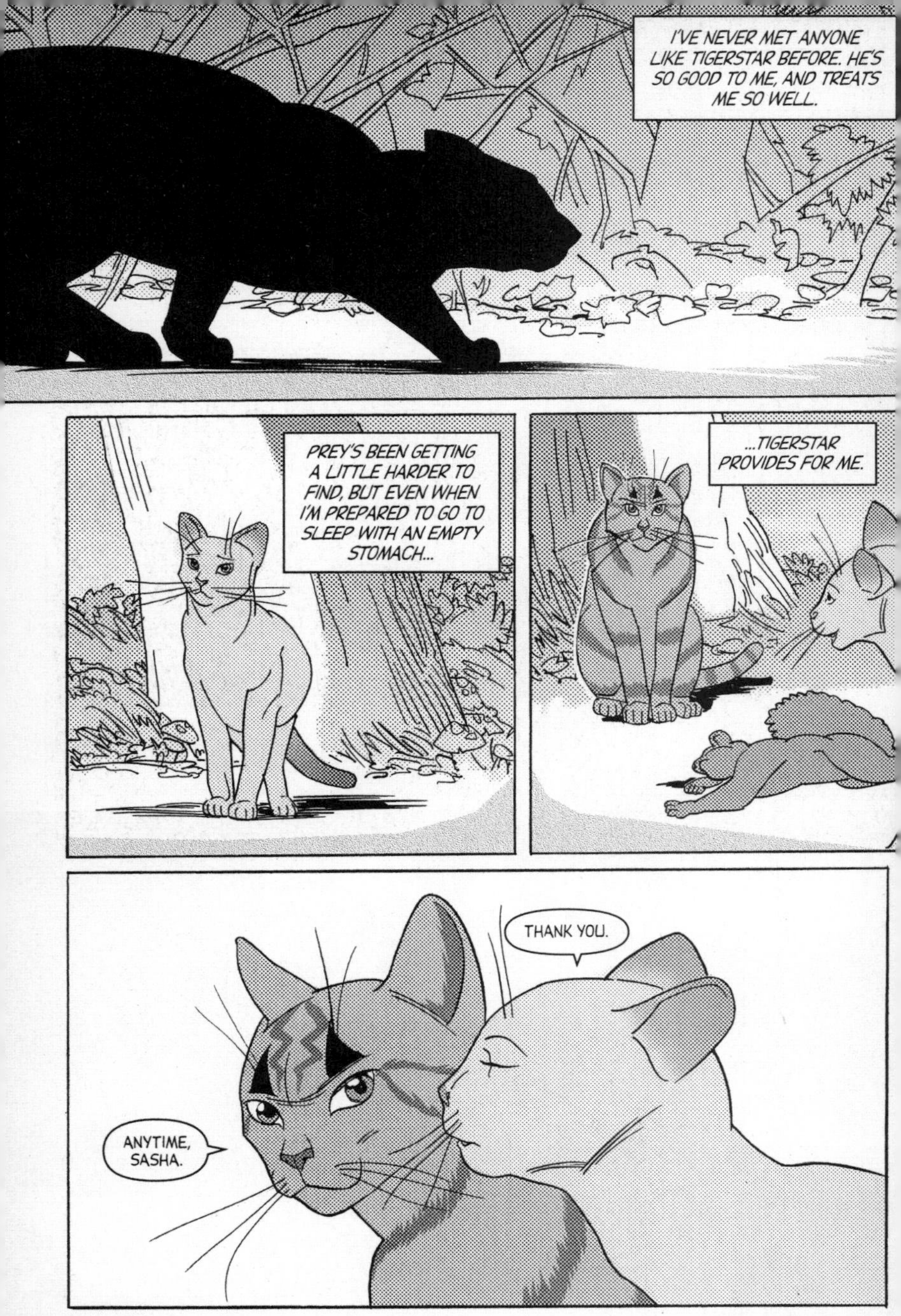
I'VE NEVER MET ANYONE LIKE TIGERSTAR BEFORE. HE'S SO GOOD TO ME, AND TREATS ME SO WELL.
PREY'S BEEN GETTING A LITTLE HARDER TO FIND, BUT EVEN WHEN I'M PREPARED TO GO TO SLEEP WITH AN EMPTY STOMACH...
...TIGERSTAR PROVIDES FOR ME.
THANK YOU.
ANYTIME, SASHA.

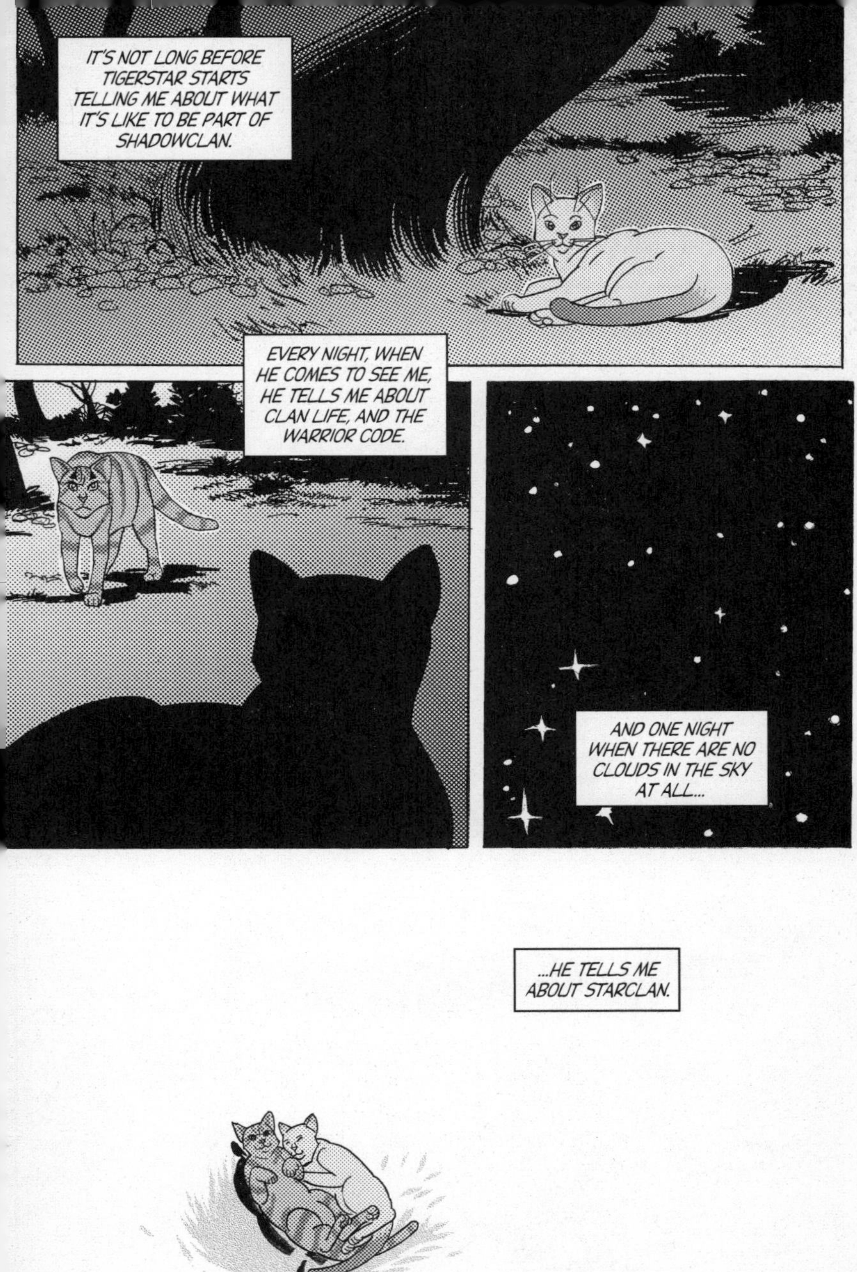
IT'S NOT LONG BEFORE TIGERSTAR STARTS TELLING ME ABOUT WHAT IT'S LIKE TO BE PART OF SHADOWCLAN.
EVERY NIGHT, WHEN HE COMES TO SEE ME, HE TELLS ME ABOUT CLAN LIFE, AND THE WARRIOR CODE.
AND ONE NIGHT WHEN THERE ARE NO CLOUDS IN THE SKY AT ALL...
...HE TELLS ME ABOUT STARCLAN.

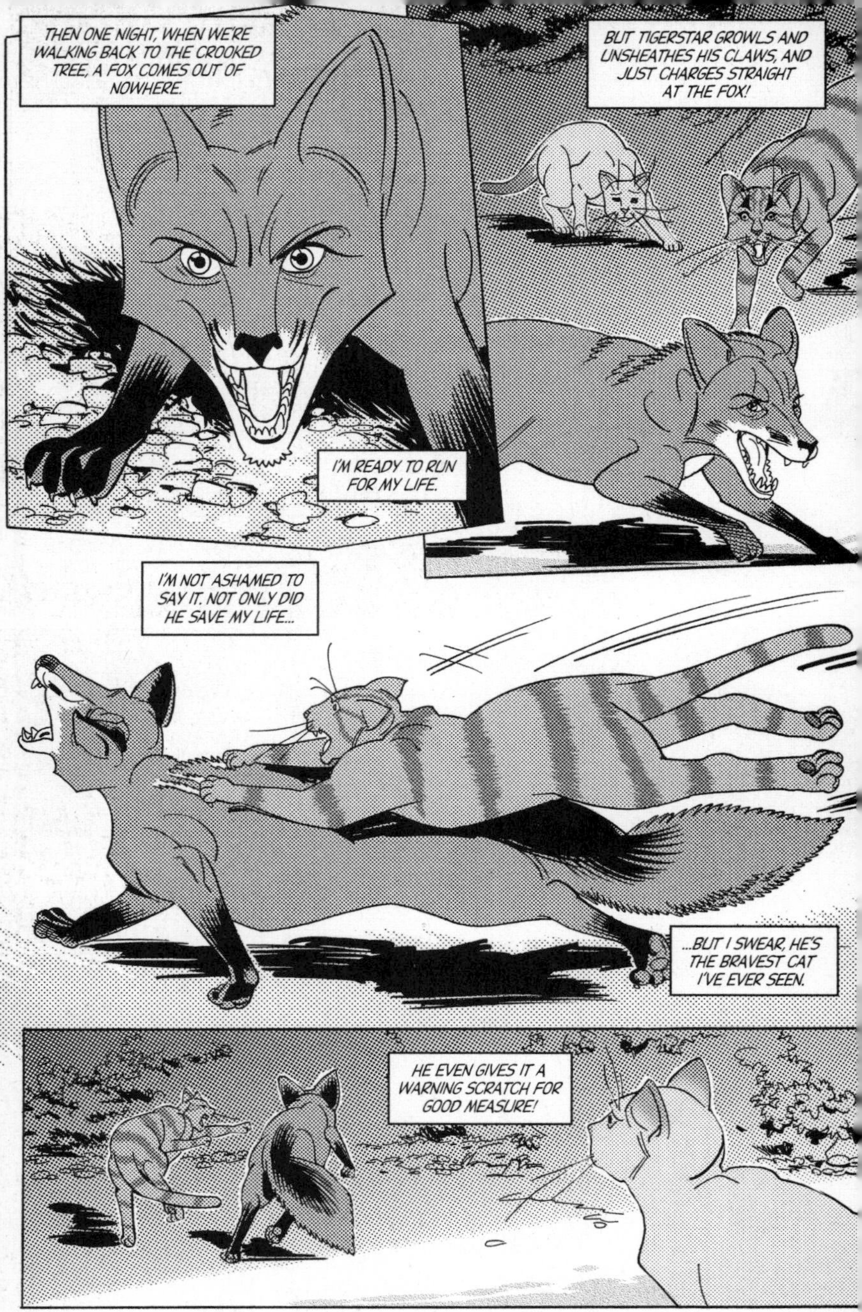
THEN ONE NIGHT, WHEN WE'RE WALKING BACK TO THE CROOKED TREE, A FOX COMES OUT OF NOWHERE.
I'M READY TO RUN FOR MY LIFE.
BUT TIGERSTAR GROWLS AND UNSHEATHES HIS CLAWS, AND JUST CHARGES STRAIGHT AT THE FOX!
I'M NOT ASHAMED TO SAY IT. NOT ONLY DID HE SAVE MY LIFE...
...BUT I SWEAR, HE'S THE BRAVEST CAT I'VE EVER SEEN.
HE EVEN GIVES IT A WARNING SCRATCH FOR GOOD MEASURE!

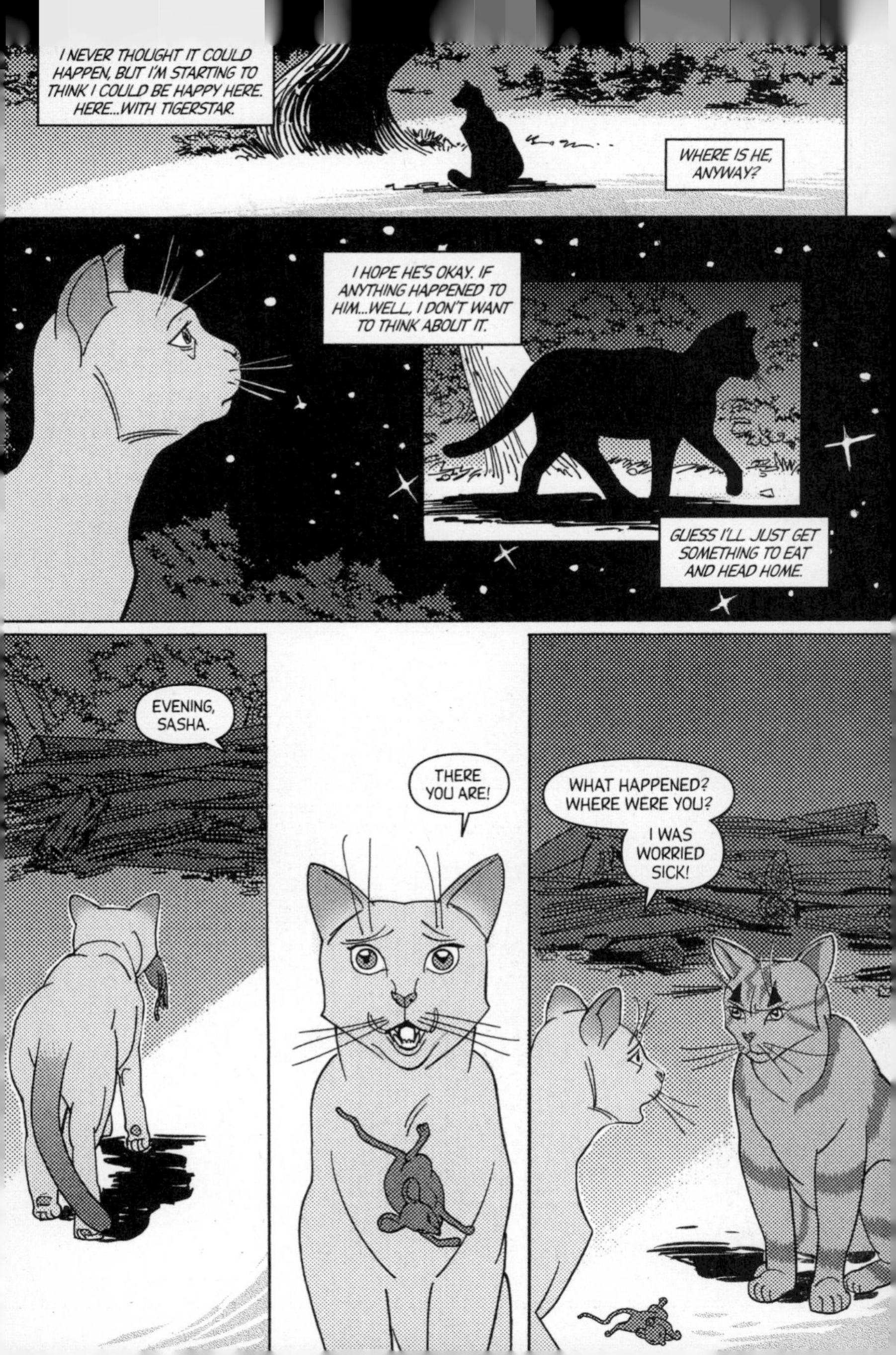

I NEVER THOUGHT IT COULD HAPPEN, BUT I'M STARTING TO THINK I COULD BE HAPPY HERE. HERE...WITH TIGERSTAR.
WHERE IS HE, ANYWAY?
I HOPE HE'S OKAY. IF ANYTHING HAPPENED TO HIM...WELL, I DON'T WANT TO THINK ABOUT IT.
GUESS I'LL JUST GET SOMETHING TO EAT AND HEAD HOME.
EVENING, SASHA.
THERE YOU ARE!
WHAT HAPPENED? WHERE WERE YOU?
I WAS WORRIED SICK!

NICE PLACE. I SHOULD'VE COME HERE EARLIER. QUIET. PEACEFUL.

SO TELL ME... ...WHEN WILL YOU BE GOING BACK TO YOUR TWOLEGS?

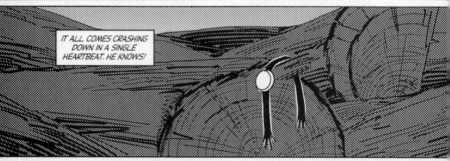

IT ALL COMES CRASHING DOWN IN A SINGLE HEARTBEAT. HE KNOWS!

WELL...WELL, WHAT GIVES YOU THE RIGHT TO GO SNOOPING IN MY DEN, ANYWAY? HUH?

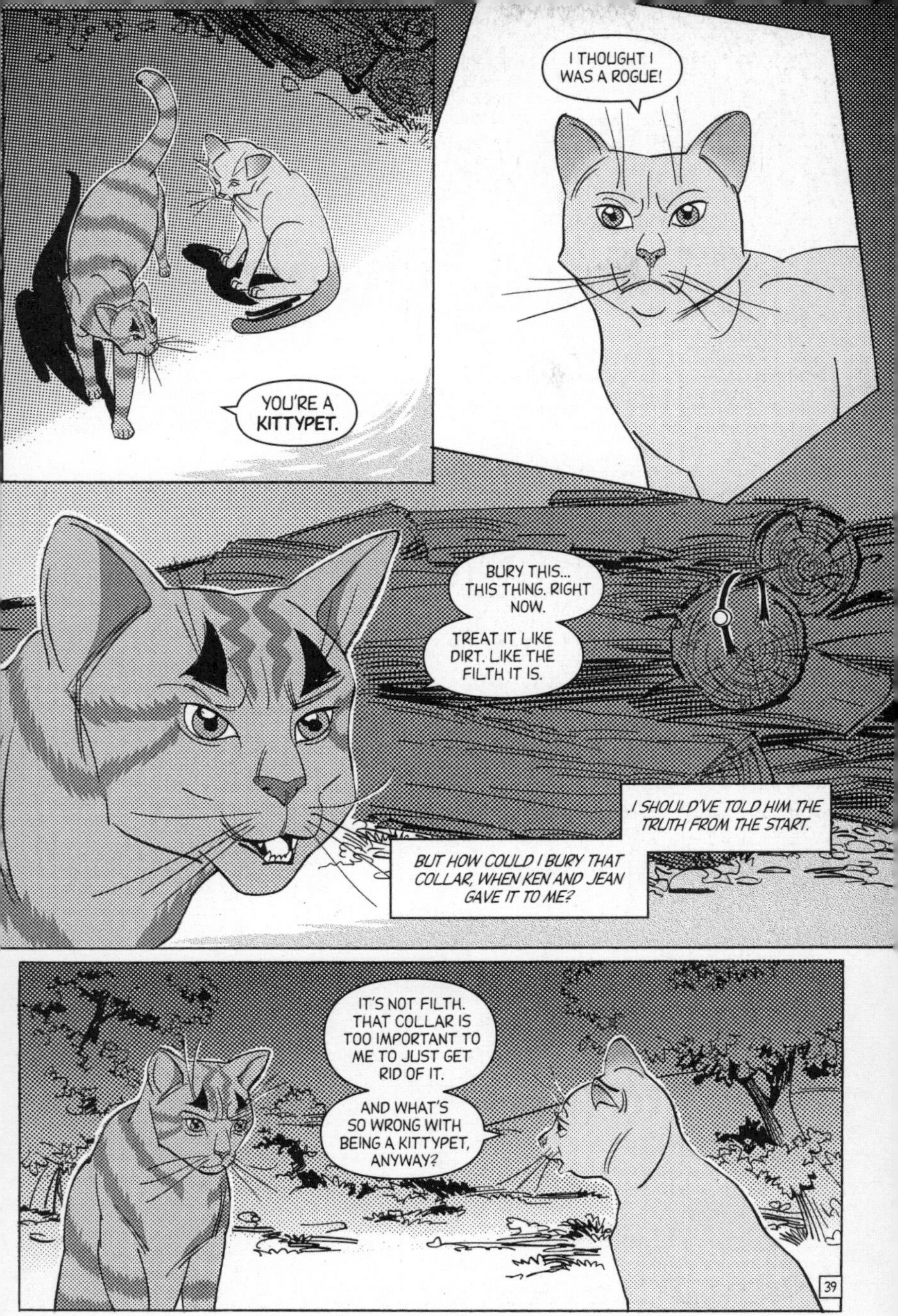
YOU'RE A KITTYPET.
I THOUGHT I WAS A ROGUE!
BURY THIS... THIS THING. RIGHT NOW.
TREAT IT LIKE DIRT. LIKE THE FILTH IT IS.
I SHOULD'VE TOLD HIM THE TRUTH FROM THE START.
BUT HOW COULD I BURY THAT COLLAR, WHEN KEN AND JEAN GAVE IT TO ME?
IT'S NOT FILTH. THAT COLLAR IS TOO IMPORTANT TO ME TO JUST GET RID OF IT.
AND WHAT'S SO WRONG WITH BEING A KITTYPET, ANYWAY?

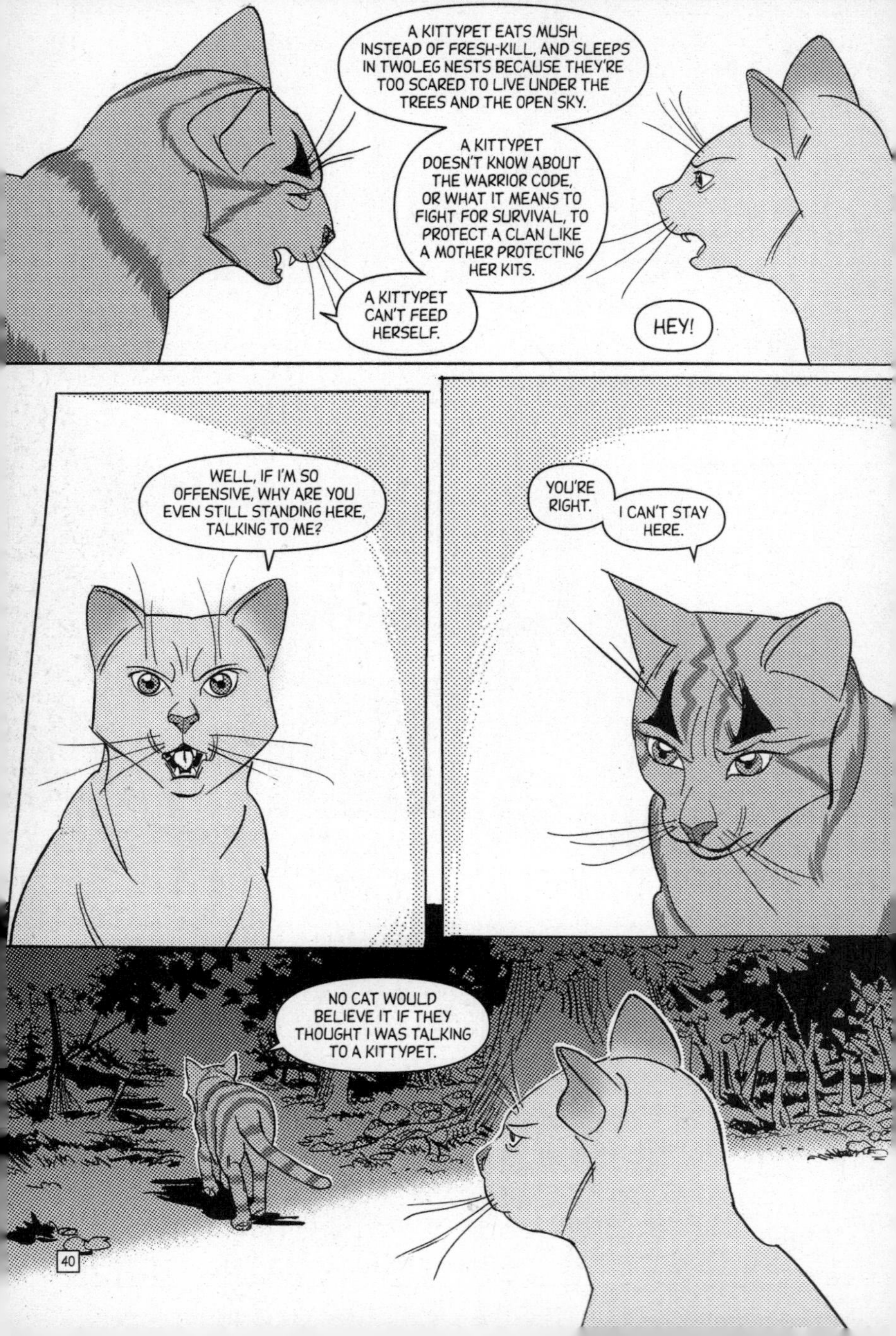
A KITTYPET EATS MUSH INSTEAD OF FRESH-KILL, AND SLEEPS IN TWOLEG NESTS BECAUSE THEY'RE TOO SCARED TO LIVE UNDER THE TREES AND THE OPEN SKY.
A KITTYPET DOESN'T KNOW ABOUT THE WARRIOR CODE, OR WHAT IT MEANS TO FIGHT FOR SURVIVAL, TO PROTECT A CLAN LIKE A MOTHER PROTECTING HER KITS.
A KITTYPET CAN'T FEED HERSELF.
HEY!
WELL, IF I'M SO OFFENSIVE, WHY ARE YOU EVEN STILL STANDING HERE, TALKING TO ME?
YOU'RE RIGHT.
I CAN'T STAY HERE.
NO CAT WOULD BELIEVE IT IF THEY THOUGHT I WAS TALKING TO A KITTYPET.

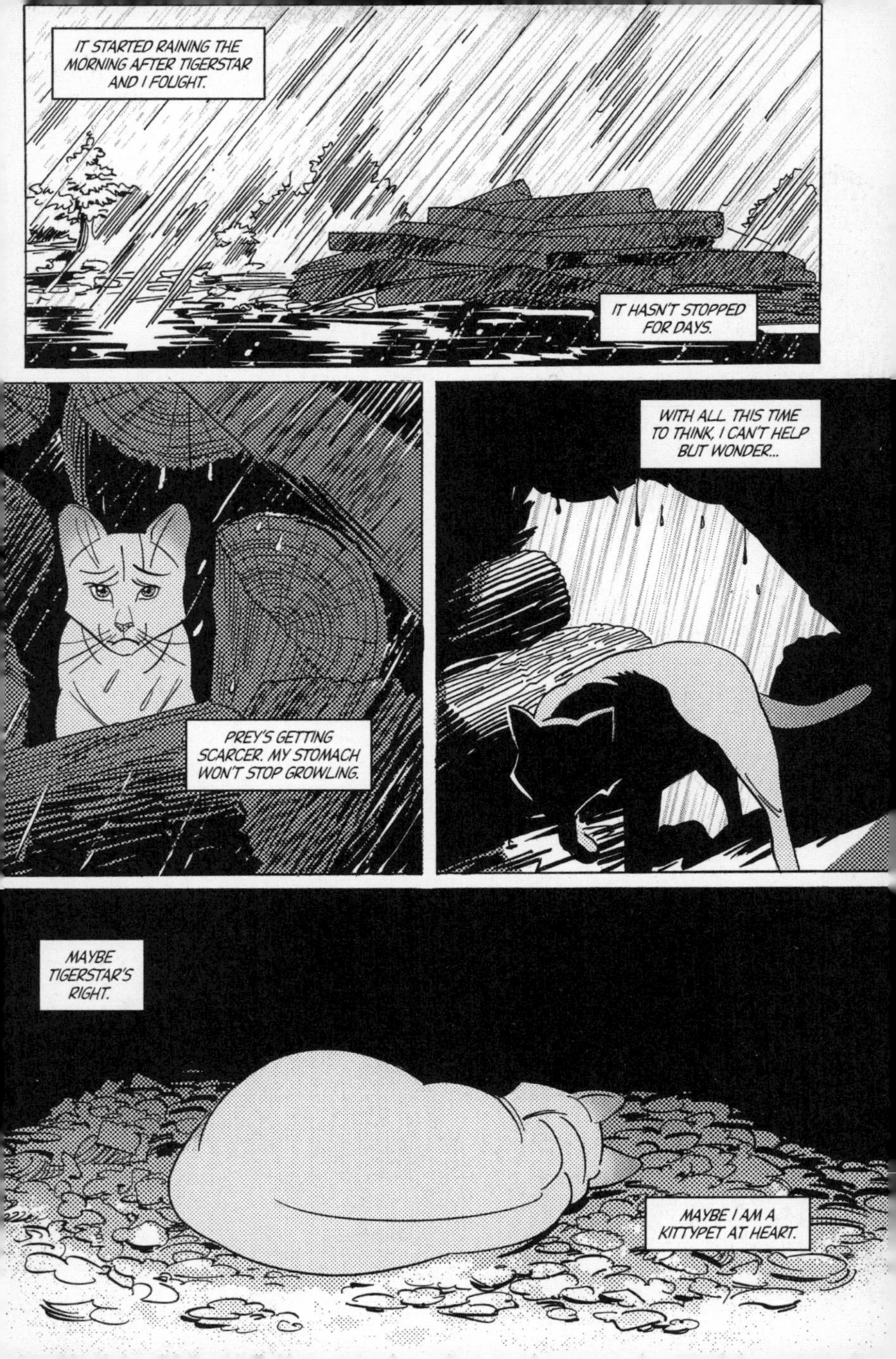
IT STARTED RAINING THE MORNING AFTER TIGERSTAR AND I FOUGHT.
IT HASN'T STOPPED FOR DAYS.
PREY'S GETTING SCARCER. MY STOMACH WON'T STOP GROWLING.
WITH ALL THIS TIME TO THINK, I CAN'T HELP BUT WONDER...
MAYBE TIGERSTAR'S RIGHT.
MAYBE I AM A KITTYPET AT HEART.

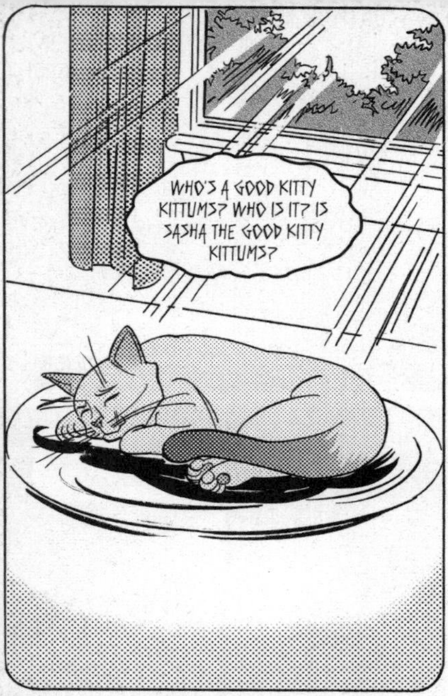
WHO'S A GOOD KITTY KITTUMS? WHO IS IT? IS SASHA THE GOOD KITTY KITTUMS?

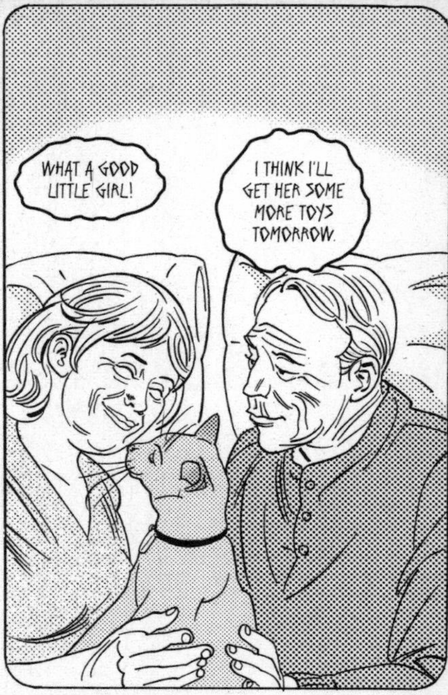
WHAT A GOOD LITTLE GIRL!
I THINK I'LL GET HER SOME MORE TOYS TOMORROW.

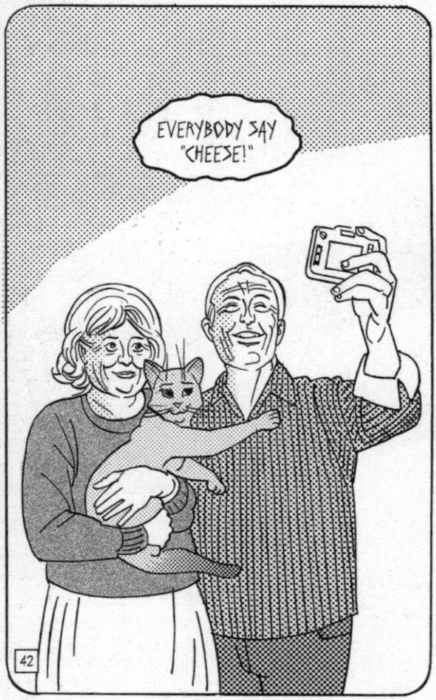
EVERYBODY SAY "CHEESE!"

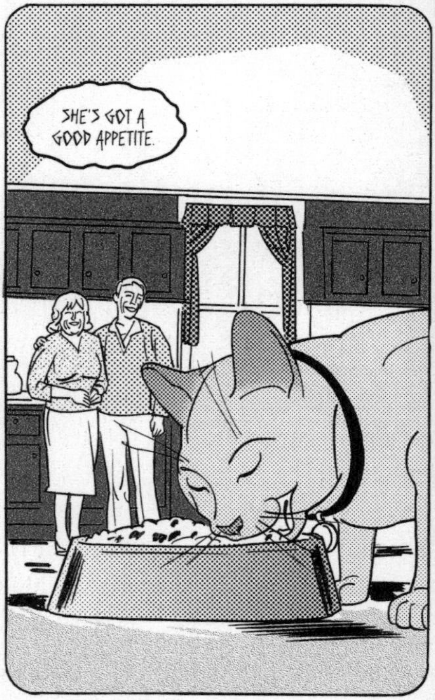
SHE'S GOT A GOOD APPETITE.

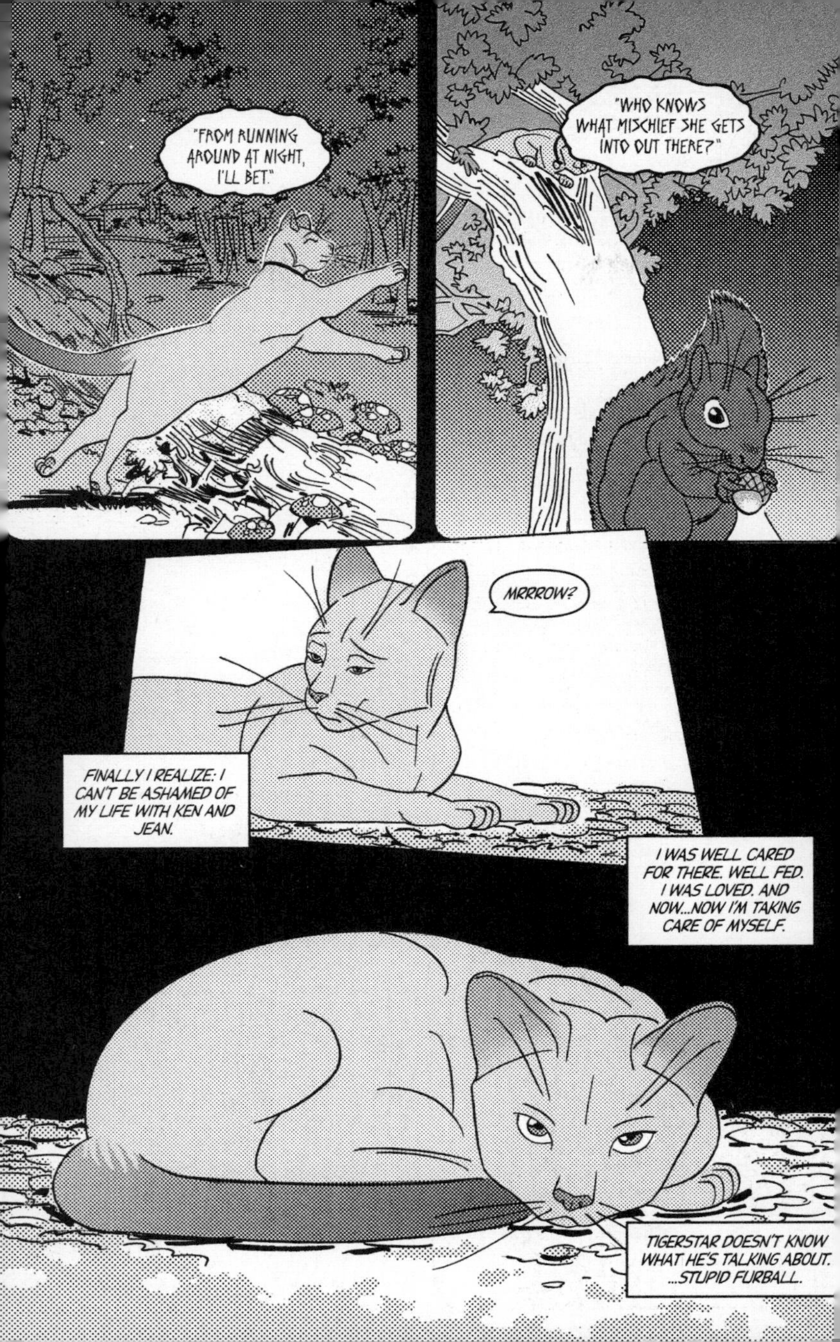
"FROM RUNNING AROUND AT NIGHT, I'LL BET."
"WHO KNOWS WHAT MISCHIEF SHE GETS INTO OUT THERE?"
MRRROW?
FINALLY I REALIZE: I CAN'T BE ASHAMED OF MY LIFE WITH KEN AND JEAN.
I WAS WELL CARED FOR THERE. WELL FED. I WAS LOVED. AND NOW...NOW I'M TAKING CARE OF MYSELF.
TIGERSTAR DOESN'T KNOW WHAT HE'S TALKING ABOUT. ...STUPID FURBALL.

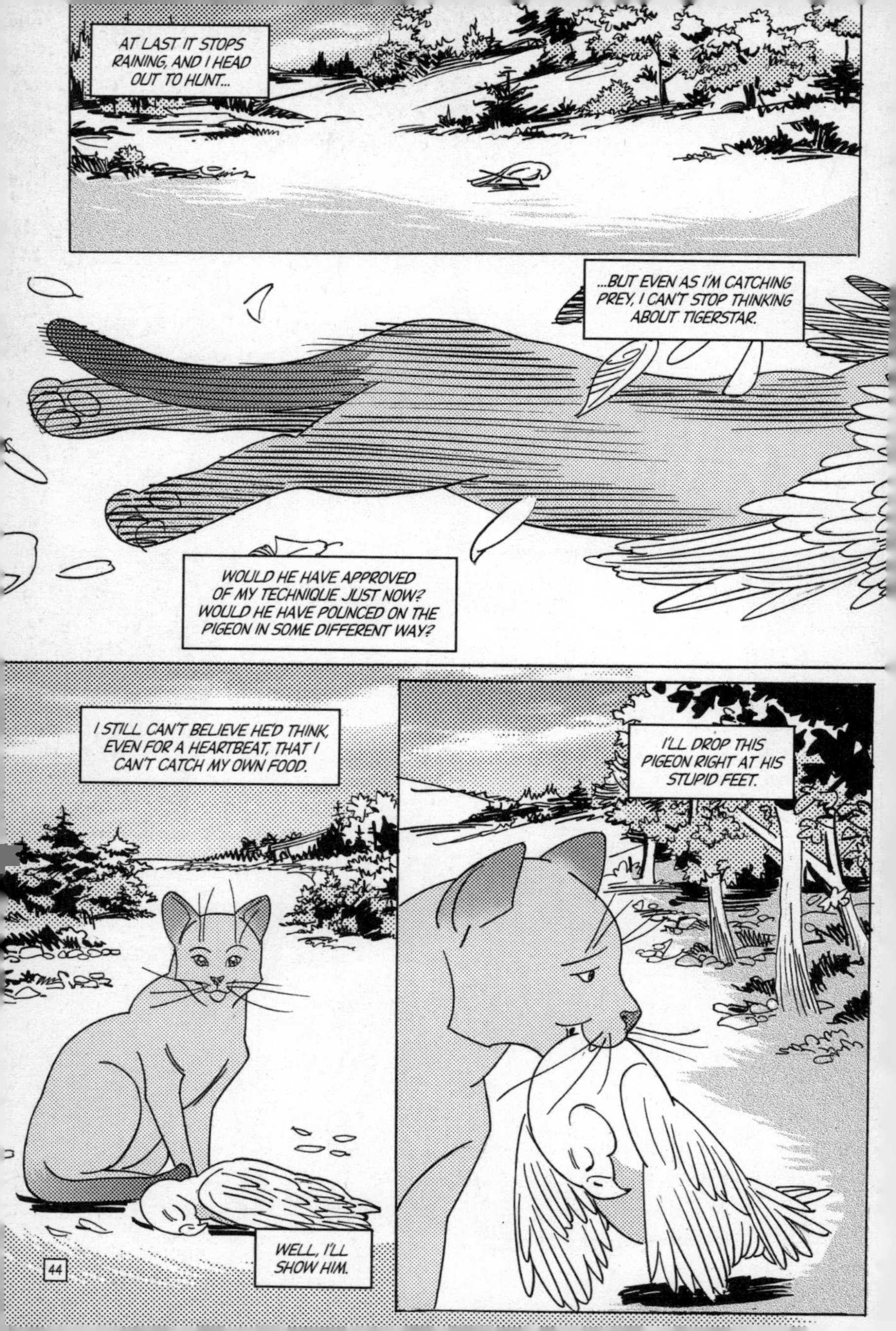
AT LAST IT STOPS RAINING, AND I HEAD OUT TO HUNT...
...BUT EVEN AS I'M CATCHING PREY, I CAN'T STOP THINKING ABOUT TIGERSTAR.
WOULD HE HAVE APPROVED OF MY TECHNIQUE JUST NOW? WOULD HE HAVE POUNCED ON THE PIGEON IN SOME DIFFERENT WAY?
I STILL CAN'T BELIEVE HE'D THINK, EVEN FOR A HEARTBEAT, THAT I CAN'T CATCH MY OWN FOOD.
WELL, I'LL SHOW HIM.
I'LL DROP THIS PIGEON RIGHT AT HIS STUPID FEET.

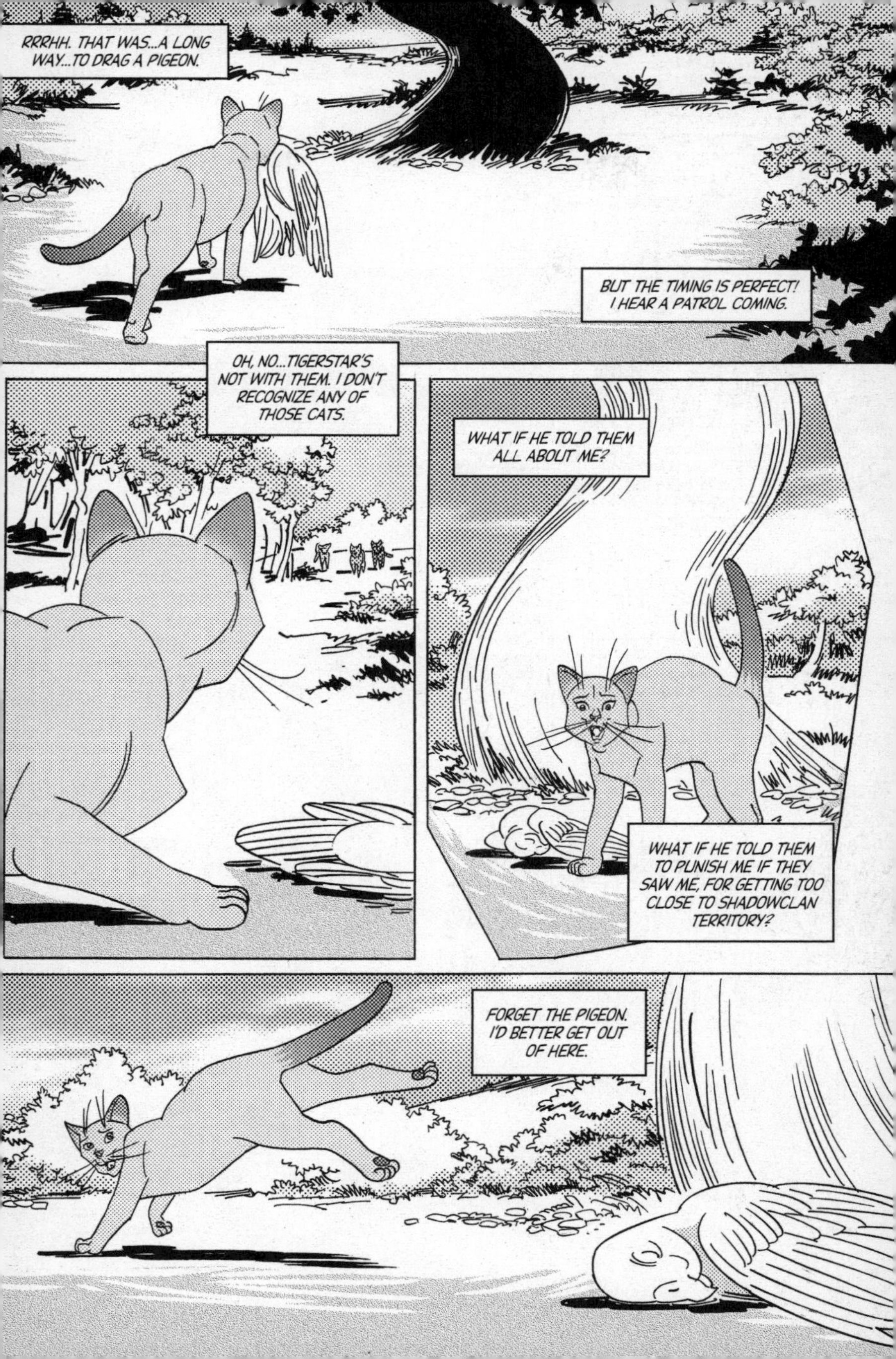
RRRHH. THAT WAS...A LONG WAY...TO DRAG A PIGEON.
BUT THE TIMING IS PERFECT! I HEAR A PATROL COMING.
OH, NO...TIGERSTAR'S NOT WITH THEM. I DON'T RECOGNIZE ANY OF THOSE CATS.
WHAT IF HE TOLD THEM ALL ABOUT ME?
WHAT IF HE TOLD THEM TO PUNISH ME IF THEY SAW ME, FOR GETTING TOO CLOSE TO SHADOWCLAN TERRITORY?
FORGET THE PIGEON. I'D BETTER GET OUT OF HERE.

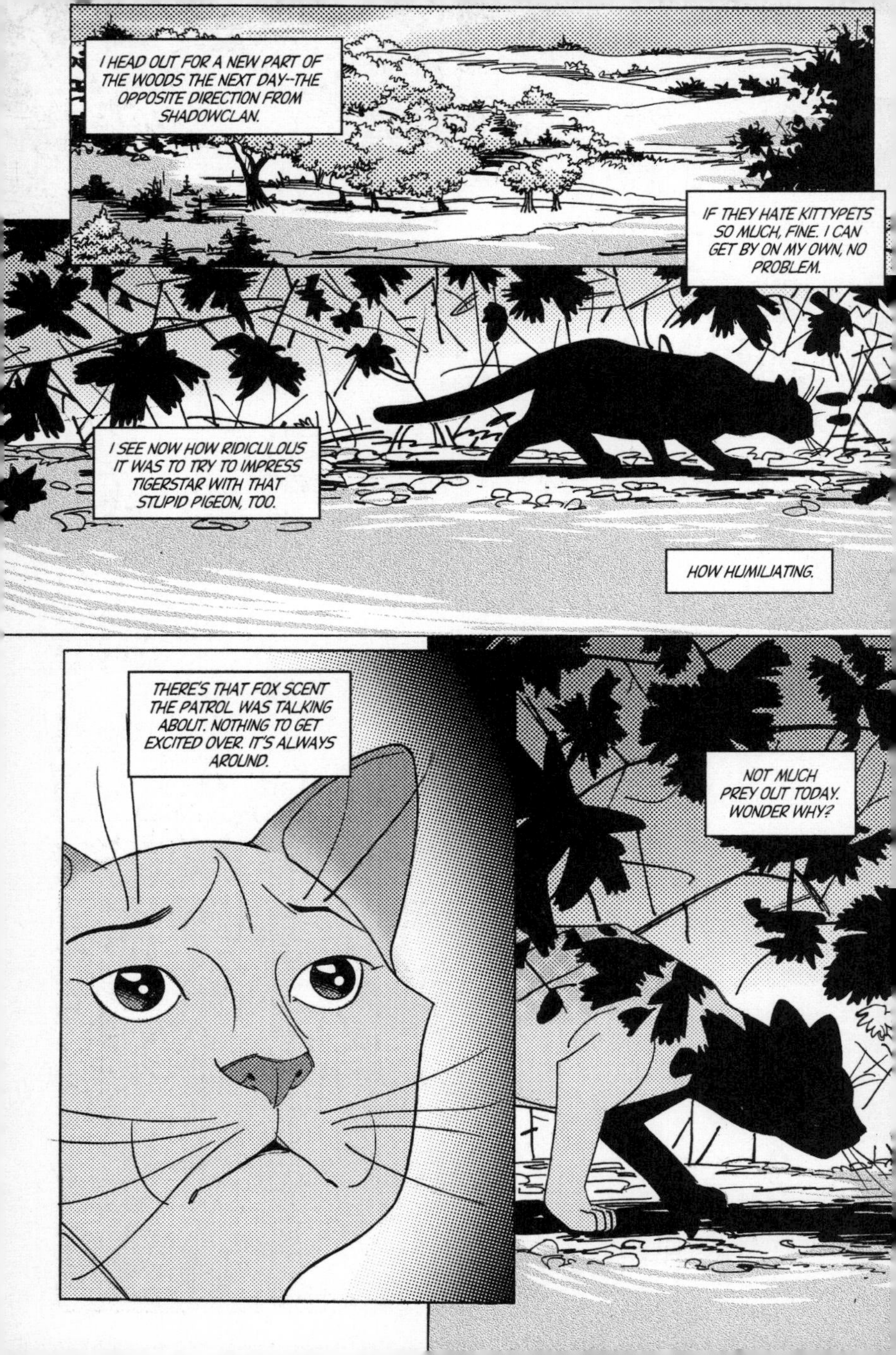
I HEAD OUT FOR A NEW PART OF THE WOODS THE NEXT DAY--THE OPPOSITE DIRECTION FROM SHADOWCLAN.
IF THEY HATE KITTYPETS SO MUCH, FINE. I CAN GET BY ON MY OWN, NO PROBLEM.
I SEE NOW HOW RIDICULOUS IT WAS TO TRY TO IMPRESS TIGERSTAR WITH THAT STUPID PIGEON, TOO.
HOW HUMILIATING.
THERE'S THAT FOX SCENT THE PATROL WAS TALKING ABOUT. NOTHING TO GET EXCITED OVER. IT'S ALWAYS AROUND.
NOT MUCH PREY OUT TODAY. WONDER WHY?

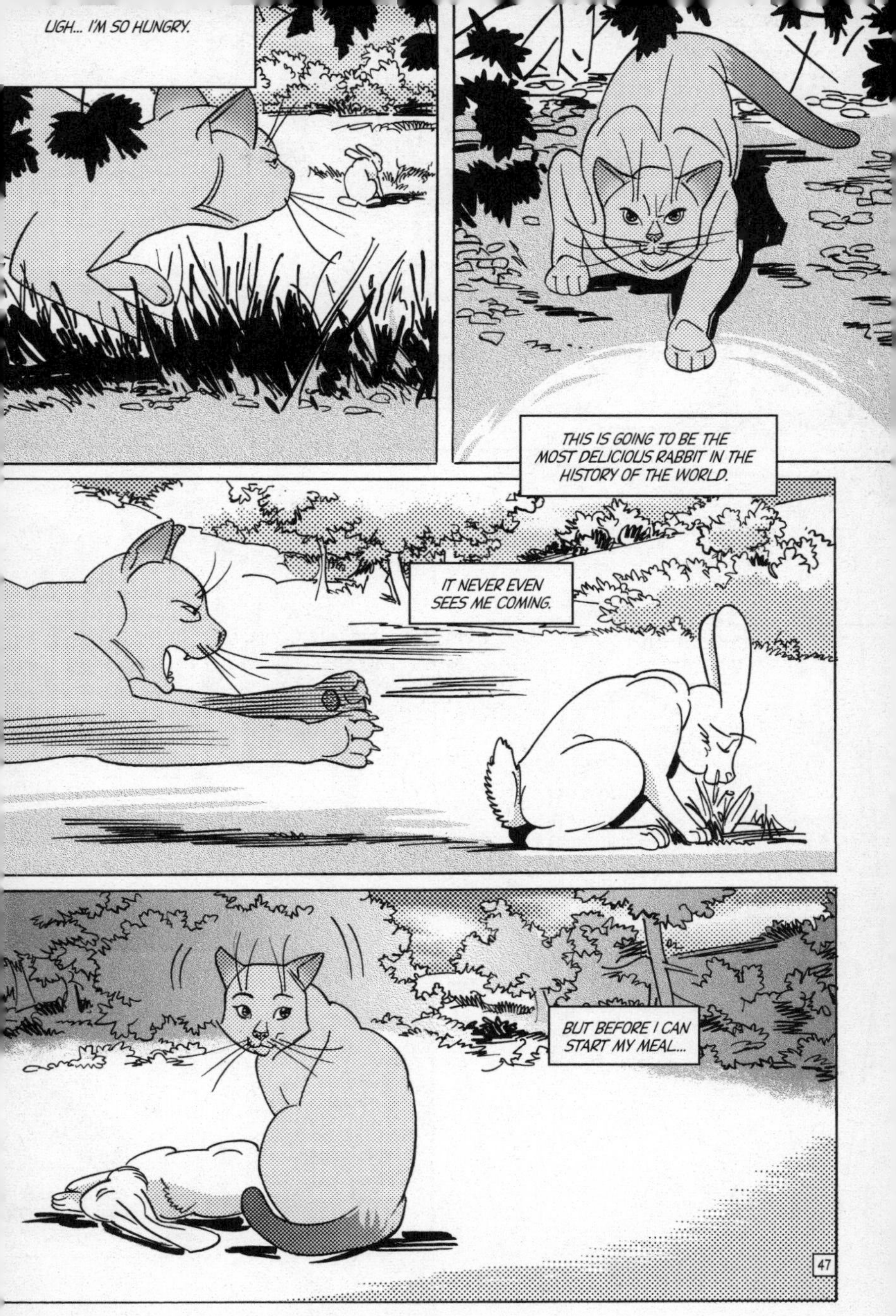
UGH... I'M SO HUNGRY.
THIS IS GOING TO BE THE MOST DELICIOUS RABBIT IN THE HISTORY OF THE WORLD.
IT NEVER EVEN SEES ME COMING.
BUT BEFORE I CAN START MY MEAL...

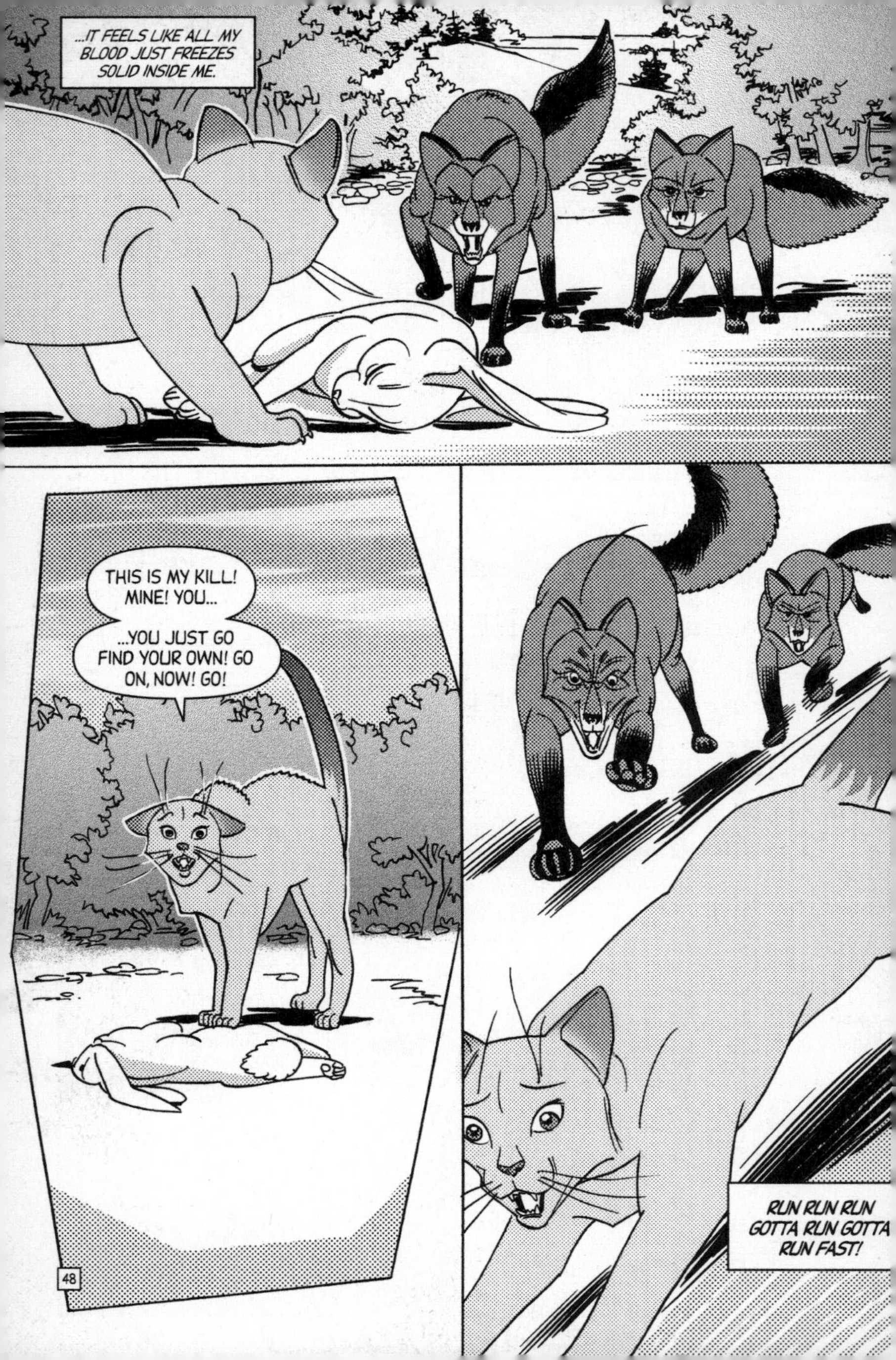
...IT FEELS LIKE ALL MY BLOOD JUST FREEZES SOLID INSIDE ME.
THIS IS MY KILL! MINE! YOU...
...YOU JUST GO FIND YOUR OWN! GO ON, NOW! GO!
RUN RUN RUN GOTTA RUN GOTTA RUN FAST!

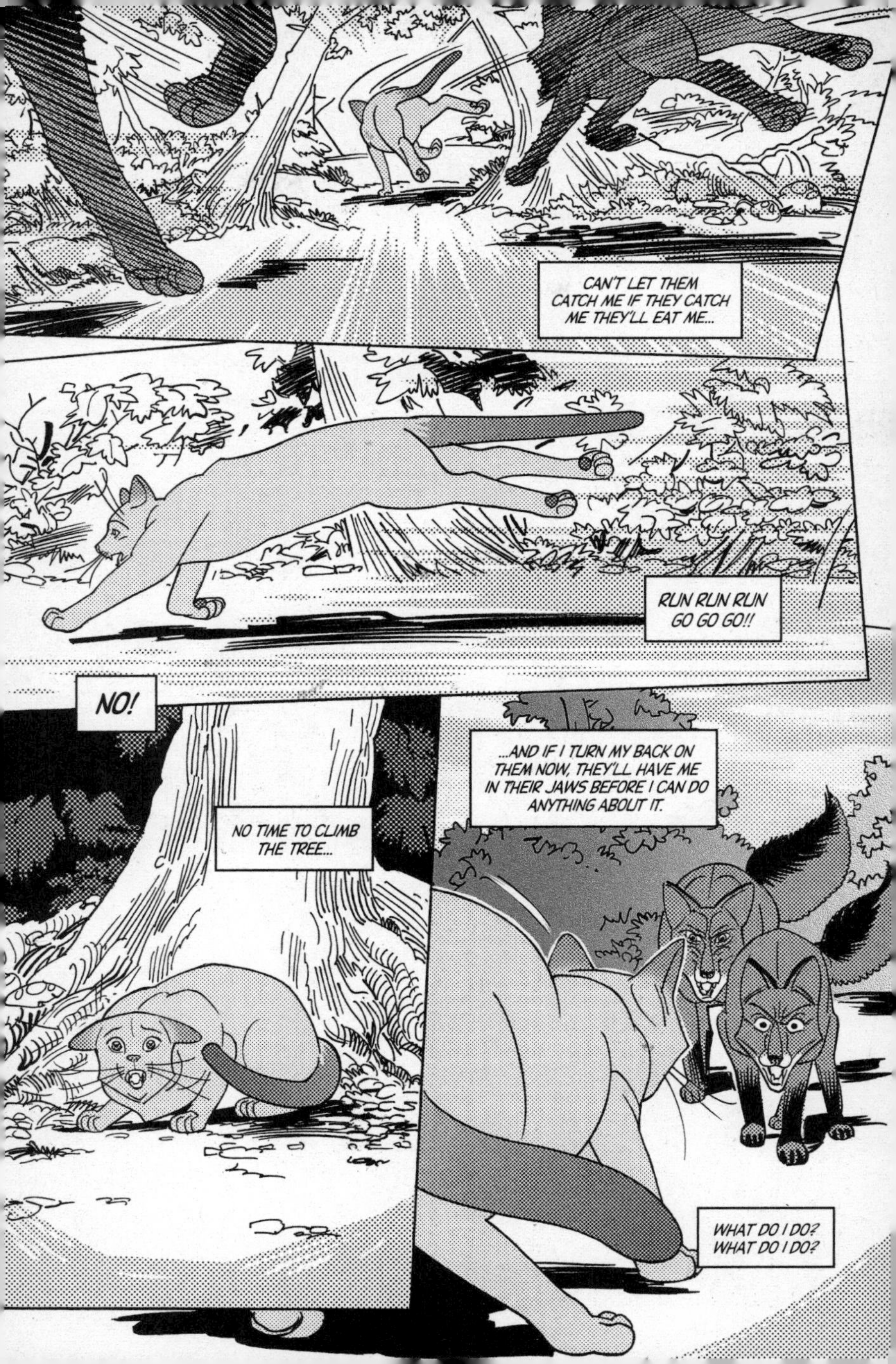
CAN'T LET THEM CATCH ME IF THEY CATCH ME THEY'LL EAT ME...
RUN RUN RUN GO GO GO!!
NO!
NO TIME TO CLIMB THE TREE...
...AND IF I TURN MY BACK ON THEM NOW, THEY'LL HAVE ME IN THEIR JAWS BEFORE I CAN DO ANYTHING ABOUT IT.
WHAT DO I DO? WHAT DO I DO?

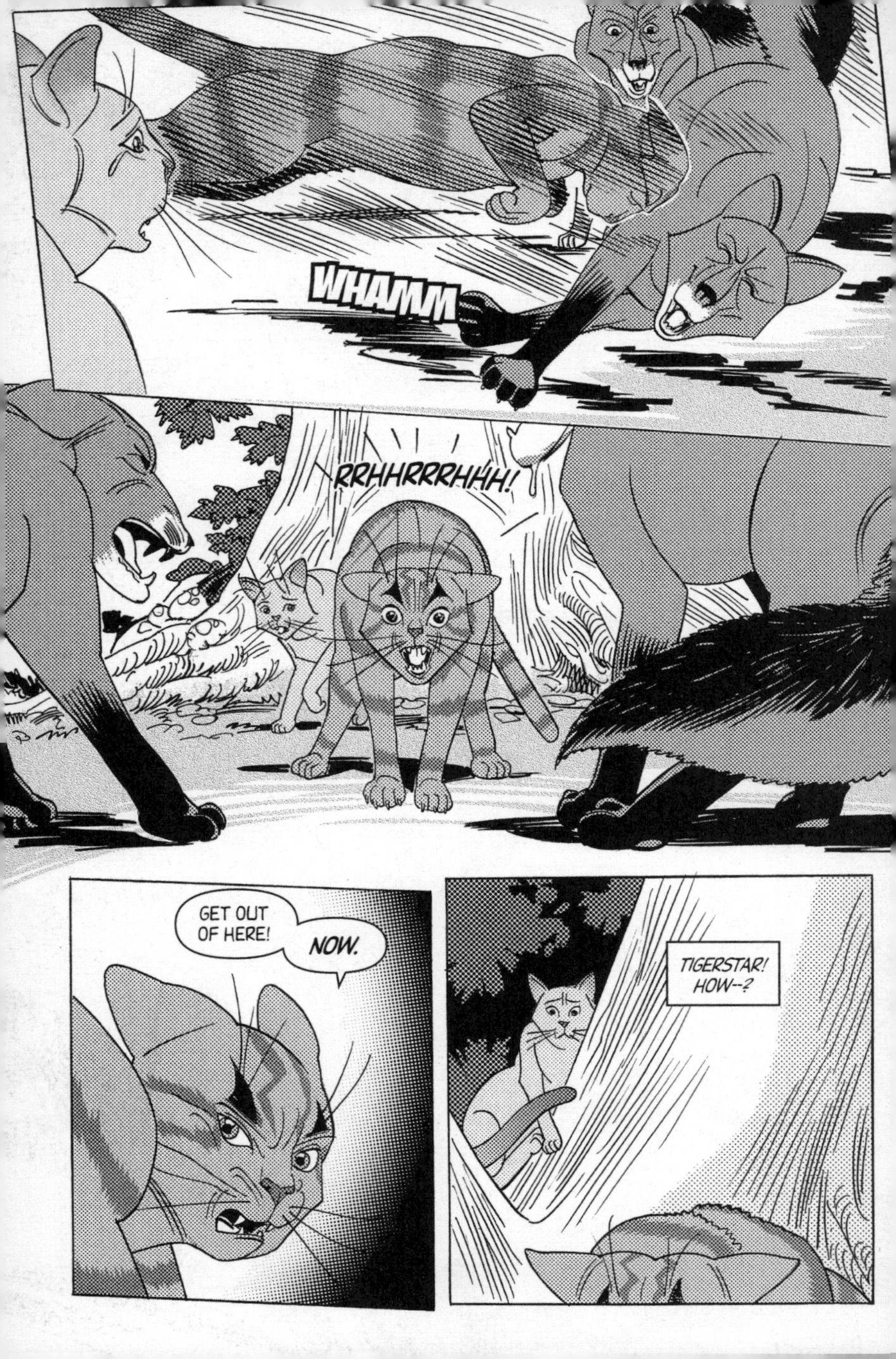
WHAMM
RRHHRRRHHH!
GET OUT OF HERE!
NOW.
TIGERSTAR! HOW--?

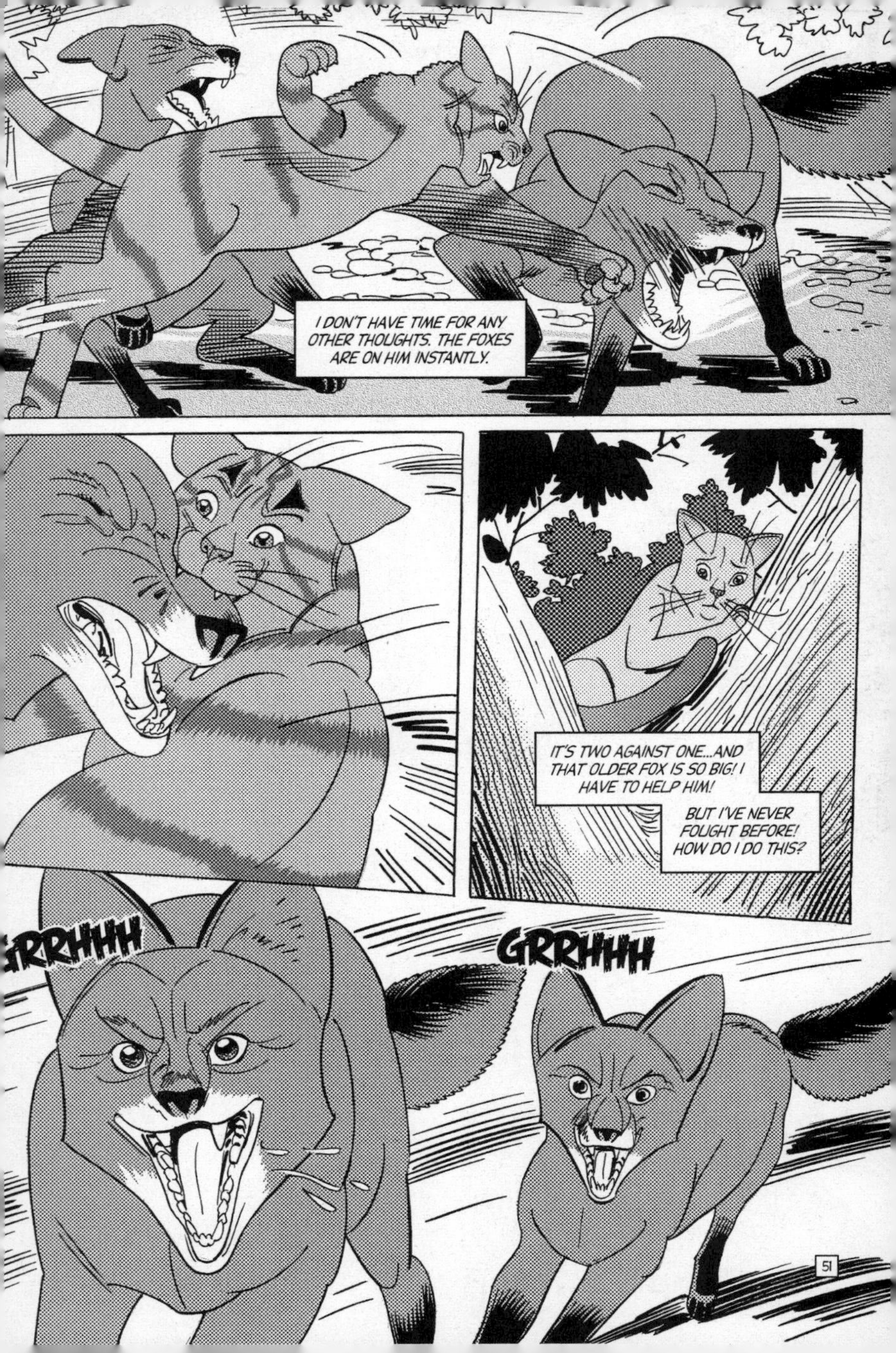

I DON'T HAVE TIME FOR ANY OTHER THOUGHTS. THE FOXES ARE ON HIM INSTANTLY.
IT'S TWO AGAINST ONE...AND THAT OLDER FOX IS SO BIG! I HAVE TO HELP HIM!
BUT I'VE NEVER FOUGHT BEFORE! HOW DO I DO THIS?
GRRHHH
GRRHHH

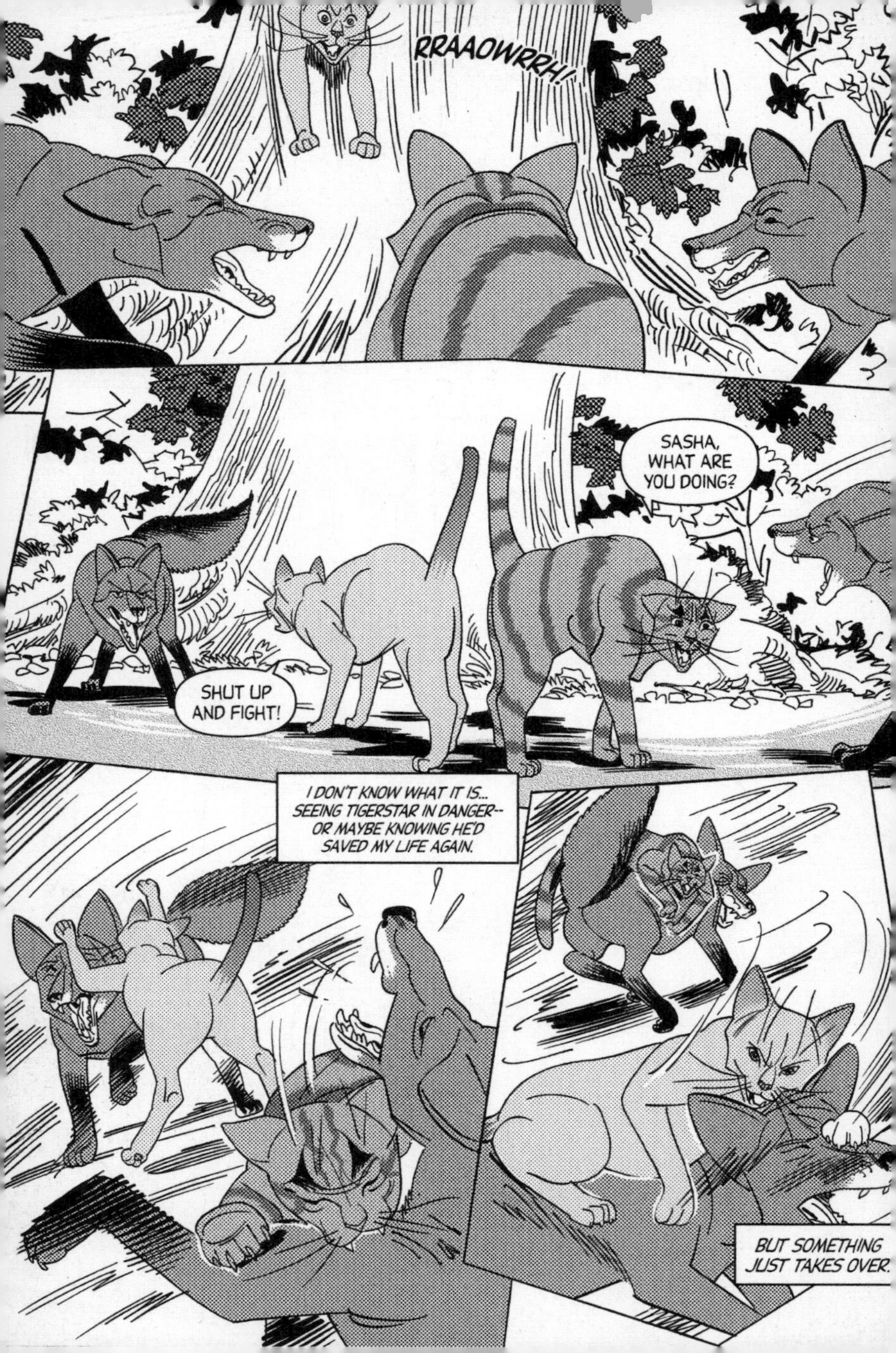
RRAAOWRRH!
SASHA, WHAT ARE YOU DOING?
SHUT UP AND FIGHT!
I DON'T KNOW WHAT IT IS... SEEING TIGERSTAR IN DANGER-- OR MAYBE KNOWING HE'D SAVED MY LIFE AGAIN.
BUT SOMETHING JUST TAKES OVER.

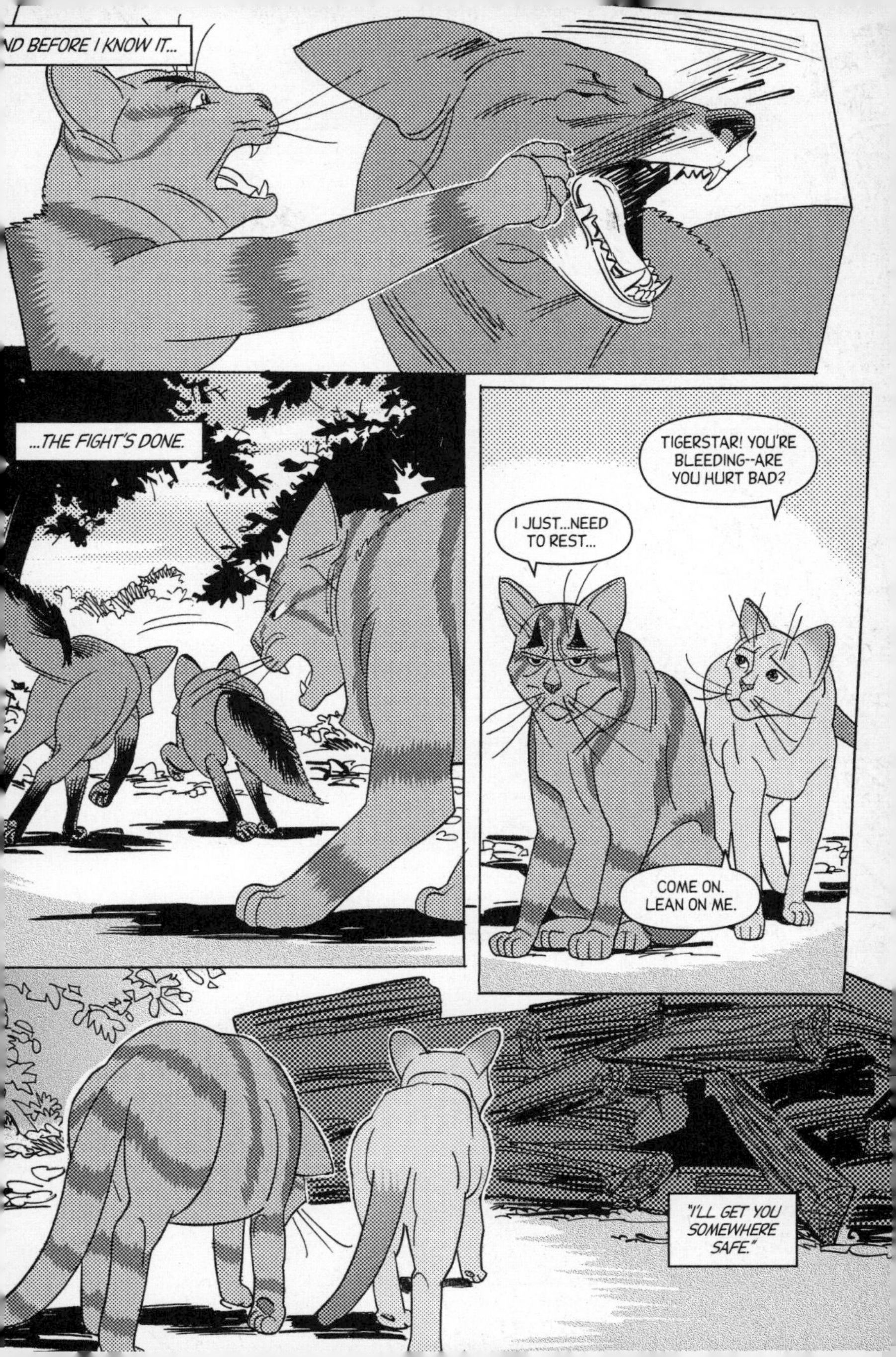

ND BEFORE I KNOW IT...
...THE FIGHT'S DONE.
TIGERSTAR! YOU'RE BLEEDING--ARE YOU HURT BAD?
I JUST...NEED TO REST...
COME ON. LEAN ON ME.
"I'LL GET YOU SOMEWHERE SAFE."

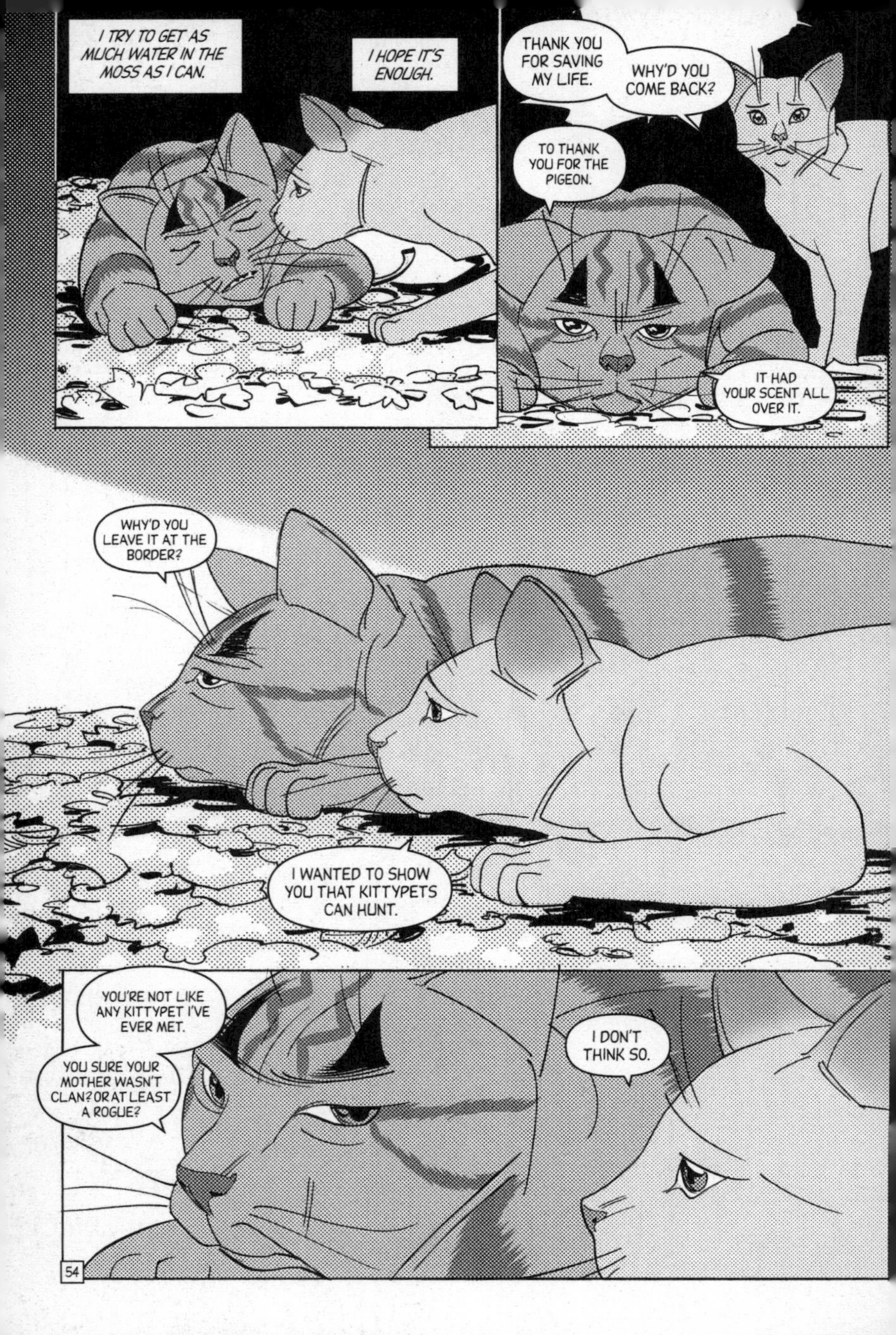
I TRY TO GET AS MUCH WATER IN THE MOSS AS I CAN.
I HOPE IT'S ENOUGH.
THANK YOU FOR SAVING MY LIFE.
WHY'D YOU COME BACK?
TO THANK YOU FOR THE PIGEON.
IT HAD YOUR SCENT ALL OVER IT.
WHY'D YOU LEAVE IT AT THE BORDER?
I WANTED TO SHOW YOU THAT KITTYPETS CAN HUNT.
YOU'RE NOT LIKE ANY KITTYPET I'VE EVER MET.
YOU SURE YOUR MOTHER WASN'T CLAN? OR AT LEAST A ROGUE?
I DON'T THINK SO.

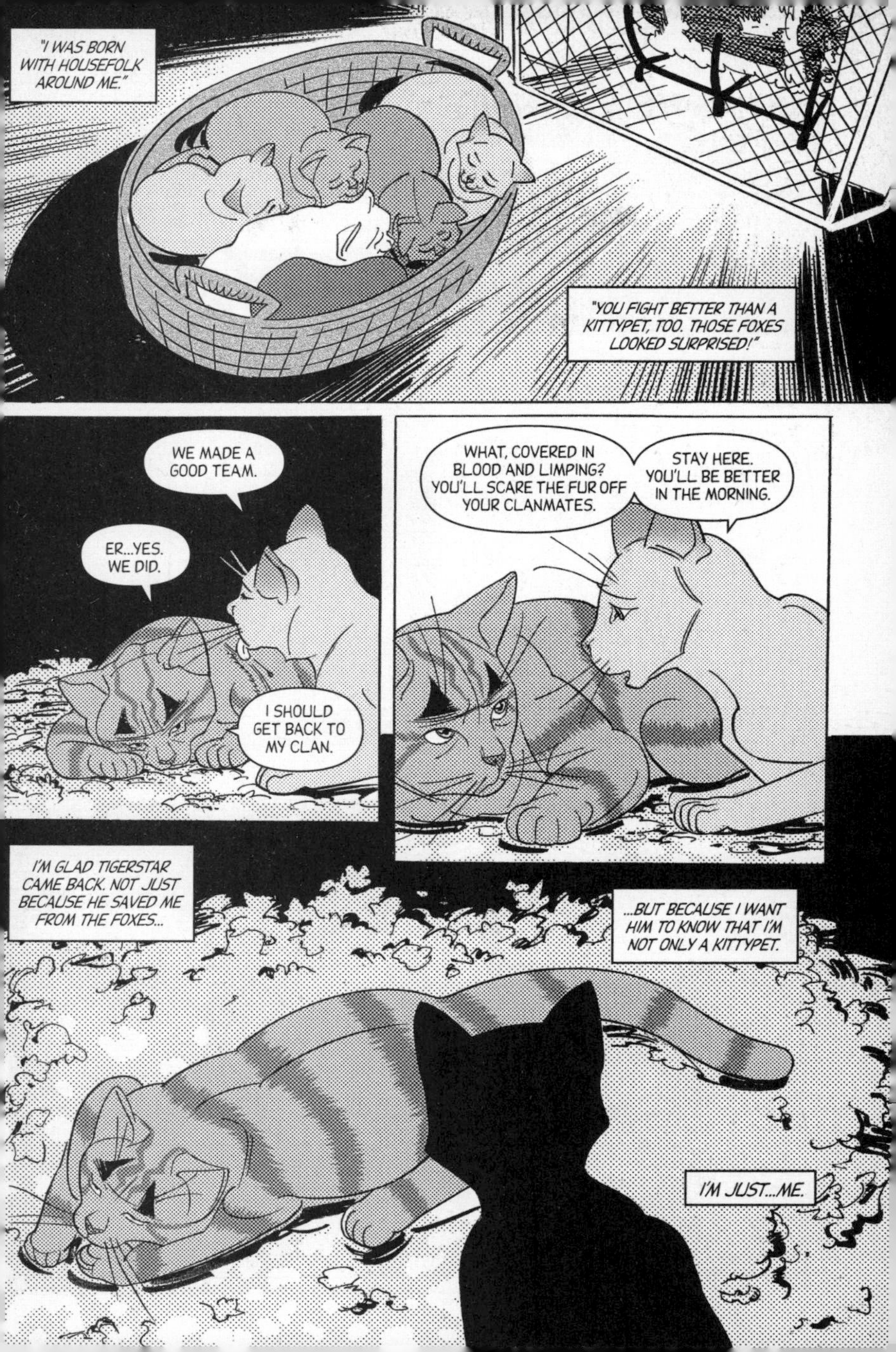
"I WAS BORN WITH HOUSEFOLK AROUND ME."
"YOU FIGHT BETTER THAN A KITTYPET, TOO. THOSE FOXES LOOKED SURPRISED!"
WE MADE A GOOD TEAM.
ER...YES. WE DID.
I SHOULD GET BACK TO MY CLAN.
WHAT, COVERED IN BLOOD AND LIMPING? YOU'LL SCARE THE FUR OFF YOUR CLANMATES.
STAY HERE. YOU'LL BE BETTER IN THE MORNING.
I'M GLAD TIGERSTAR CAME BACK. NOT JUST BECAUSE HE SAVED ME FROM THE FOXES...
...BUT BECAUSE I WANT HIM TO KNOW THAT I'M NOT ONLY A KITTYPET.
I'M JUST...ME.

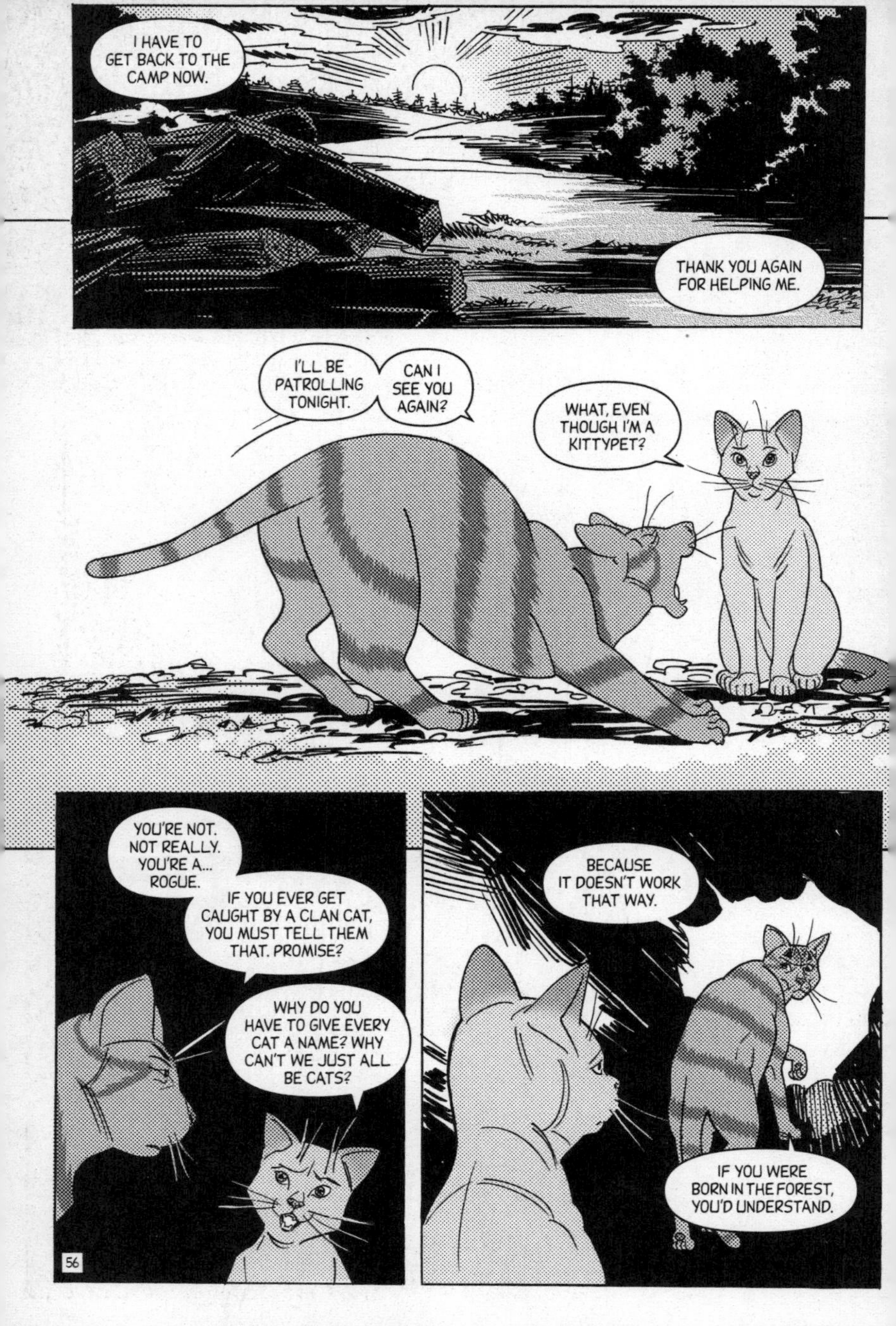
I HAVE TO GET BACK TO THE CAMP NOW.
THANK YOU AGAIN FOR HELPING ME.
I'LL BE PATROLLING TONIGHT.
CAN I SEE YOU AGAIN?
WHAT, EVEN THOUGH I'M A KITTYPET?
YOU'RE NOT. NOT REALLY. YOU'RE A... ROGUE.
IF YOU EVER GET CAUGHT BY A CLAN CAT, YOU MUST TELL THEM THAT. PROMISE?
WHY DO YOU HAVE TO GIVE EVERY CAT A NAME? WHY CAN'T WE JUST ALL BE CATS?
BECAUSE IT DOESN'T WORK THAT WAY.
IF YOU WERE BORN IN THE FOREST, YOU'D UNDERSTAND.

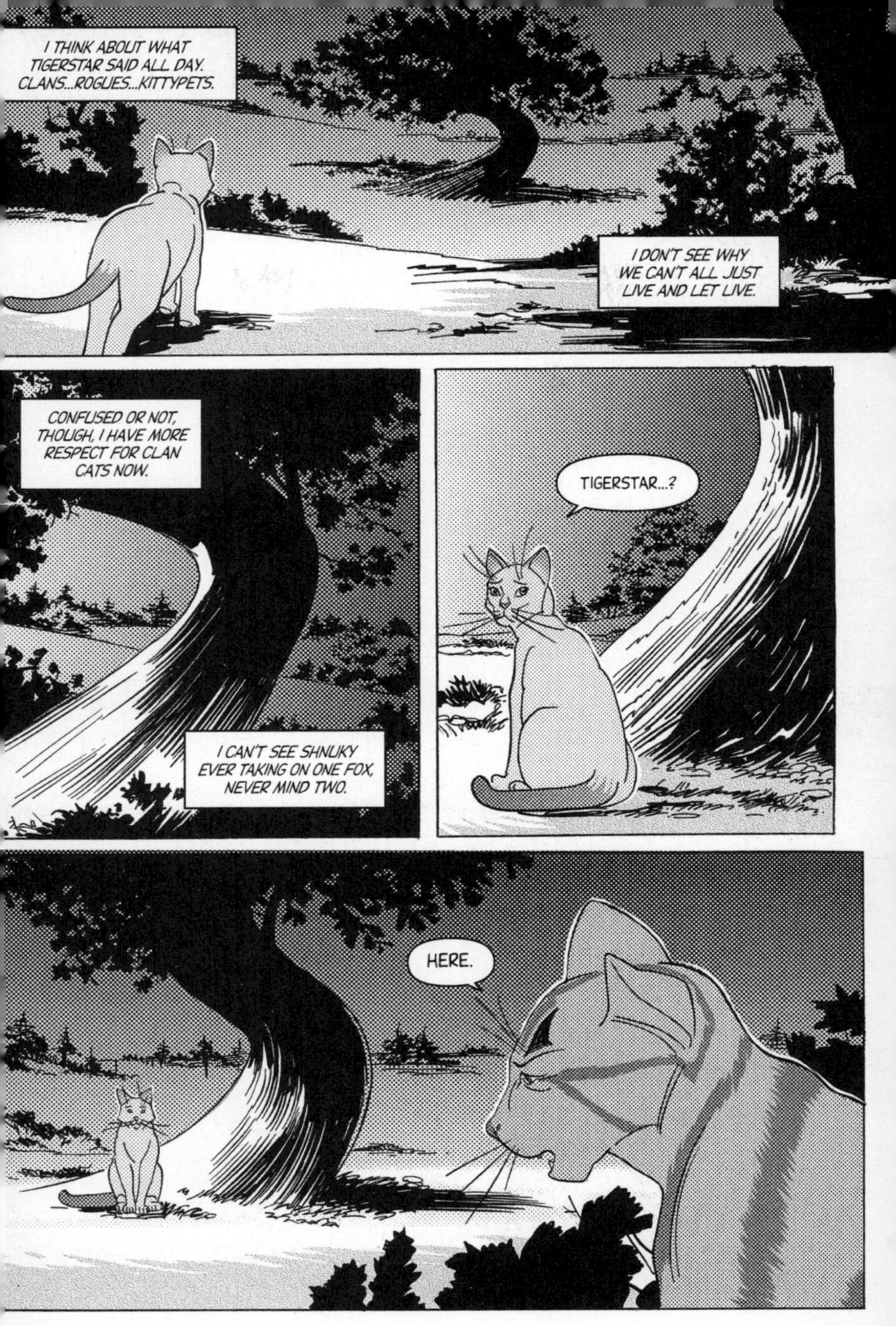
I THINK ABOUT WHAT TIGERSTAR SAID ALL DAY. CLANS...ROGUES...KITTYPETS.
I DON'T SEE WHY WE CAN'T ALL JUST LIVE AND LET LIVE.
CONFUSED OR NOT, THOUGH, I HAVE MORE RESPECT FOR CLAN CATS NOW.
I CAN'T SEE SHNUKY EVER TAKING ON ONE FOX, NEVER MIND TWO.
TIGERSTAR...?
HERE.

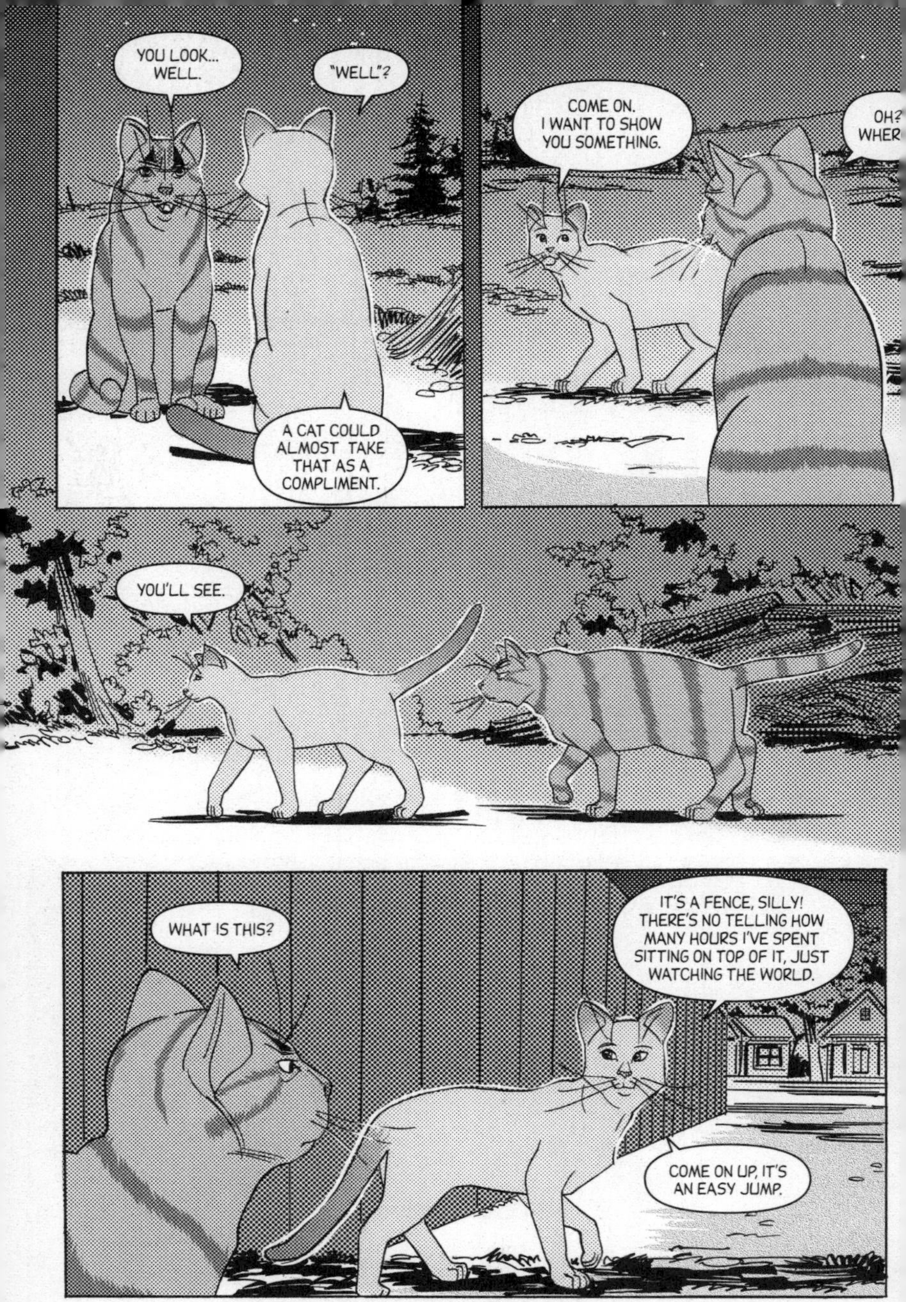
YOU LOOK... WELL.
"WELL"?
A CAT COULD ALMOST TAKE THAT AS A COMPLIMENT.
COME ON. I WANT TO SHOW YOU SOMETHING.
OH? WHER
YOU'LL SEE.
WHAT IS THIS?
IT'S A FENCE, SILLY! THERE'S NO TELLING HOW MANY HOURS I'VE SPENT SITTING ON TOP OF IT, JUST WATCHING THE WORLD.
COME ON UP, IT'S AN EASY JUMP.

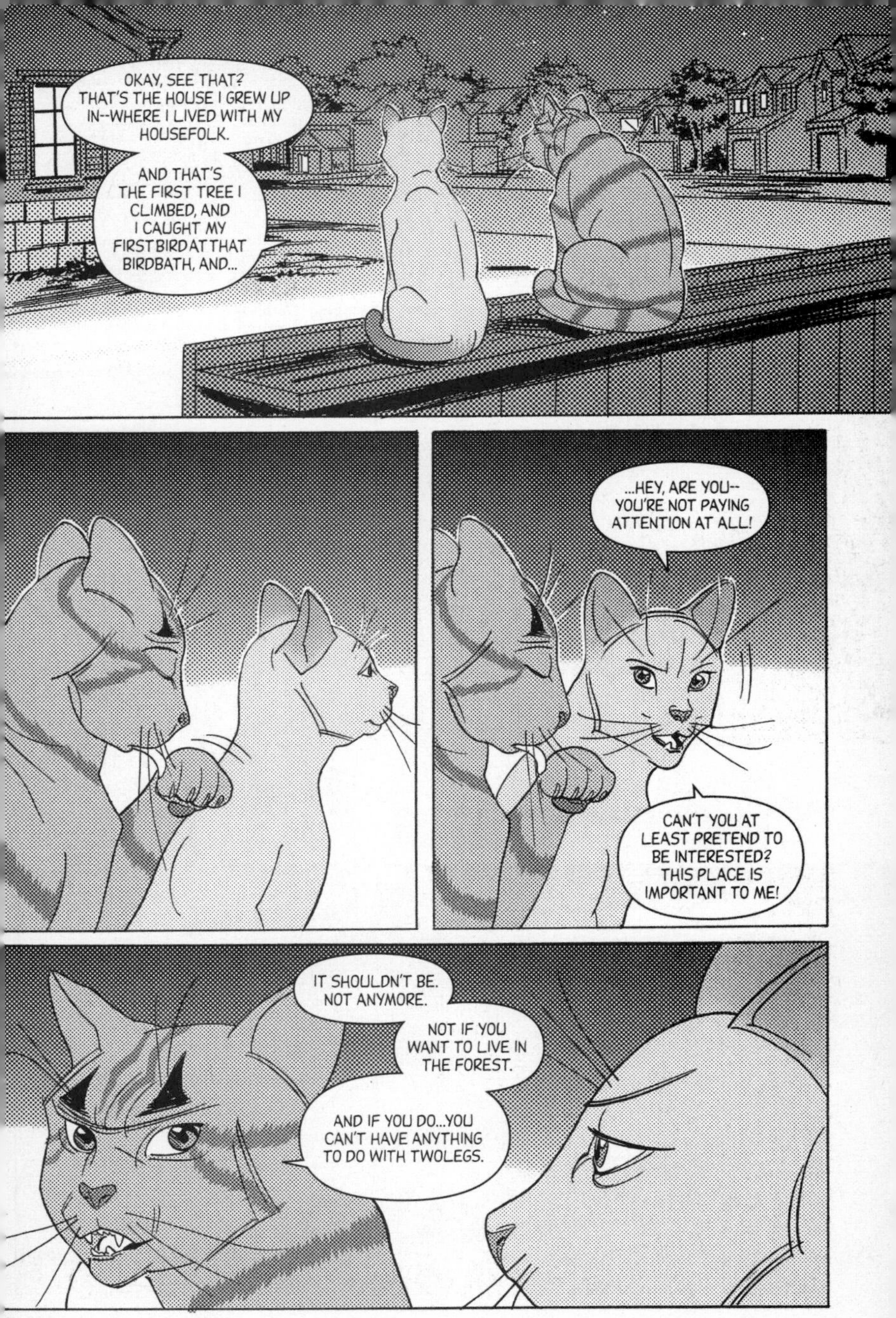
OKAY, SEE THAT? THAT'S THE HOUSE I GREW UP IN--WHERE I LIVED WITH MY HOUSEFOLK.
AND THAT'S THE FIRST TREE I CLIMBED, AND I CAUGHT MY FIRST BIRD AT THAT BIRDBATH, AND...
...HEY, ARE YOU-- YOU'RE NOT PAYING ATTENTION AT ALL!
CAN'T YOU AT LEAST PRETEND TO BE INTERESTED? THIS PLACE IS IMPORTANT TO ME!
IT SHOULDN'T BE. NOT ANYMORE.
NOT IF YOU WANT TO LIVE IN THE FOREST.
AND IF YOU DO...YOU CAN'T HAVE ANYTHING TO DO WITH TWOLEGS.

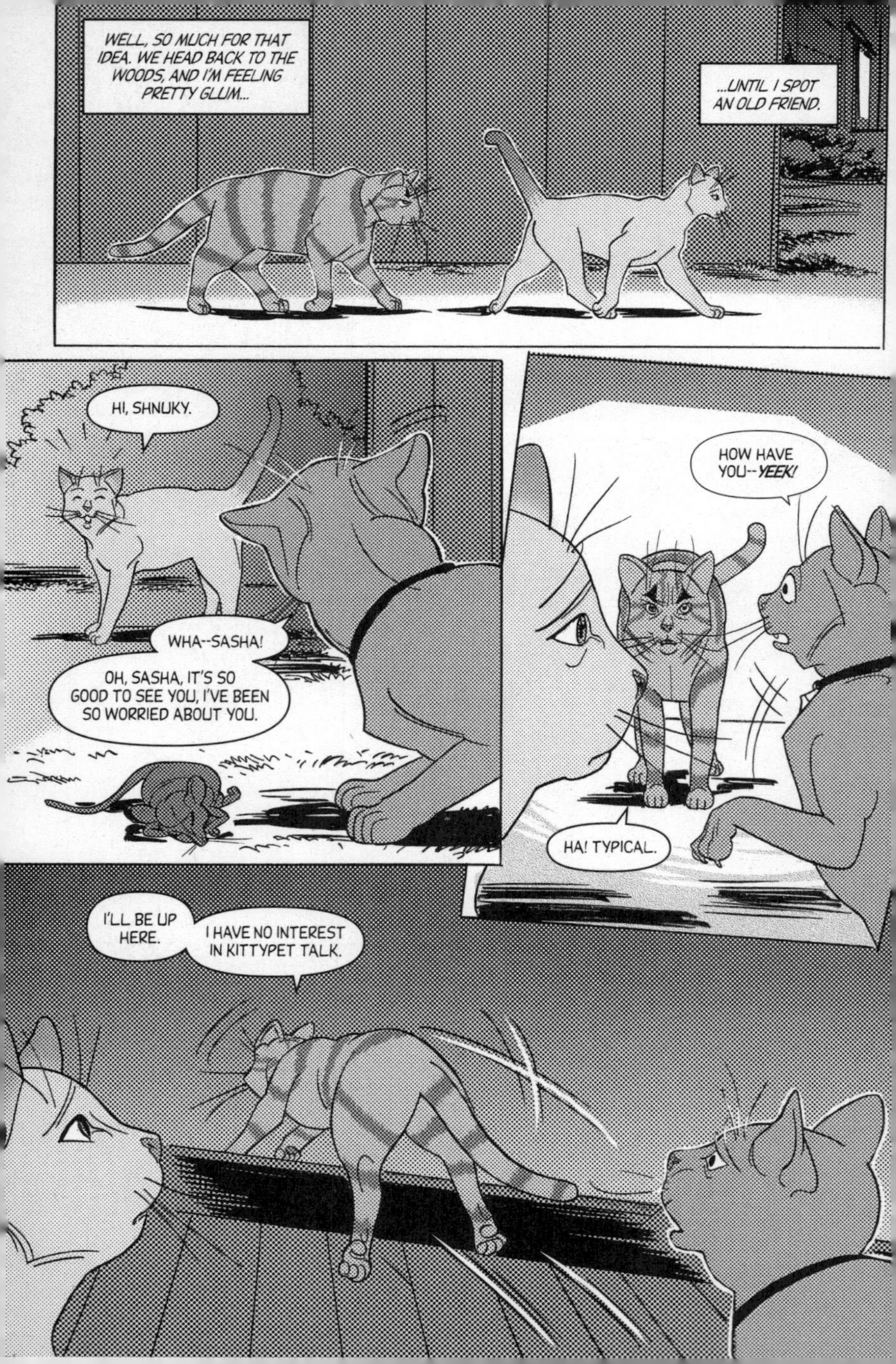
WELL, SO MUCH FOR THAT IDEA. WE HEAD BACK TO THE WOODS, AND I'M FEELING PRETTY GLUM...
...UNTIL I SPOT AN OLD FRIEND.
HI, SHNUKY.
WHA--SASHA!
OH, SASHA, IT'S SO GOOD TO SEE YOU, I'VE BEEN SO WORRIED ABOUT YOU.
HOW HAVE YOU--*YEEK!*
HA! TYPICAL.
I'LL BE UP HERE.
I HAVE NO INTEREST IN KITTYPET TALK.

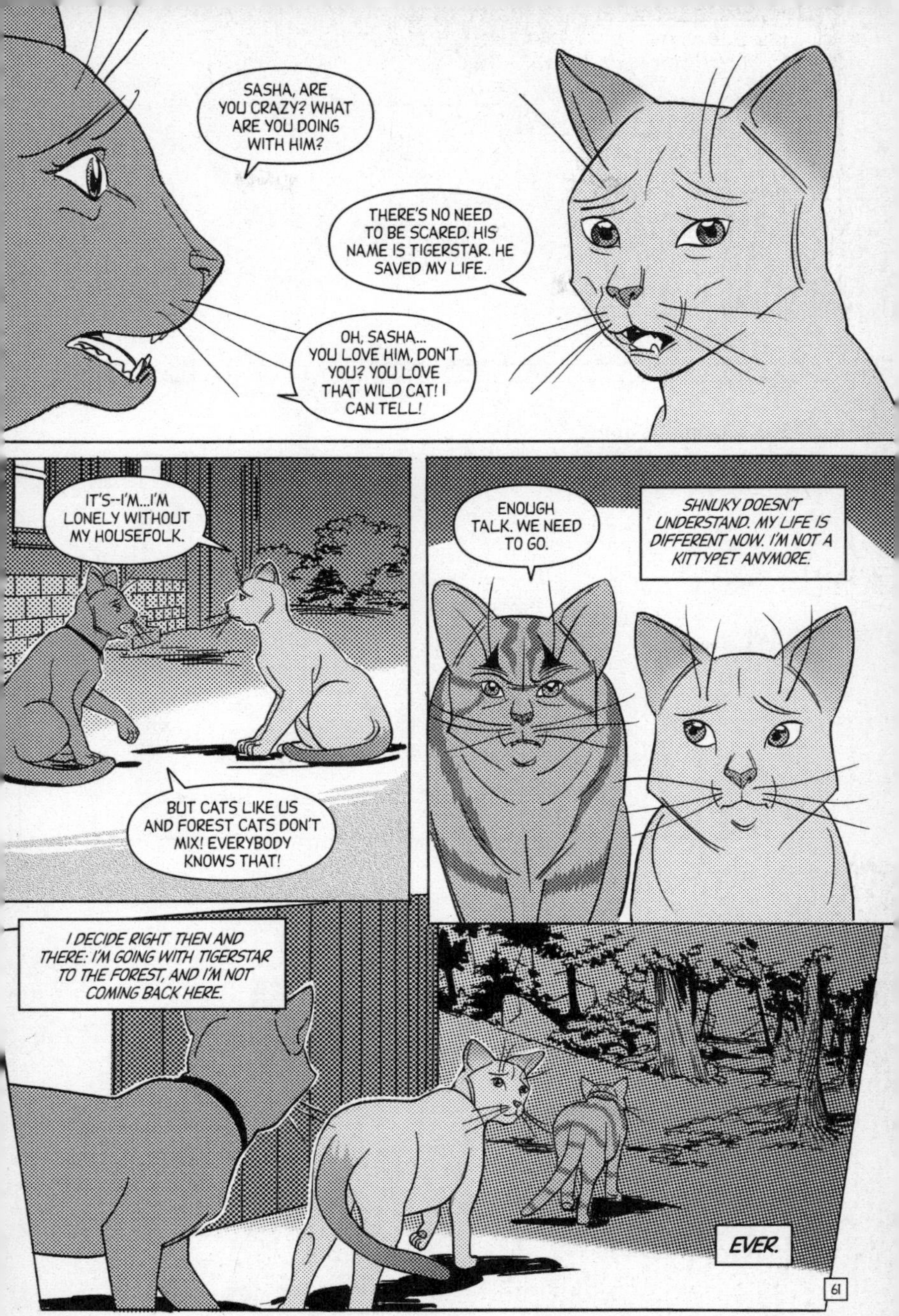

SASHA, ARE YOU CRAZY? WHAT ARE YOU DOING WITH HIM?
THERE'S NO NEED TO BE SCARED. HIS NAME IS TIGERSTAR. HE SAVED MY LIFE.
OH, SASHA... YOU LOVE HIM, DON'T YOU? YOU LOVE THAT WILD CAT! I CAN TELL!
IT'S--I'M...I'M LONELY WITHOUT MY HOUSEFOLK.
BUT CATS LIKE US AND FOREST CATS DON'T MIX! EVERYBODY KNOWS THAT!
ENOUGH TALK. WE NEED TO GO.
SHNUKY DOESN'T UNDERSTAND. MY LIFE IS DIFFERENT NOW. I'M NOT A KITTYPET ANYMORE.
I DECIDE RIGHT THEN AND THERE: I'M GOING WITH TIGERSTAR TO THE FOREST, AND I'M NOT COMING BACK HERE.
EVER.

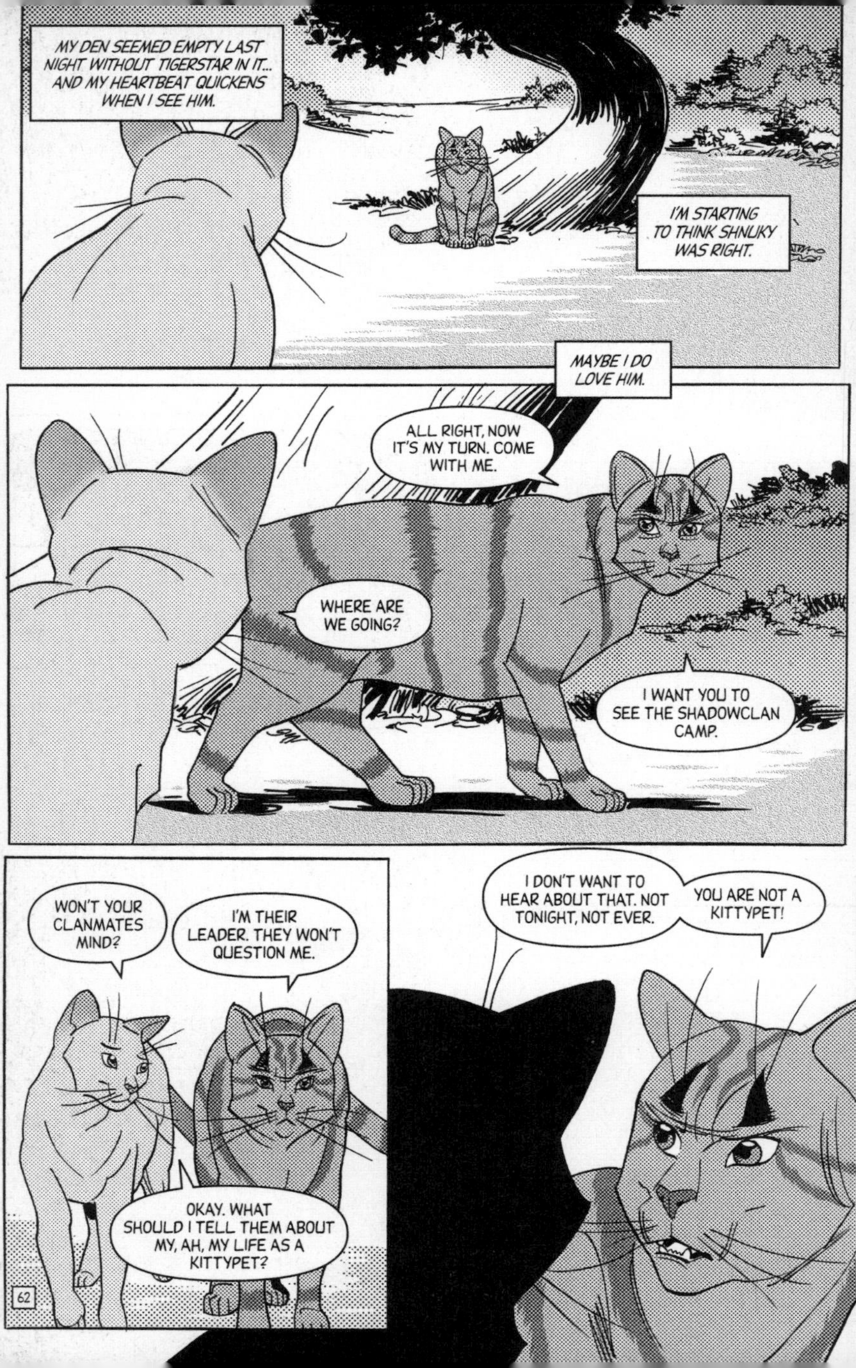

MY DEN SEEMED EMPTY LAST NIGHT WITHOUT TIGERSTAR IN IT... AND MY HEARTBEAT QUICKENS WHEN I SEE HIM.
I'M STARTING TO THINK SHNUKY WAS RIGHT.
MAYBE I DO LOVE HIM.
ALL RIGHT, NOW IT'S MY TURN. COME WITH ME.
WHERE ARE WE GOING?
I WANT YOU TO SEE THE SHADOWCLAN CAMP.
WON'T YOUR CLANMATES MIND?
I'M THEIR LEADER. THEY WON'T QUESTION ME.
OKAY. WHAT SHOULD I TELL THEM ABOUT MY, AH, MY LIFE AS A KITTYPET?
I DON'T WANT TO HEAR ABOUT THAT. NOT TONIGHT, NOT EVER.
YOU ARE NOT A KITTYPET!

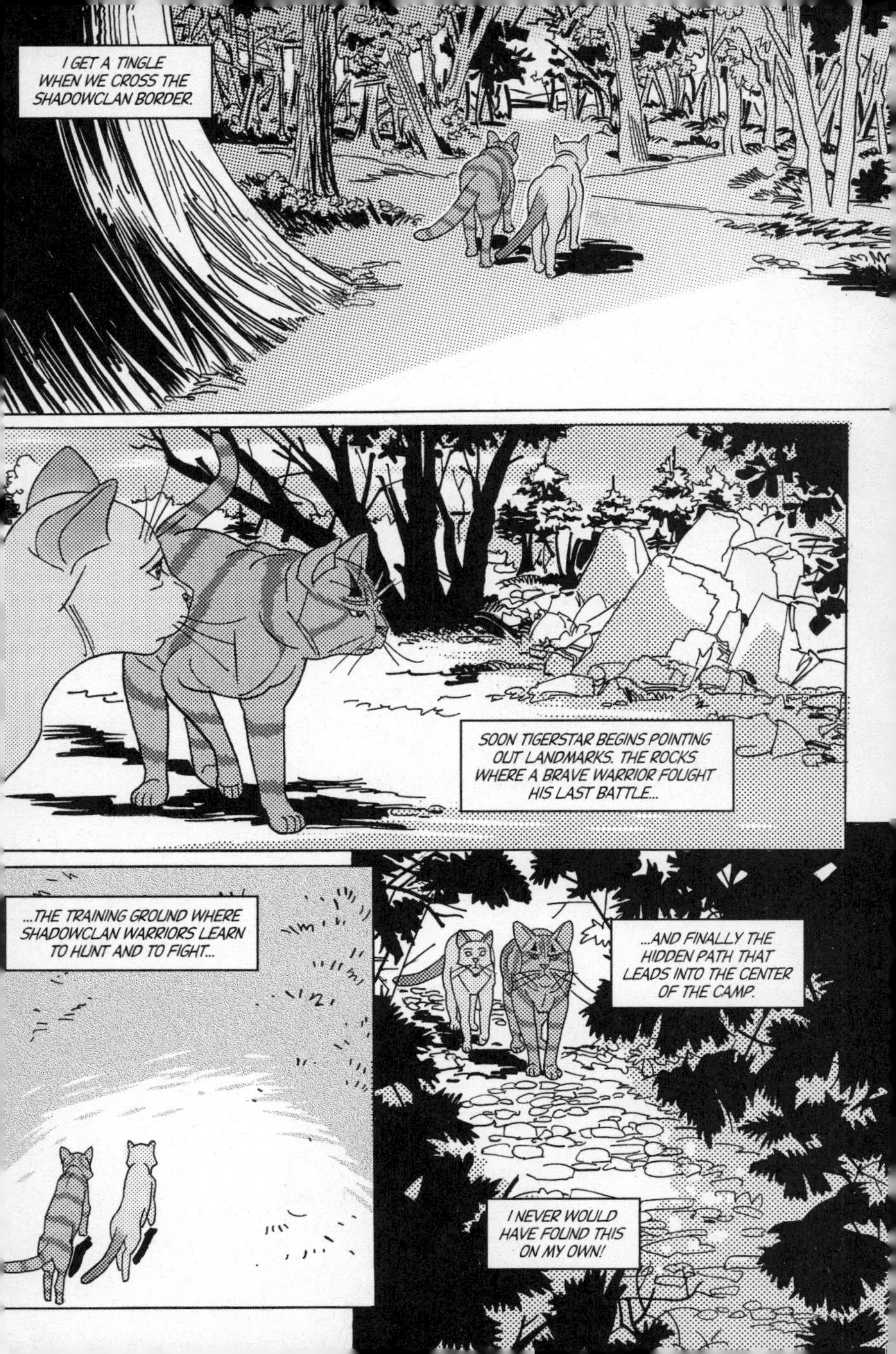
I GET A TINGLE WHEN WE CROSS THE SHADOWCLAN BORDER.
SOON TIGERSTAR BEGINS POINTING OUT LANDMARKS. THE ROCKS WHERE A BRAVE WARRIOR FOUGHT HIS LAST BATTLE...
...THE TRAINING GROUND WHERE SHADOWCLAN WARRIORS LEARN TO HUNT AND TO FIGHT...
...AND FINALLY THE HIDDEN PATH THAT LEADS INTO THE CENTER OF THE CAMP.
I NEVER WOULD HAVE FOUND THIS ON MY OWN!

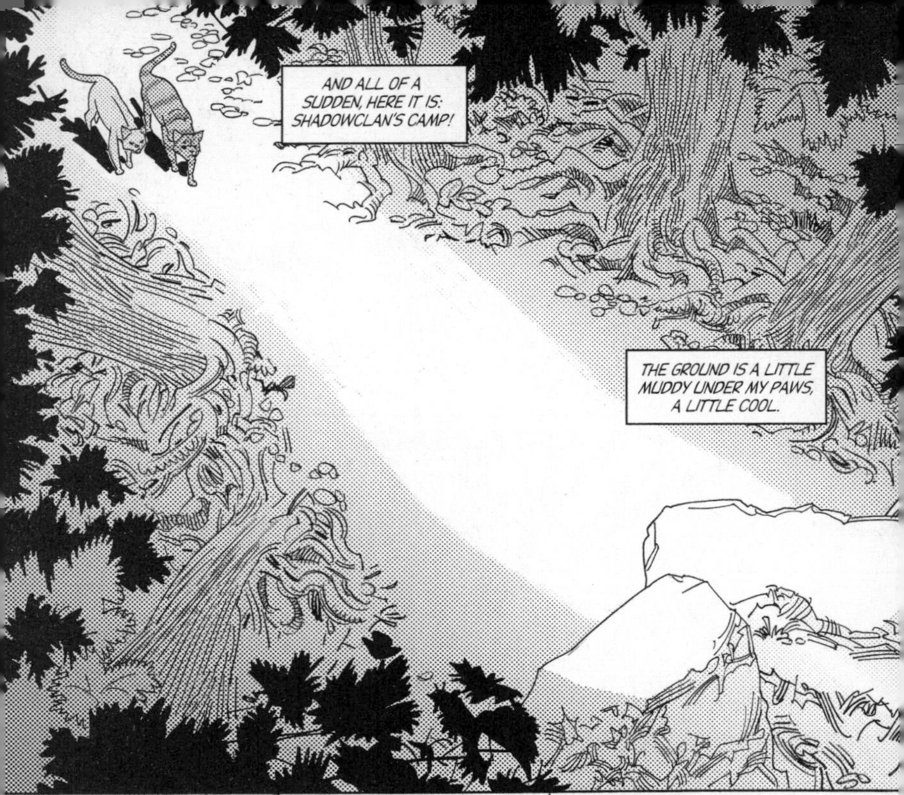
AND ALL OF A SUDDEN, HERE IT IS: SHADOWCLAN'S CAMP!
THE GROUND IS A LITTLE MUDDY UNDER MY PAWS, A LITTLE COOL.
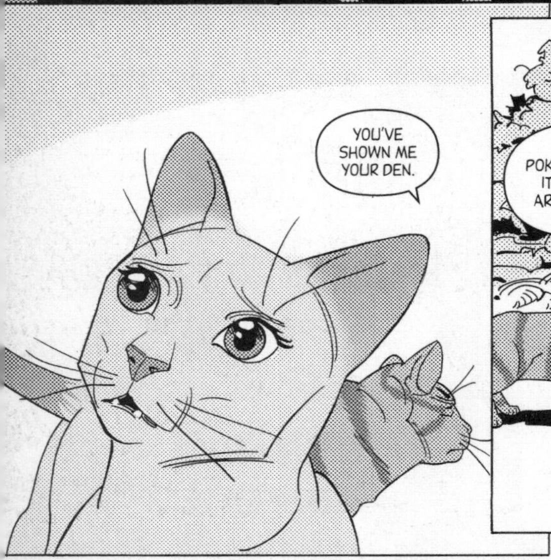
YOU'VE SHOWN ME YOUR DEN.
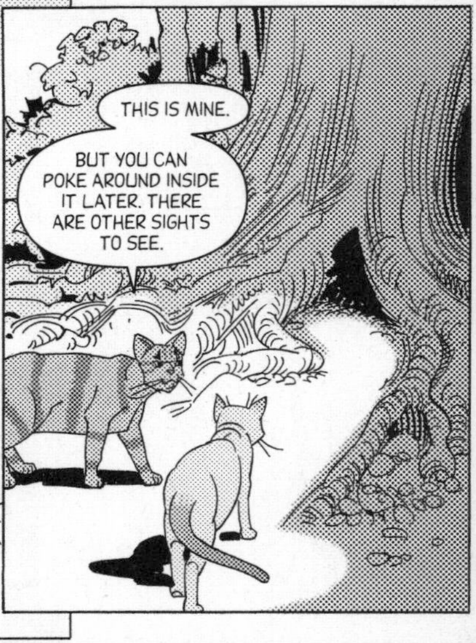
THIS IS MINE.
BUT YOU CAN POKE AROUND INSIDE IT LATER. THERE ARE OTHER SIGHTS TO SEE.

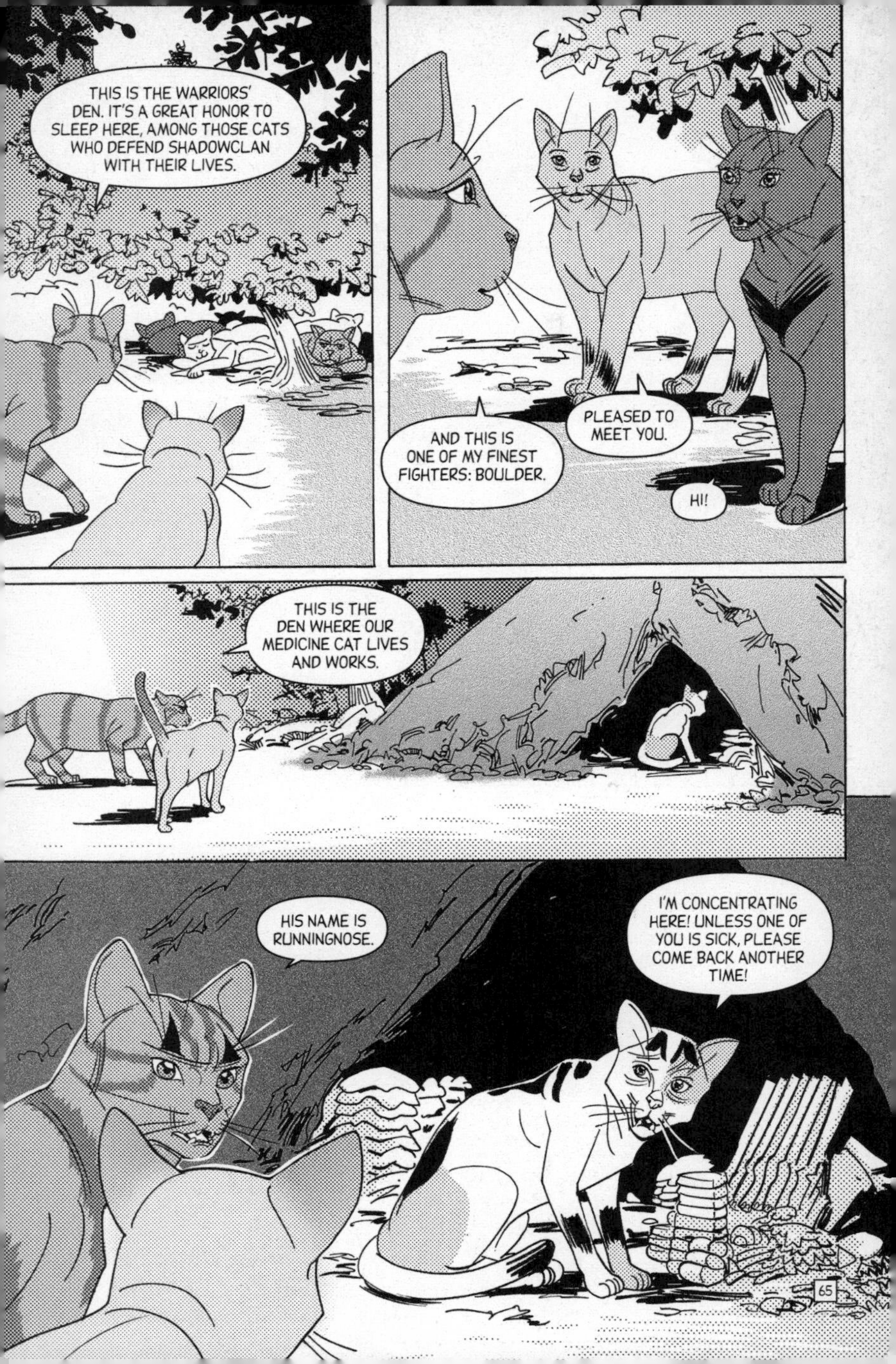
THIS IS THE WARRIORS' DEN. IT'S A GREAT HONOR TO SLEEP HERE, AMONG THOSE CATS WHO DEFEND SHADOWCLAN WITH THEIR LIVES.
AND THIS IS ONE OF MY FINEST FIGHTERS: BOULDER.
PLEASED TO MEET YOU.
HI!
THIS IS THE DEN WHERE OUR MEDICINE CAT LIVES AND WORKS.
HIS NAME IS RUNNINGNOSE.
I'M CONCENTRATING HERE! UNLESS ONE OF YOU IS SICK, PLEASE COME BACK ANOTHER TIME!

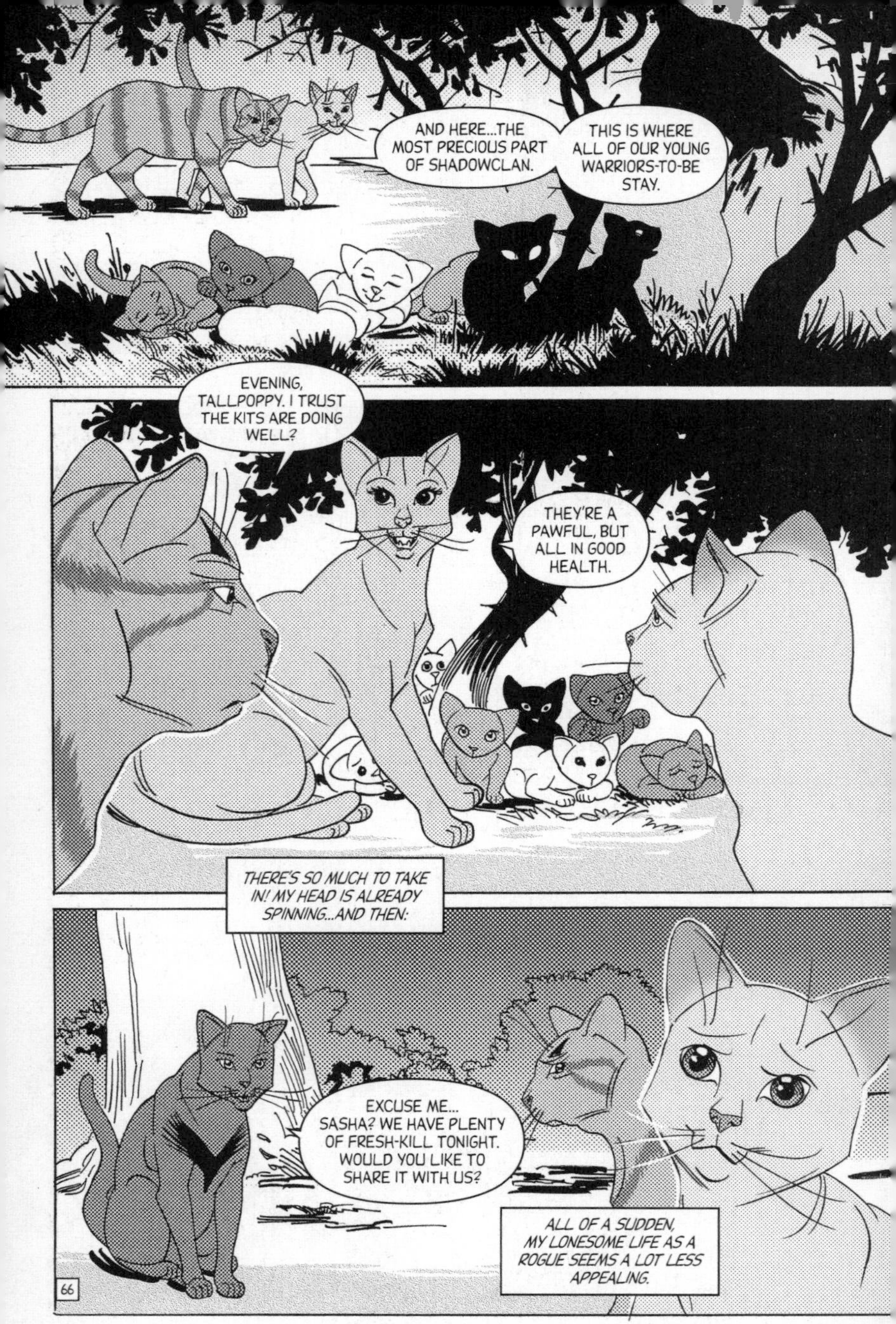
AND HERE...THE MOST PRECIOUS PART OF SHADOWCLAN.
THIS IS WHERE ALL OF OUR YOUNG WARRIORS-TO-BE STAY.
EVENING, TALLPOPPY. I TRUST THE KITS ARE DOING WELL?
THEY'RE A PAWFUL, BUT ALL IN GOOD HEALTH.
THERE'S SO MUCH TO TAKE IN! MY HEAD IS ALREADY SPINNING...AND THEN:
EXCUSE ME... SASHA? WE HAVE PLENTY OF FRESH-KILL TONIGHT. WOULD YOU LIKE TO SHARE IT WITH US?
ALL OF A SUDDEN, MY LONESOME LIFE AS A ROGUE SEEMS A LOT LESS APPEALING.

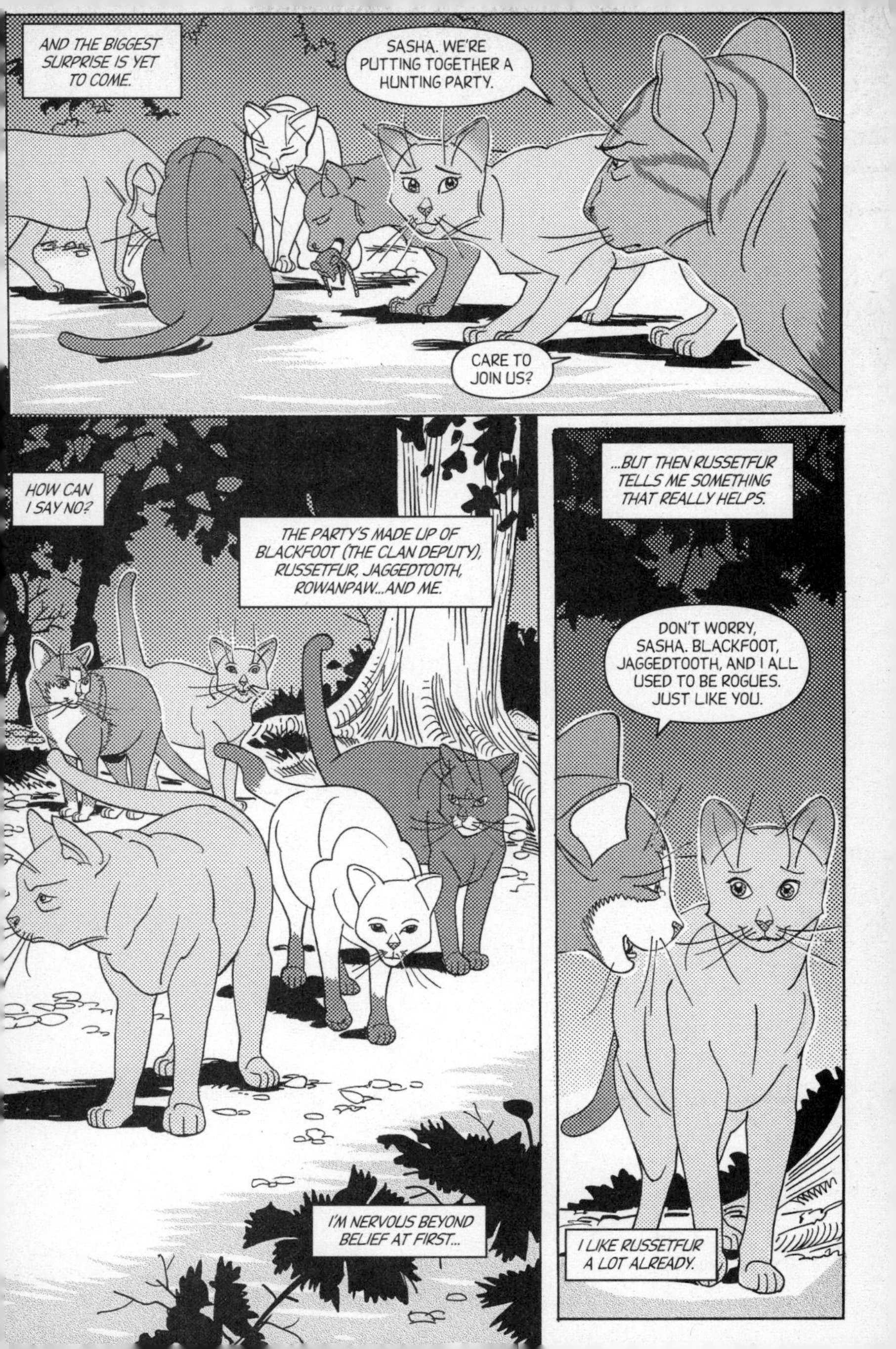
AND THE BIGGEST SURPRISE IS YET TO COME.
SASHA. WE'RE PUTTING TOGETHER A HUNTING PARTY.
CARE TO JOIN US?
HOW CAN I SAY NO?
THE PARTY'S MADE UP OF BLACKFOOT (THE CLAN DEPUTY), RUSSETFUR, JAGGEDTOOTH, ROWANPAW...AND ME.
I'M NERVOUS BEYOND BELIEF AT FIRST...
...BUT THEN RUSSETFUR TELLS ME SOMETHING THAT REALLY HELPS.
DON'T WORRY, SASHA. BLACKFOOT, JAGGEDTOOTH, AND I ALL USED TO BE ROGUES. JUST LIKE YOU.
I LIKE RUSSETFUR A LOT ALREADY.

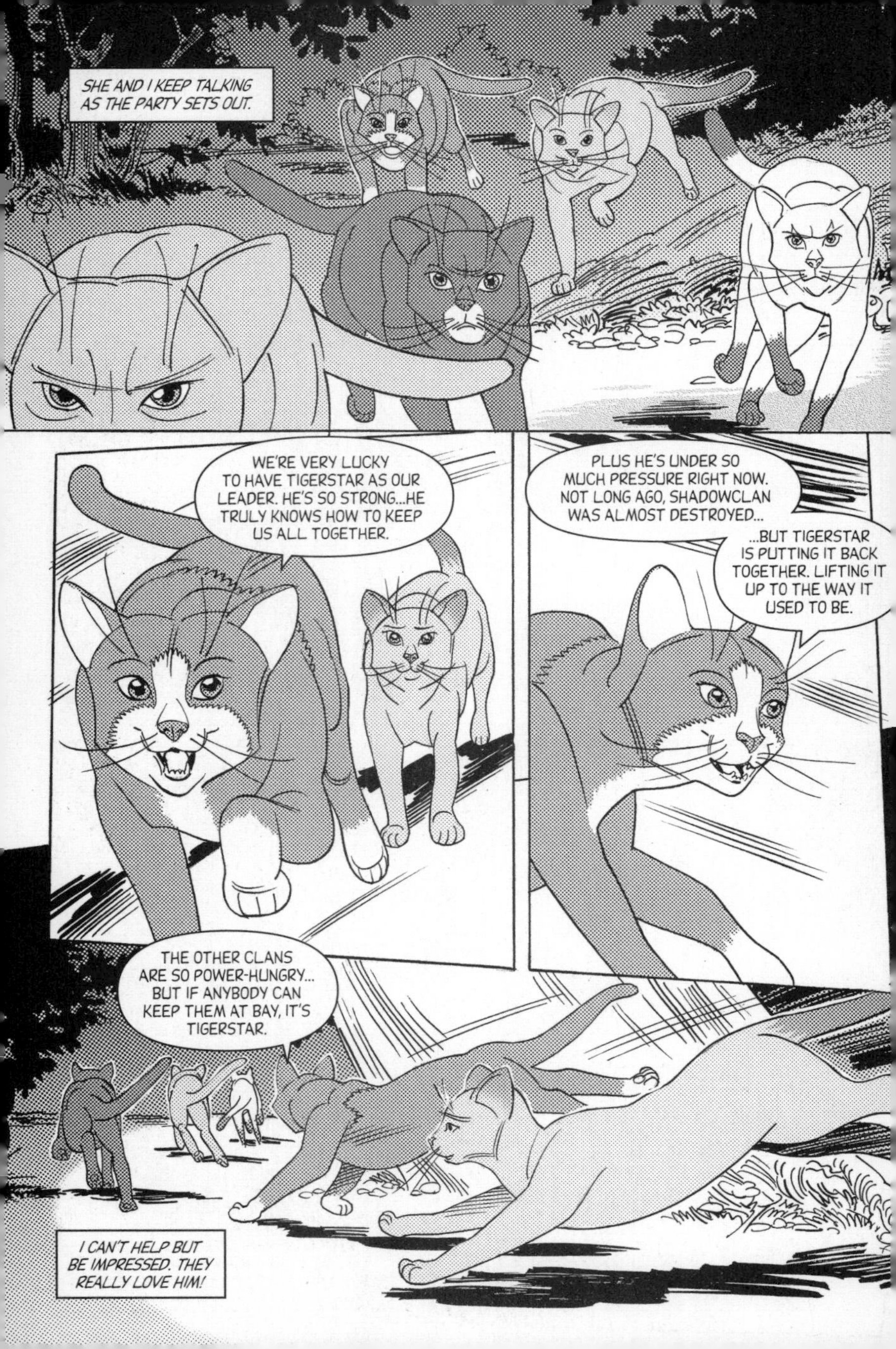
SHE AND I KEEP TALKING AS THE PARTY SETS OUT.
WE'RE VERY LUCKY TO HAVE TIGERSTAR AS OUR LEADER. HE'S SO STRONG...HE TRULY KNOWS HOW TO KEEP US ALL TOGETHER.
PLUS HE'S UNDER SO MUCH PRESSURE RIGHT NOW. NOT LONG AGO, SHADOWCLAN WAS ALMOST DESTROYED...
...BUT TIGERSTAR IS PUTTING IT BACK TOGETHER. LIFTING IT UP TO THE WAY IT USED TO BE.
THE OTHER CLANS ARE SO POWER-HUNGRY... BUT IF ANYBODY CAN KEEP THEM AT BAY, IT'S TIGERSTAR.
I CAN'T HELP BUT BE IMPRESSED. THEY REALLY LOVE HIM!

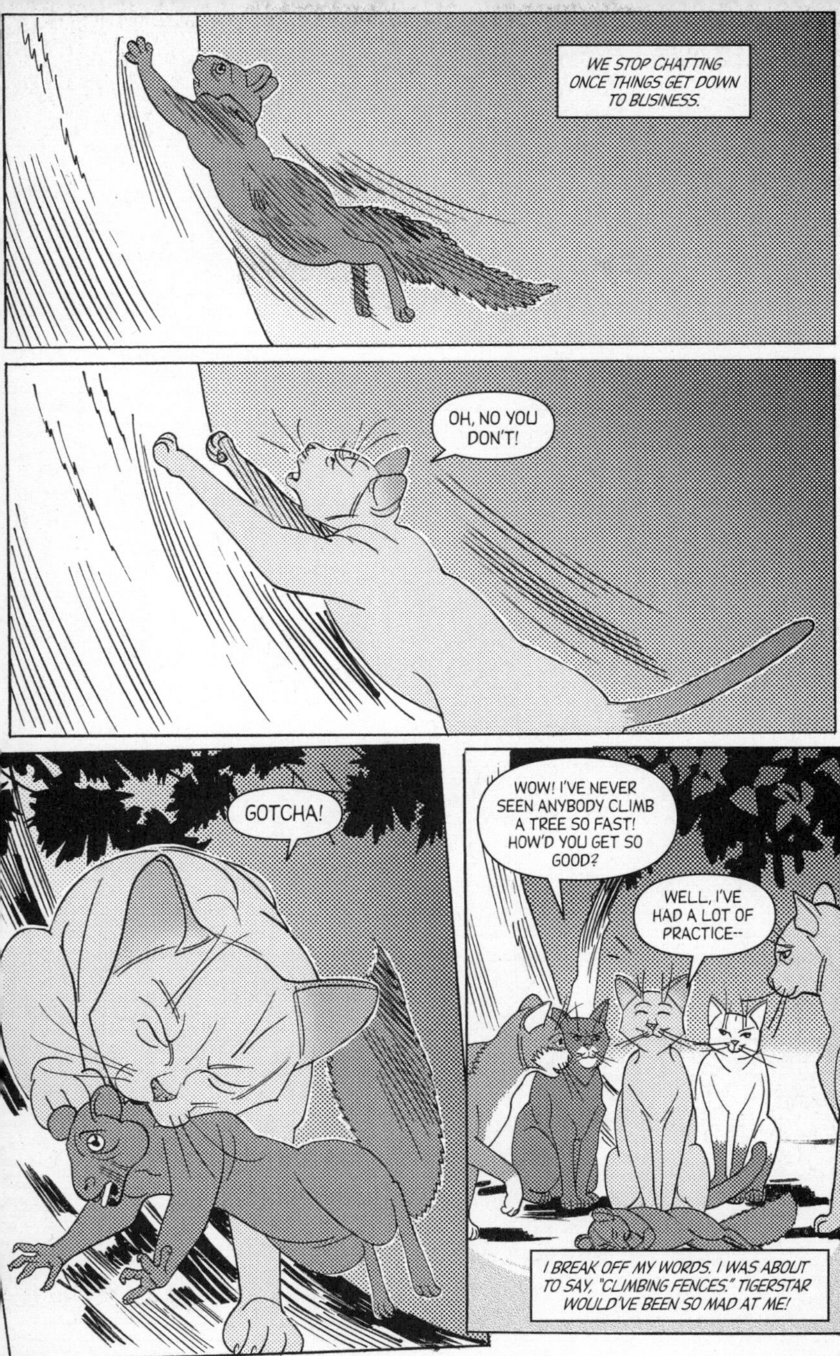
WE STOP CHATTING ONCE THINGS GET DOWN TO BUSINESS.
OH, NO YOU DON'T!
GOTCHA!
WOW! I'VE NEVER SEEN ANYBODY CLIMB A TREE SO FAST! HOW'D YOU GET SO GOOD?
WELL, I'VE HAD A LOT OF PRACTICE--
I BREAK OFF MY WORDS. I WAS ABOUT TO SAY, "CLIMBING FENCES." TIGERSTAR WOULD'VE BEEN SO MAD AT ME!

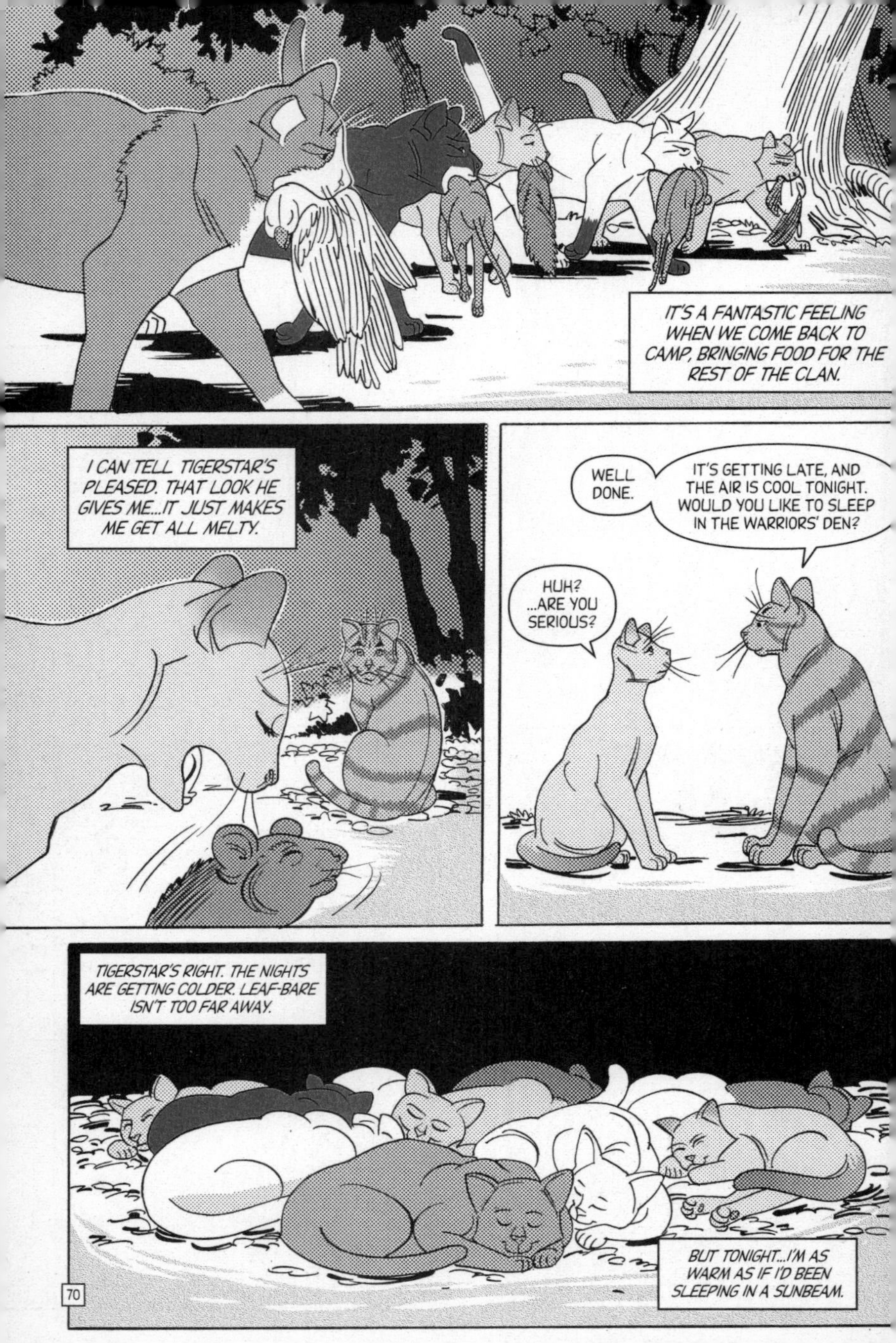
IT'S A FANTASTIC FEELING WHEN WE COME BACK TO CAMP, BRINGING FOOD FOR THE REST OF THE CLAN.
I CAN TELL TIGERSTAR'S PLEASED. THAT LOOK HE GIVES ME...IT JUST MAKES ME GET ALL MELTY.
WELL DONE.
IT'S GETTING LATE, AND THE AIR IS COOL TONIGHT. WOULD YOU LIKE TO SLEEP IN THE WARRIORS' DEN?
HUH? ...ARE YOU SERIOUS?
TIGERSTAR'S RIGHT. THE NIGHTS ARE GETTING COLDER. LEAF-BARE ISN'T TOO FAR AWAY.
BUT TONIGHT...I'M AS WARM AS IF I'D BEEN SLEEPING IN A SUNBEAM.

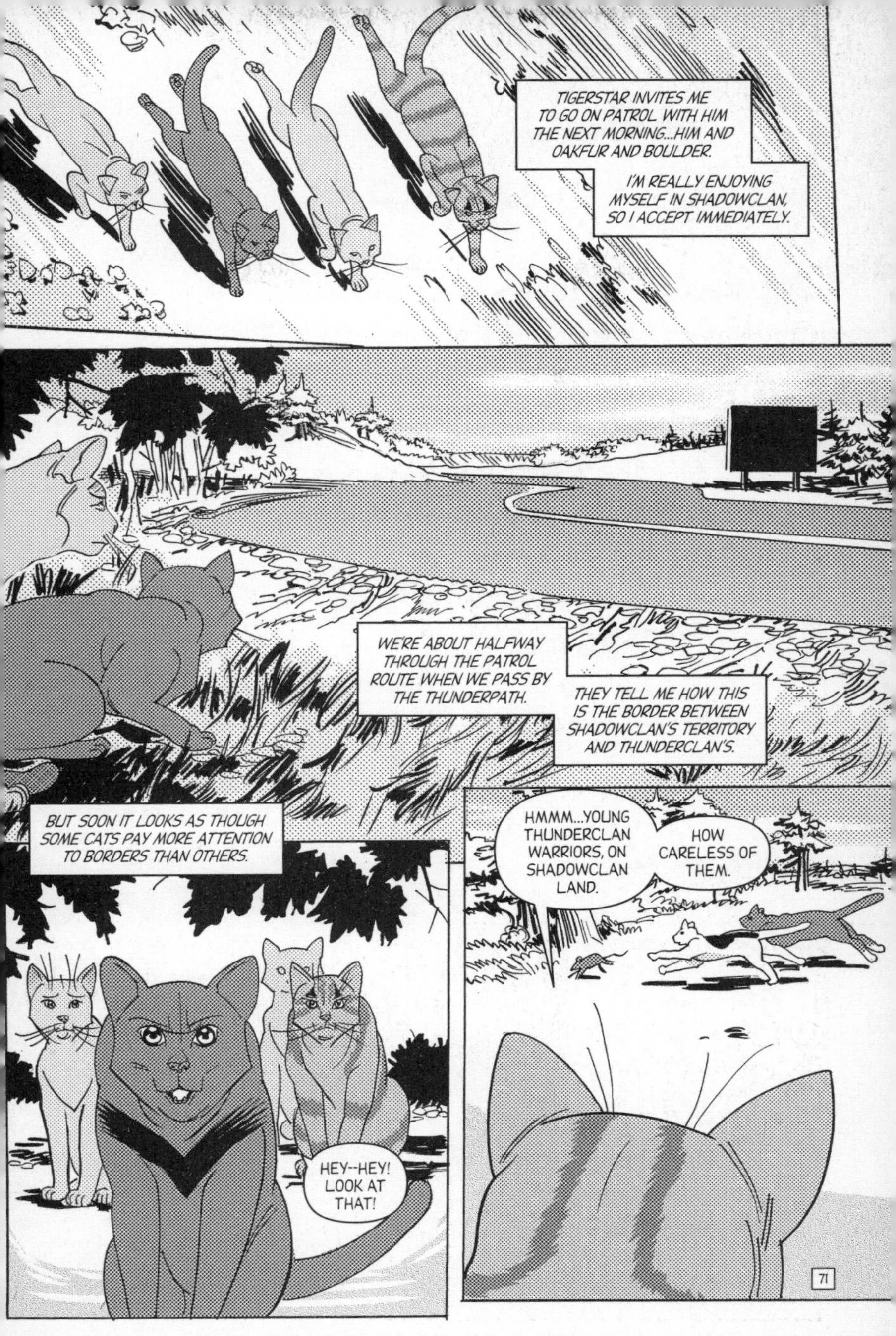
TIGERSTAR INVITES ME TO GO ON PATROL WITH HIM THE NEXT MORNING...HIM AND OAKFUR AND BOULDER.
I'M REALLY ENJOYING MYSELF IN SHADOWCLAN, SO I ACCEPT IMMEDIATELY.
WE'RE ABOUT HALFWAY THROUGH THE PATROL ROUTE WHEN WE PASS BY THE THUNDERPATH.
THEY TELL ME HOW THIS IS THE BORDER BETWEEN SHADOWCLAN'S TERRITORY AND THUNDERCLAN'S.
BUT SOON IT LOOKS AS THOUGH SOME CATS PAY MORE ATTENTION TO BORDERS THAN OTHERS.
HEY--HEY! LOOK AT THAT!
HMMM...YOUNG THUNDERCLAN WARRIORS, ON SHADOWCLAN LAND.
HOW CARELESS OF THEM.

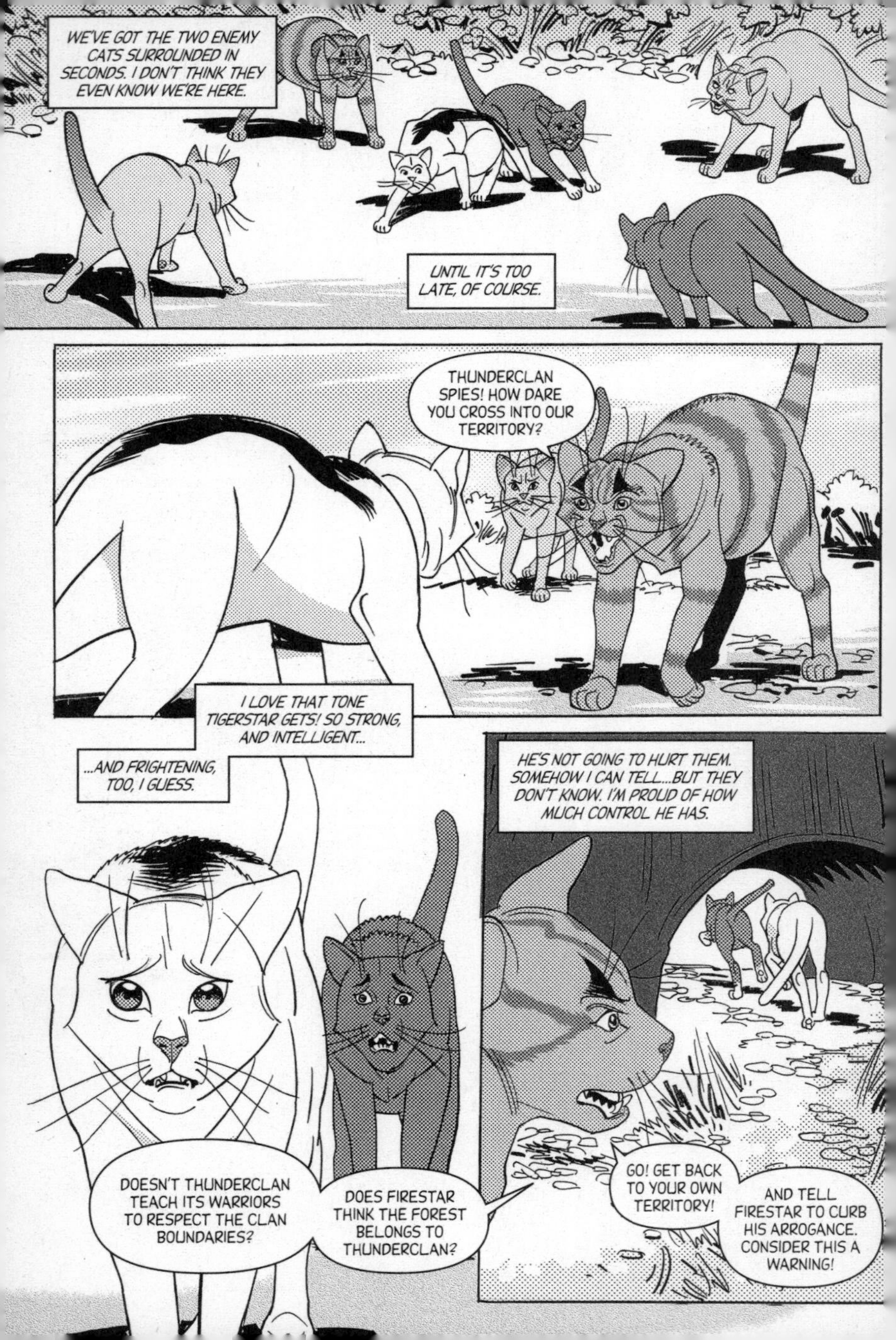
WE'VE GOT THE TWO ENEMY CATS SURROUNDED IN SECONDS. I DON'T THINK THEY EVEN KNOW WE'RE HERE.
UNTIL IT'S TOO LATE, OF COURSE.
THUNDERCLAN SPIES! HOW DARE YOU CROSS INTO OUR TERRITORY?
I LOVE THAT TONE TIGERSTAR GETS! SO STRONG, AND INTELLIGENT...
...AND FRIGHTENING, TOO, I GUESS.
DOESN'T THUNDERCLAN TEACH ITS WARRIORS TO RESPECT THE CLAN BOUNDARIES?
DOES FIRESTAR THINK THE FOREST BELONGS TO THUNDERCLAN?
HE'S NOT GOING TO HURT THEM. SOMEHOW I CAN TELL...BUT THEY DON'T KNOW. I'M PROUD OF HOW MUCH CONTROL HE HAS.
GO! GET BACK TO YOUR OWN TERRITORY!
AND TELL FIRESTAR TO CURB HIS ARROGANCE. CONSIDER THIS A WARNING!

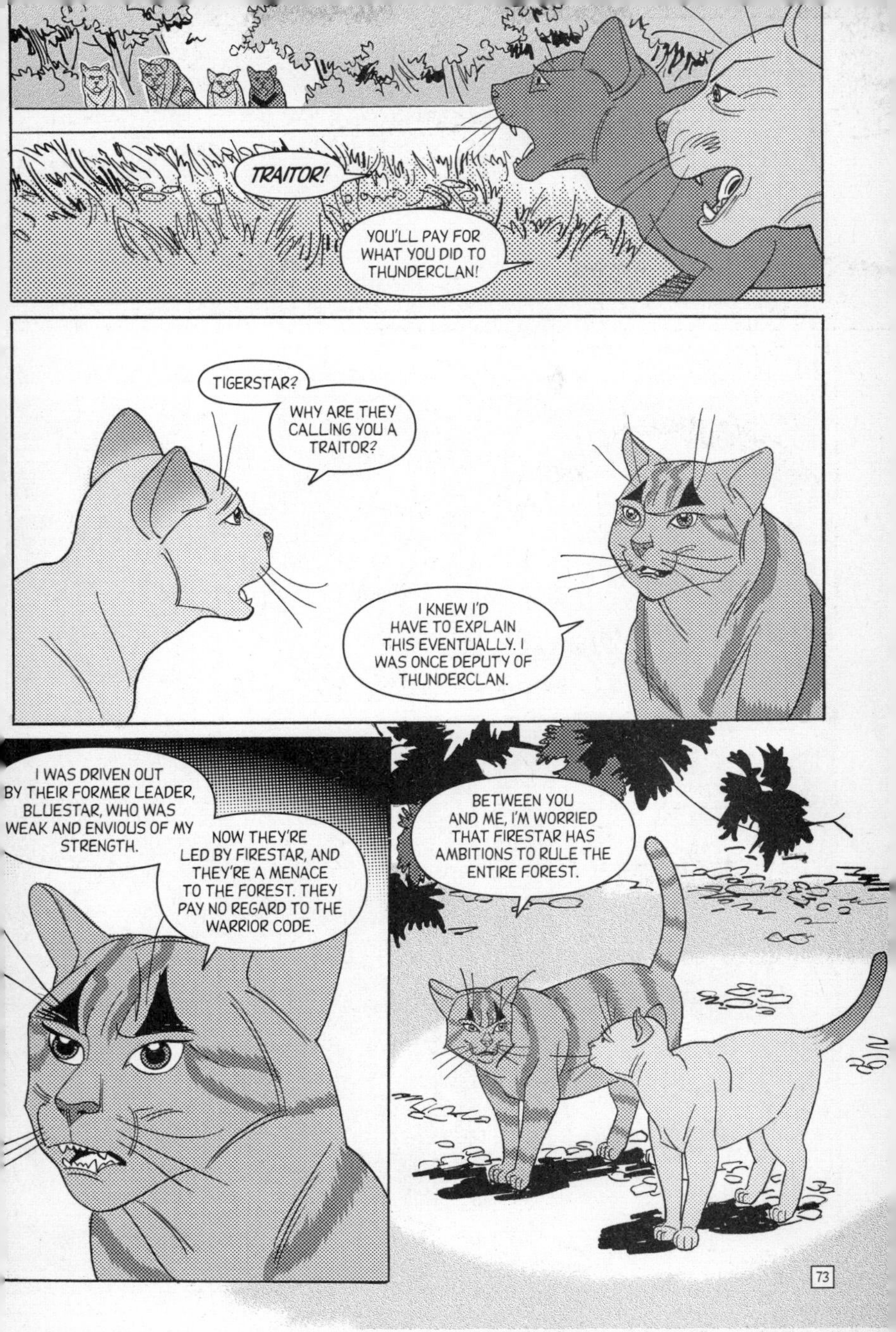
TRAITOR!
YOU'LL PAY FOR WHAT YOU DID TO THUNDERCLAN!
TIGERSTAR?
WHY ARE THEY CALLING YOU A TRAITOR?
I KNEW I'D HAVE TO EXPLAIN THIS EVENTUALLY. I WAS ONCE DEPUTY OF THUNDERCLAN.
I WAS DRIVEN OUT BY THEIR FORMER LEADER, BLUESTAR, WHO WAS WEAK AND ENVIOUS OF MY STRENGTH.
NOW THEY'RE LED BY FIRESTAR, AND THEY'RE A MENACE TO THE FOREST. THEY PAY NO REGARD TO THE WARRIOR CODE.
BETWEEN YOU AND ME, I'M WORRIED THAT FIRESTAR HAS AMBITIONS TO RULE THE ENTIRE FOREST.

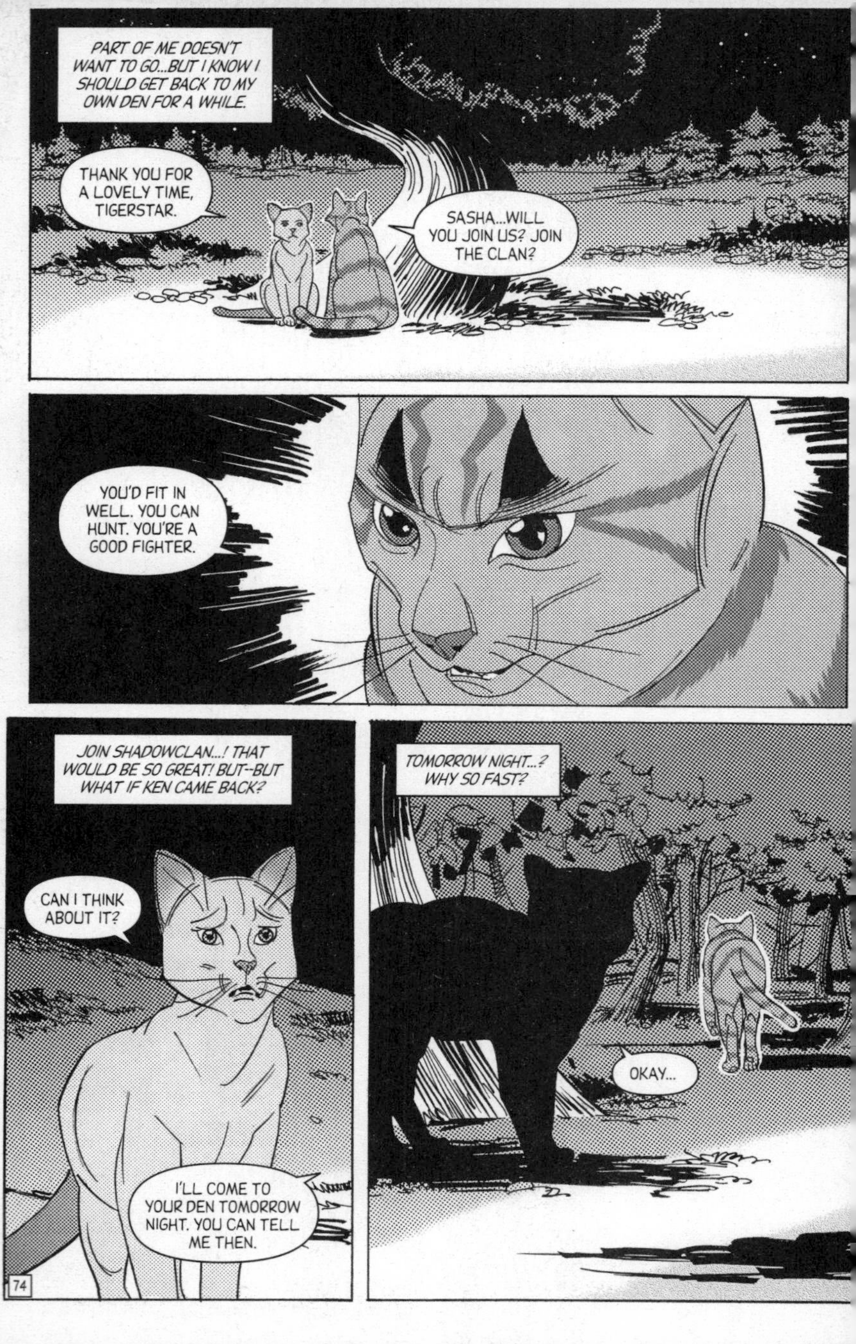
PART OF ME DOESN'T WANT TO GO...BUT I KNOW I SHOULD GET BACK TO MY OWN DEN FOR A WHILE.
THANK YOU FOR A LOVELY TIME, TIGERSTAR.
SASHA...WILL YOU JOIN US? JOIN THE CLAN?
YOU'D FIT IN WELL. YOU CAN HUNT. YOU'RE A GOOD FIGHTER.
JOIN SHADOWCLAN...! THAT WOULD BE SO GREAT! BUT--BUT WHAT IF KEN CAME BACK?
CAN I THINK ABOUT IT?
I'LL COME TO YOUR DEN TOMORROW NIGHT. YOU CAN TELL ME THEN.
TOMORROW NIGHT...? WHY SO FAST?
OKAY...

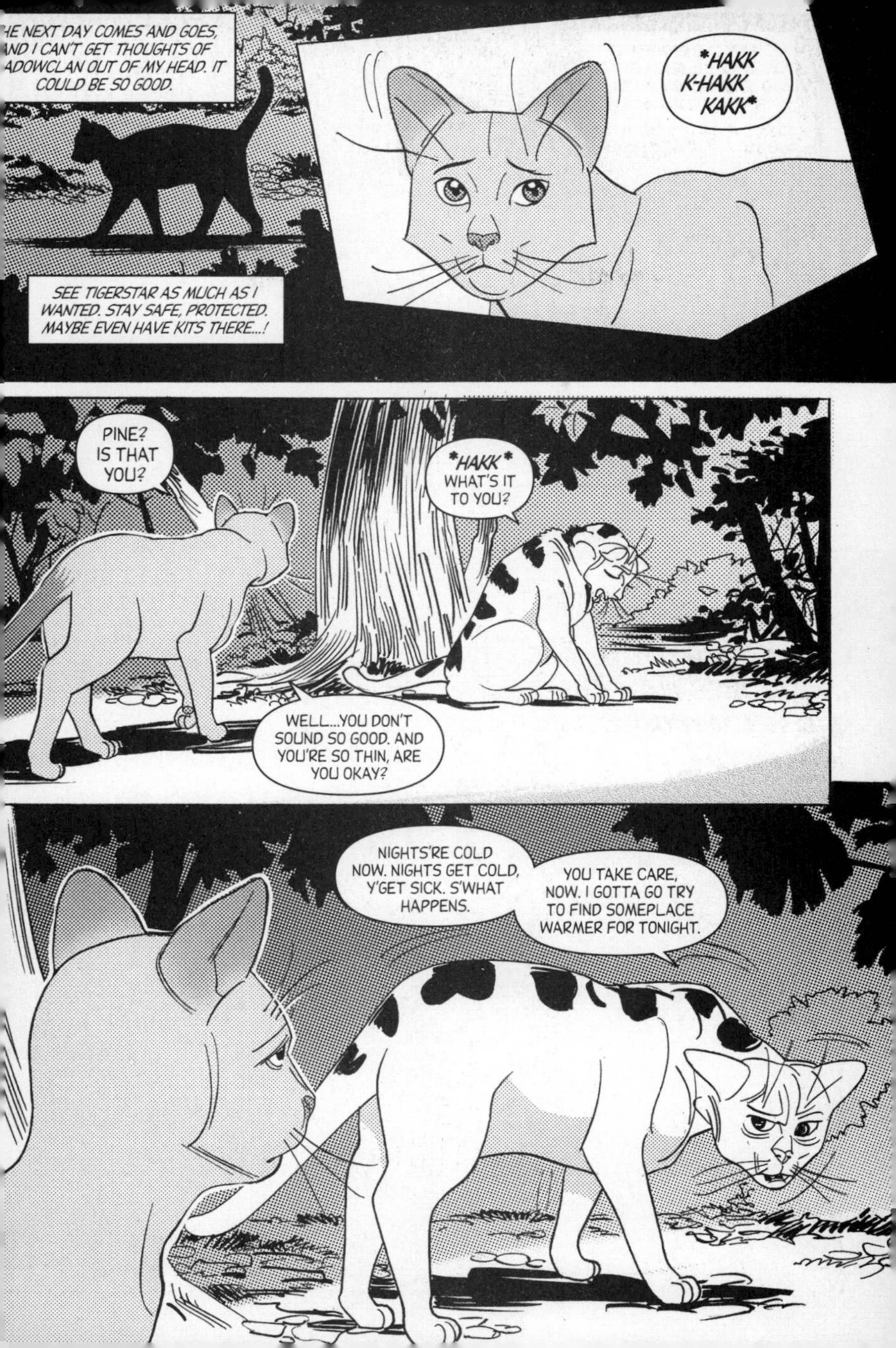
HE NEXT DAY COMES AND GOES, ND I CAN'T GET THOUGHTS OF ADOWCLAN OUT OF MY HEAD. IT COULD BE SO GOOD.
SEE TIGERSTAR AS MUCH AS I WANTED. STAY SAFE, PROTECTED. MAYBE EVEN HAVE KITS THERE...!
HAKK K-HAKK KAKK
PINE? IS THAT YOU?
HAKK WHAT'S IT TO YOU?
WELL...YOU DON'T SOUND SO GOOD. AND YOU'RE SO THIN, ARE YOU OKAY?
NIGHTS'RE COLD NOW. NIGHTS GET COLD, Y'GET SICK. S'WHAT HAPPENS.
YOU TAKE CARE, NOW. I GOTTA GO TRY TO FIND SOMEPLACE WARMER FOR TONIGHT.

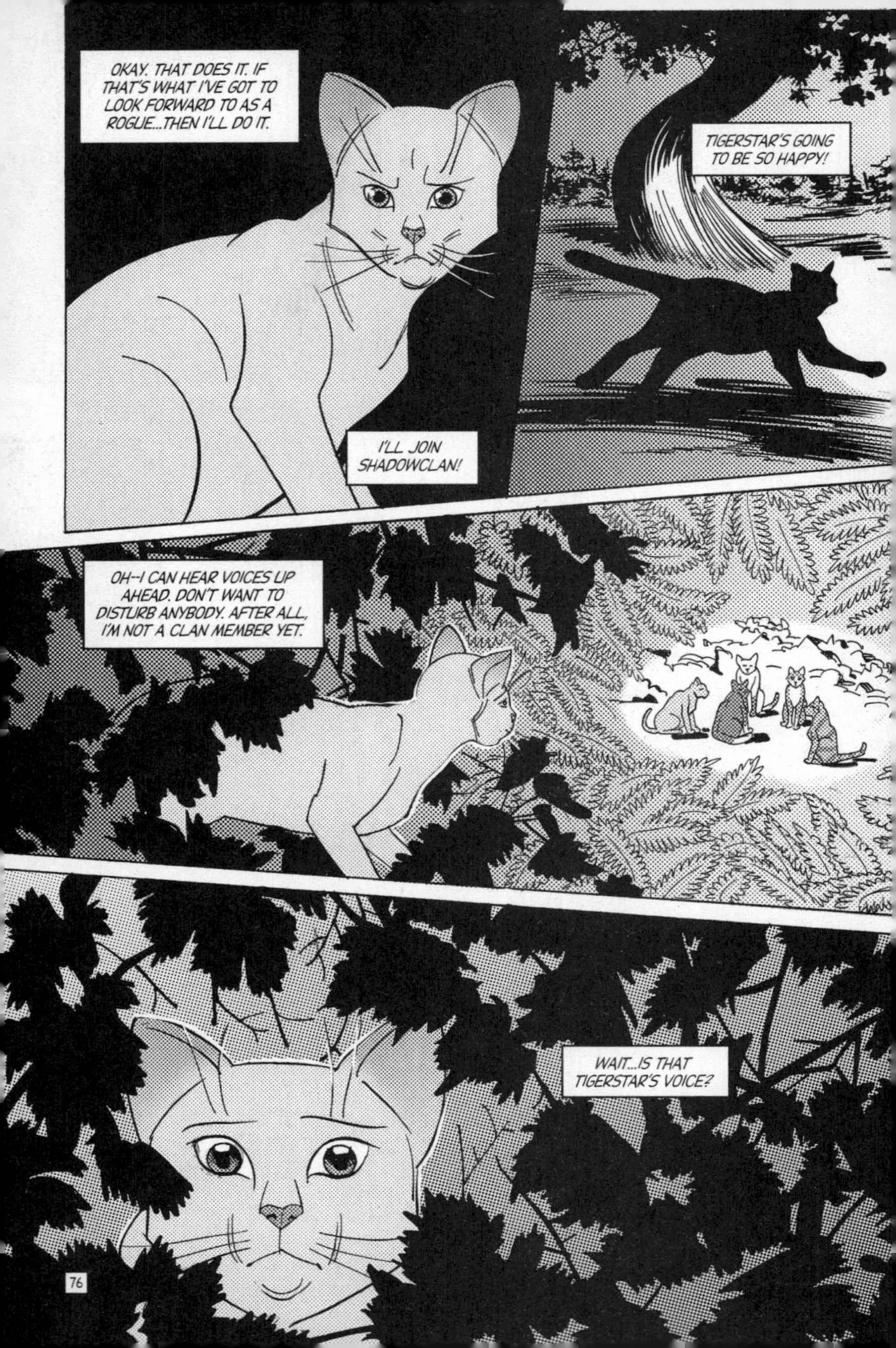
OKAY. THAT DOES IT. IF THAT'S WHAT I'VE GOT TO LOOK FORWARD TO AS A ROGUE...THEN I'LL DO IT.
I'LL JOIN SHADOWCLAN!
TIGERSTAR'S GOING TO BE SO HAPPY!
OH--I CAN HEAR VOICES UP AHEAD. DON'T WANT TO DISTURB ANYBODY. AFTER ALL, I'M NOT A CLAN MEMBER YET.
WAIT...IS THAT TIGERSTAR'S VOICE?

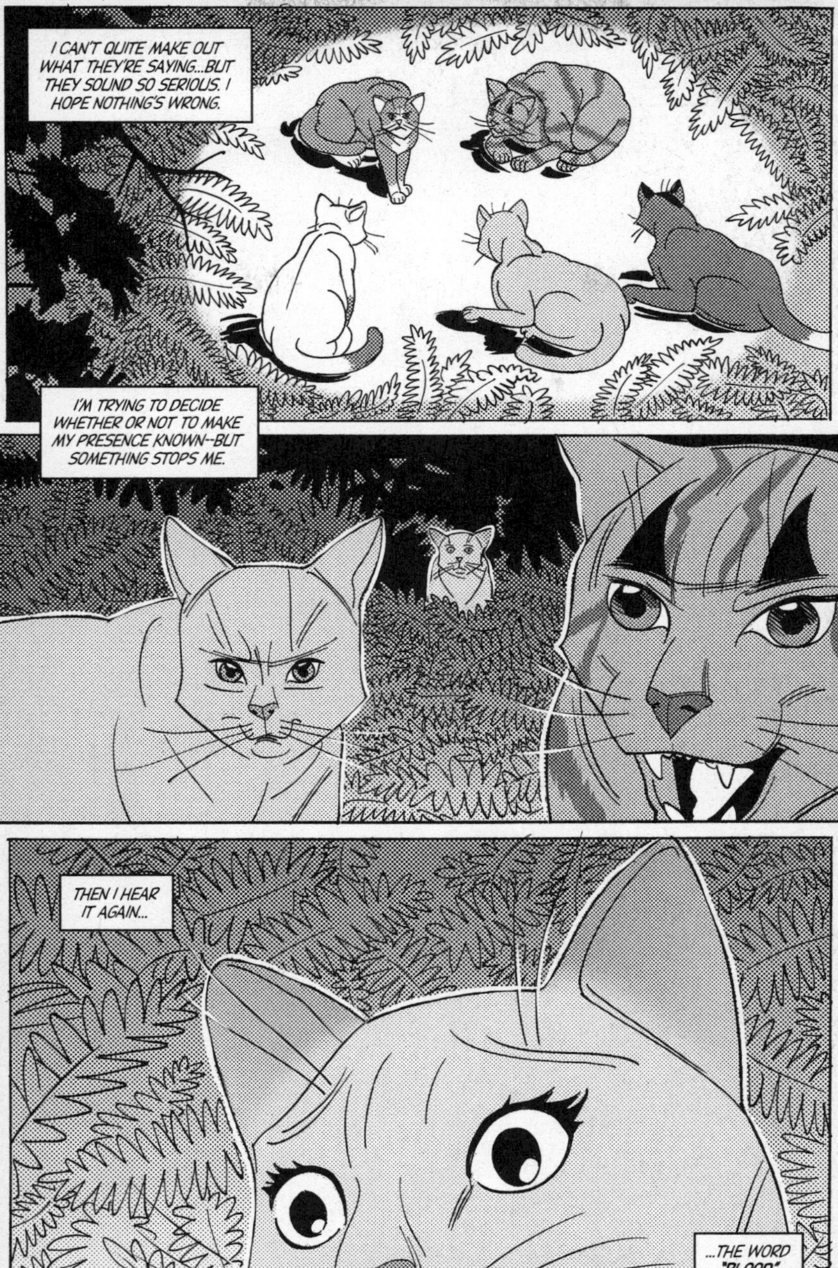
I CAN'T QUITE MAKE OUT WHAT THEY'RE SAYING...BUT THEY SOUND SO SERIOUS. I HOPE NOTHING'S WRONG.
I'M TRYING TO DECIDE WHETHER OR NOT TO MAKE MY PRESENCE KNOWN--BUT SOMETHING STOPS ME.
THEN I HEAR IT AGAIN...
...THE WORD "BLOOD."

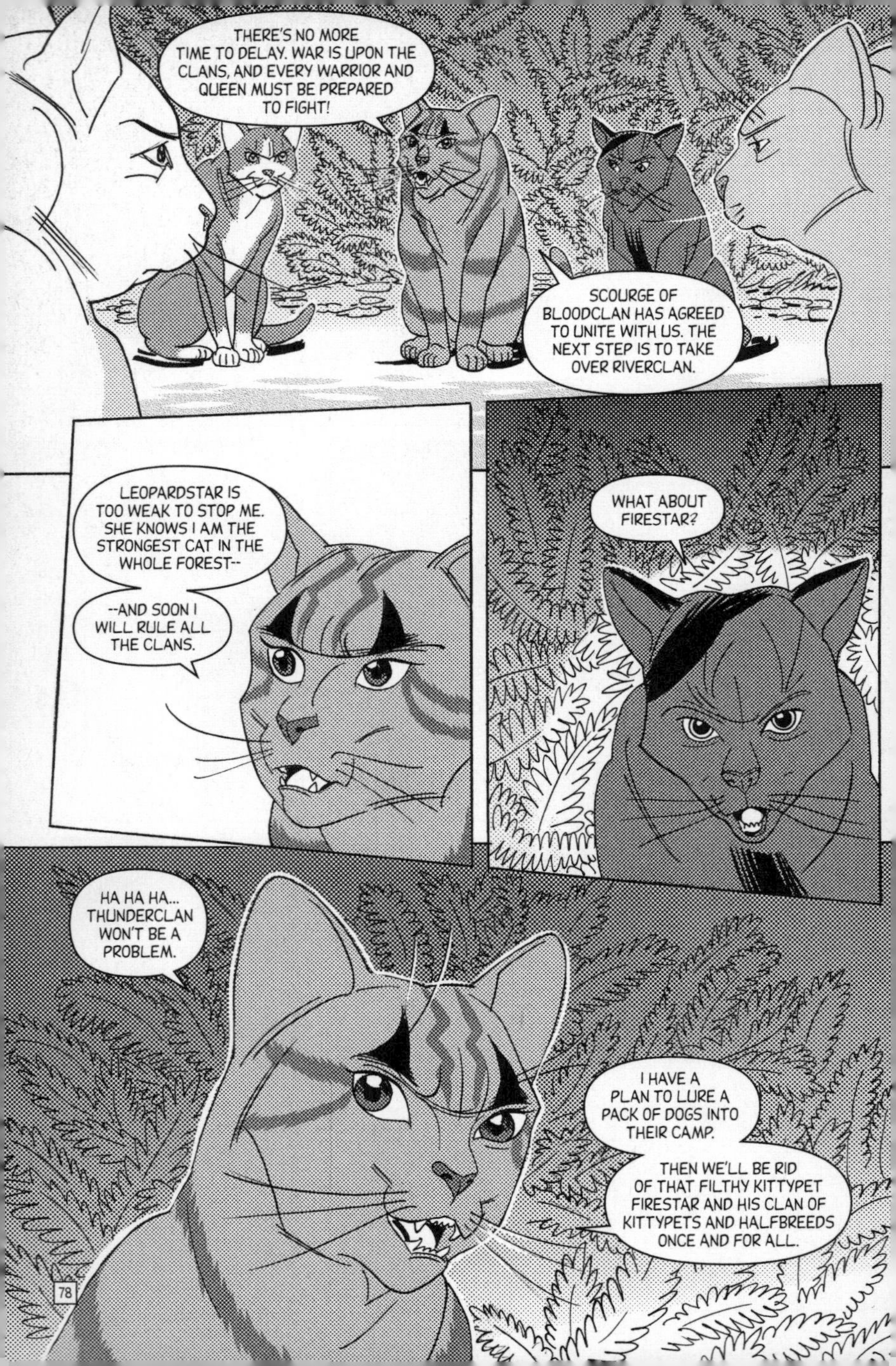
THERE'S NO MORE TIME TO DELAY. WAR IS UPON THE CLANS, AND EVERY WARRIOR AND QUEEN MUST BE PREPARED TO FIGHT!
SCOURGE OF BLOODCLAN HAS AGREED TO UNITE WITH US. THE NEXT STEP IS TO TAKE OVER RIVERCLAN.
LEOPARDSTAR IS TOO WEAK TO STOP ME. SHE KNOWS I AM THE STRONGEST CAT IN THE WHOLE FOREST--
--AND SOON I WILL RULE ALL THE CLANS.
WHAT ABOUT FIRESTAR?
HA HA HA... THUNDERCLAN WON'T BE A PROBLEM.
I HAVE A PLAN TO LURE A PACK OF DOGS INTO THEIR CAMP.
THEN WE'LL BE RID OF THAT FILTHY KITTYPET FIRESTAR AND HIS CLAN OF KITTYPETS AND HALFBREEDS ONCE AND FOR ALL.

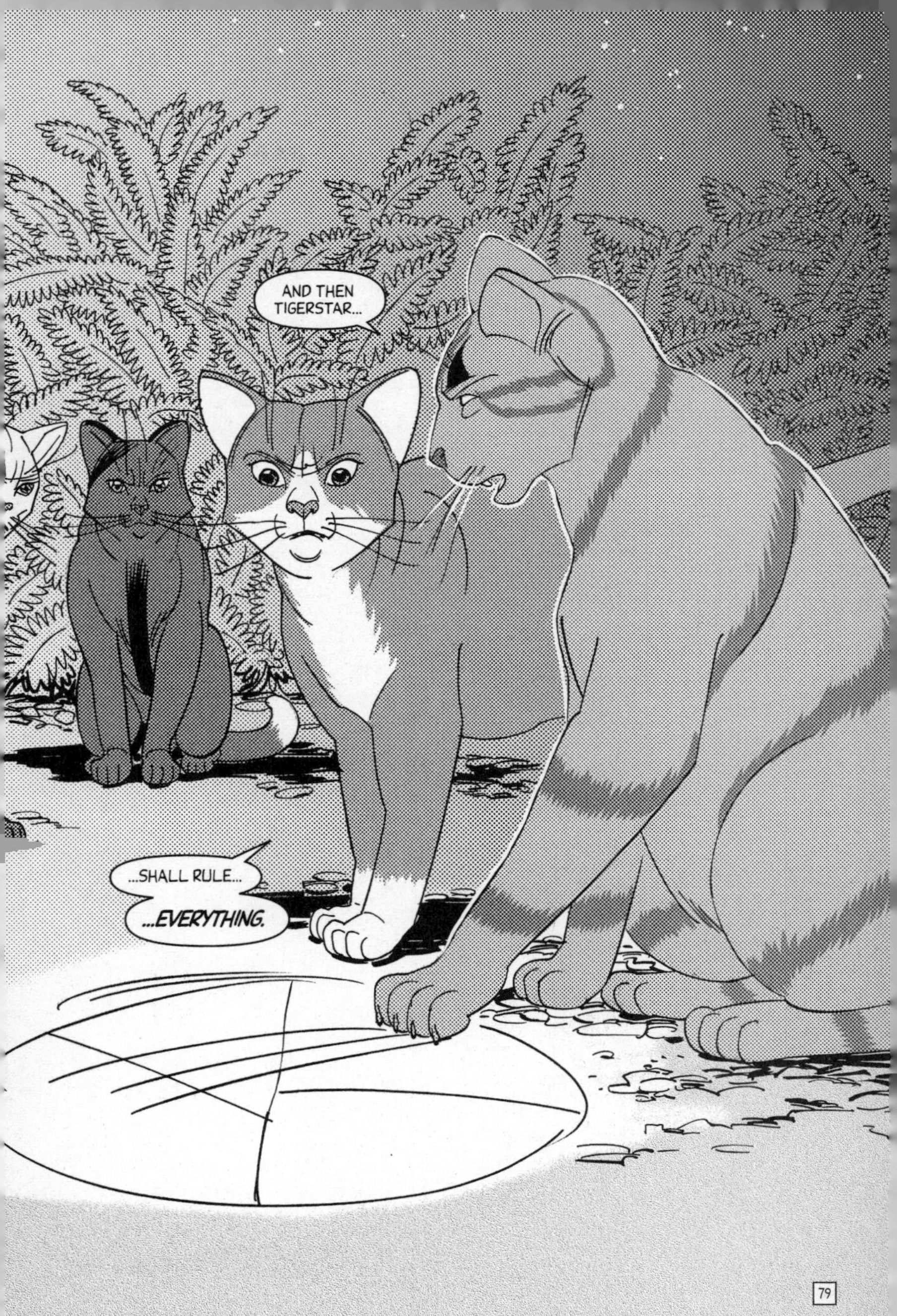
AND THEN TIGERSTAR...
...SHALL RULE...
...EVERYTHING.

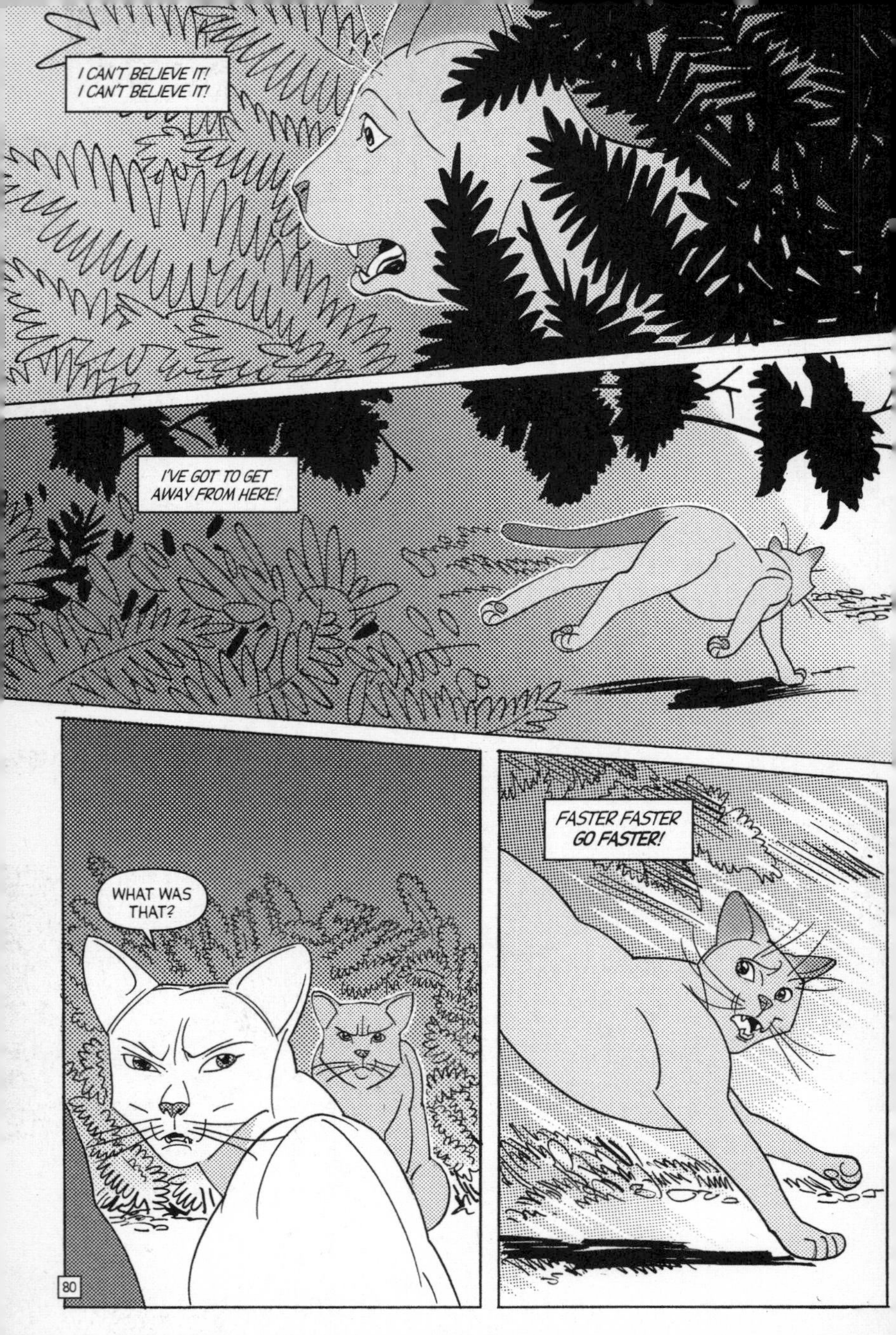
I CAN'T BELIEVE IT! I CAN'T BELIEVE IT!
I'VE GOT TO GET AWAY FROM HERE!
WHAT WAS THAT?
FASTER FASTER GO FASTER!

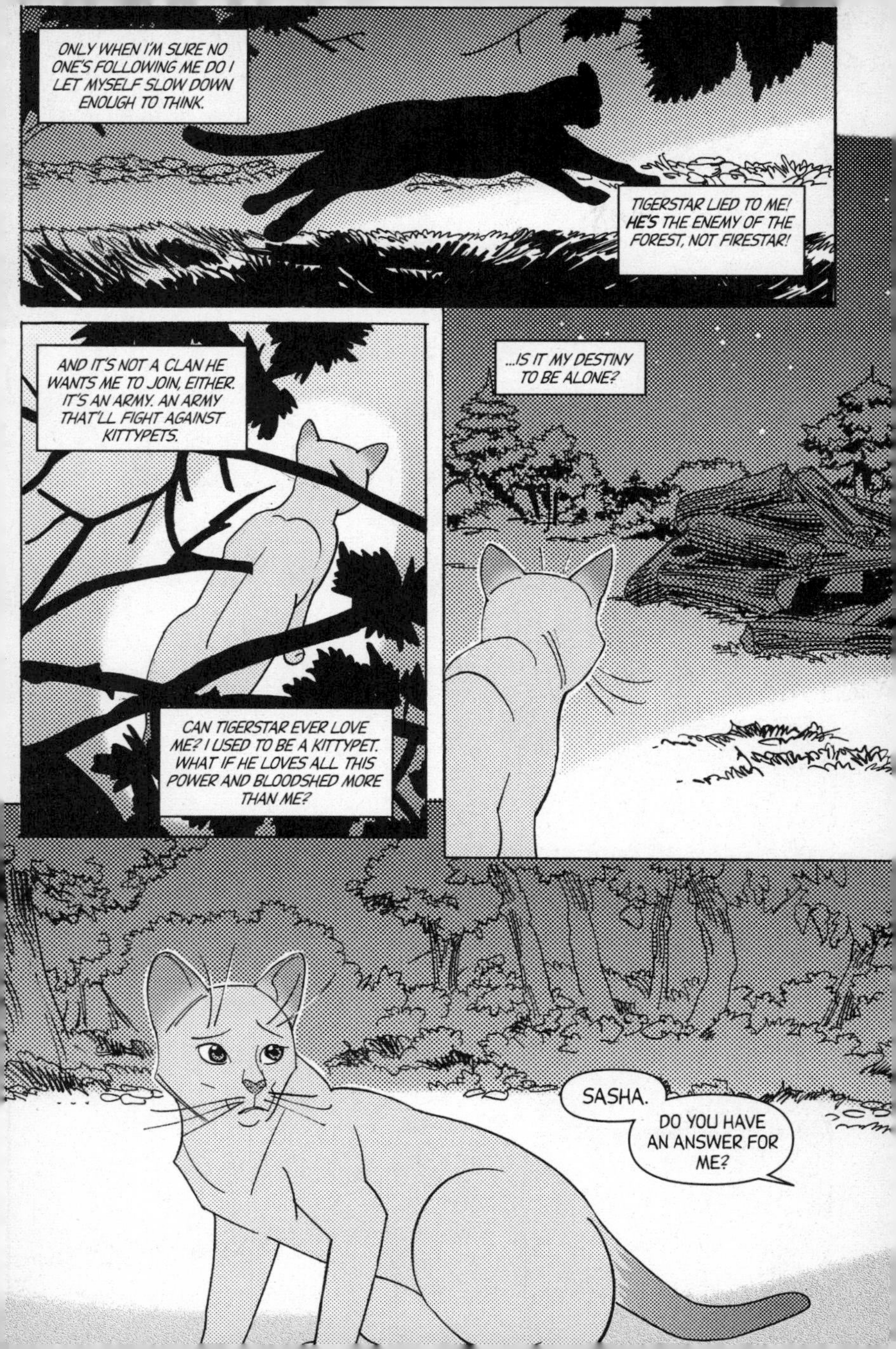
ONLY WHEN I'M SURE NO ONE'S FOLLOWING ME DO I LET MYSELF SLOW DOWN ENOUGH TO THINK.
TIGERSTAR LIED TO ME! HE'S THE ENEMY OF THE FOREST, NOT FIRESTAR!
AND IT'S NOT A CLAN HE WANTS ME TO JOIN, EITHER. IT'S AN ARMY. AN ARMY THAT'LL FIGHT AGAINST KITTYPETS.
CAN TIGERSTAR EVER LOVE ME? I USED TO BE A KITTYPET. WHAT IF HE LOVES ALL THIS POWER AND BLOODSHED MORE THAN ME?
...IS IT MY DESTINY TO BE ALONE?
SASHA.
DO YOU HAVE AN ANSWER FOR ME?

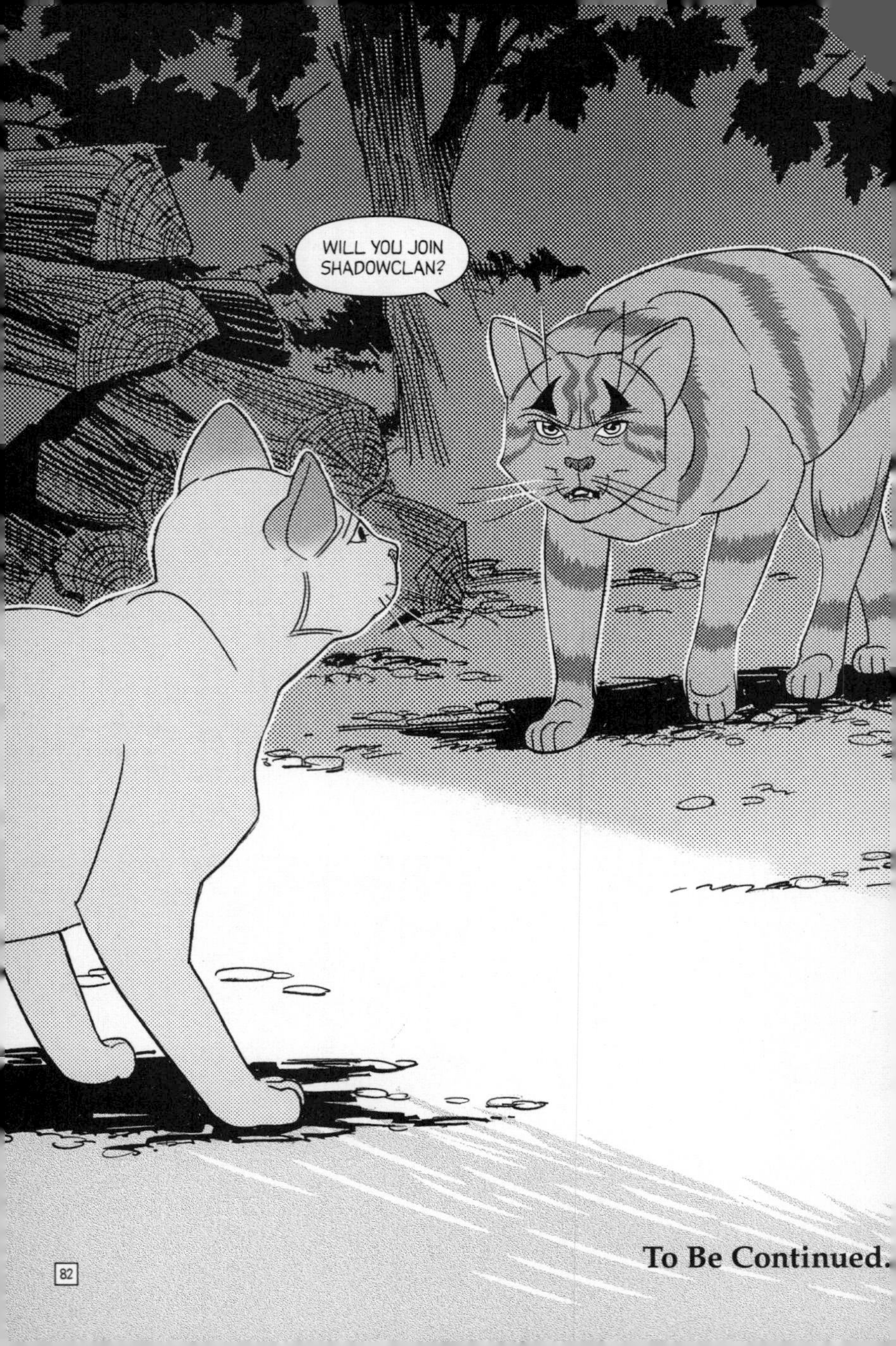
WILL YOU JOIN SHADOWCLAN?

To Be Continued.

ERIN
HUNTER

is inspired by a love of cats and a fascination with the ferocity of the natural world. As well as having great respect for nature in all its forms, Erin enjoys creating rich mythical explanations for animal behavior, shaped by her interest in astrology and standing stones. She is also the author of the Seekers series.

Visit the Clans online
and play the Warriors Quest game at
www.warriorcats.com.

For exclusive information on your
favorite authors and artists, visit
www.authortracker.com.

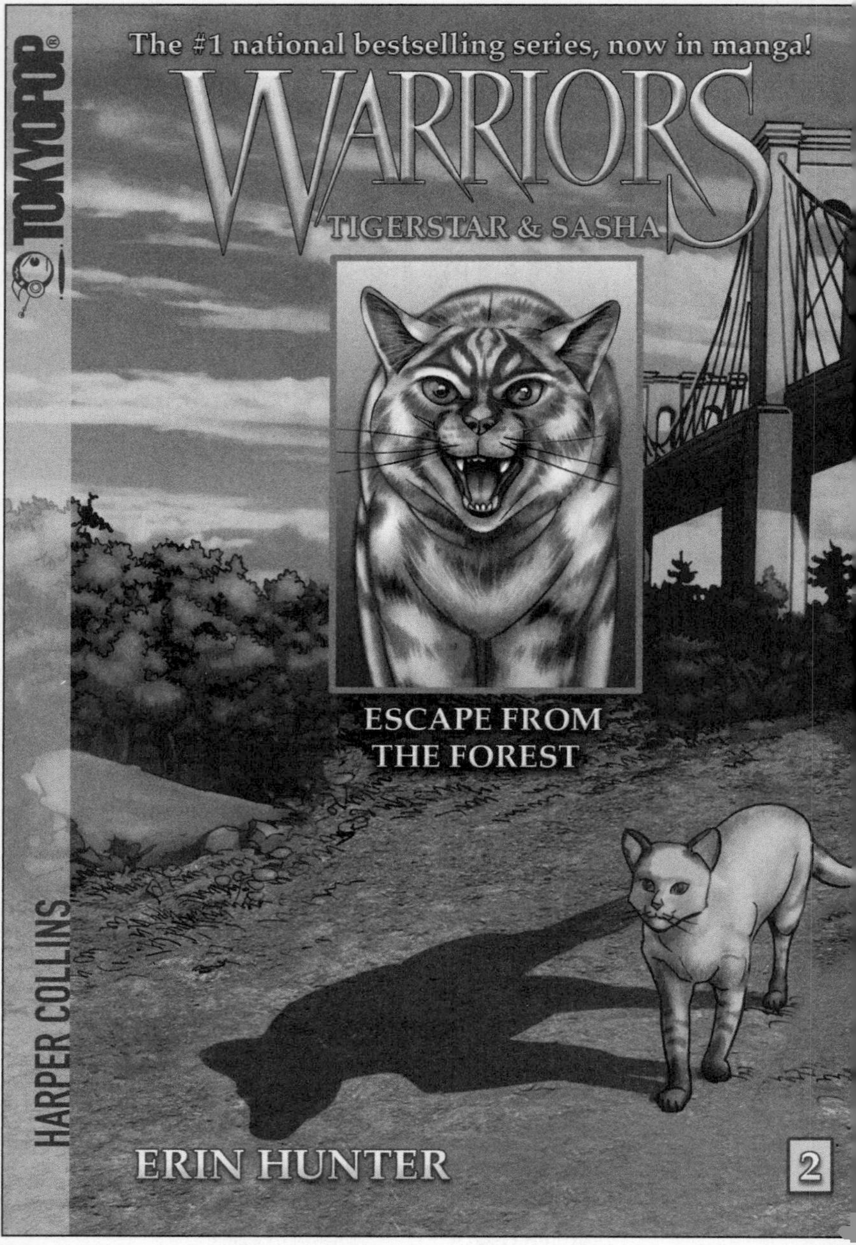
TOKYOPOP
The #1 national bestselling series, now in manga!
WARRIORS
TIGERSTAR & SASHA
ESCAPE FROM THE FOREST
HARPER COLLINS
ERIN HUNTER
2

KEEP WATCH FOR

WARRIORS

TIGERSTAR & SASHA
#2: ESCAPE FROM
THE FOREST

Sasha must make the hardest decision of her life: Stay
with Tigerstar and join ShadowClan, or forge a new life
on her own.

The nationally bestselling series, now in manga!
WARRIORS
THE LOST WARRIOR
TOKYOPOP
HARPER COLLINS
ERIN HUNTER
1

The #1 national bestselling series, now in manga!
WARRIORS
WARRIOR'S REFUGE
TOKYOPOP
HARPER COLLINS
ERIN HUNTER
2

The #1 national bestselling series, now in manga!
WARRIORS
TOKYOPOP
HARPER COLLINS
ERIN HUNTER
3

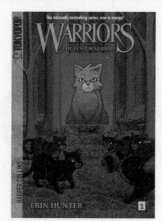

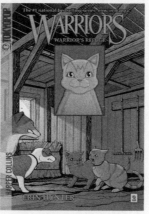

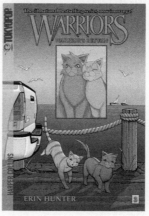

DON'T MISS THE
FIRST MANGA TRILOGY

WARRIORS

THE LOST WARRIOR

WARRIOR'S REFUGE

WARRIOR'S RETURN

Find out what really happened to Graystripe when he was captured by Twolegs, and follow him and Millie on their torturous journey through the old forest territory and Twolegplace as they search for ThunderClan.

WARRIORS

THE RISE OF SCOURGE

TOKYOPOP®

HARPER COLLINS

ERIN HUNTER

NO WARRIORS MANGA COLLECTION IS COMPLETE WITHOUT:

WARRIORS

THE RISE OF SCOURGE

Black-and-white Tiny may be the runt of the litter, but he's also the most curious about what lies beyond the backyard fence. When he crosses paths with some wild cats defending their territory, Tiny is left with scars—and a bitter, deep-seated grudge—that he carries with him back to Twolegplace. As his reputation grows among the strays and loners that live in the dirty brick alleyways, Tiny leaves behind his name, his kittypet past, and everything that was once important to him—except his deadly desire for revenge.

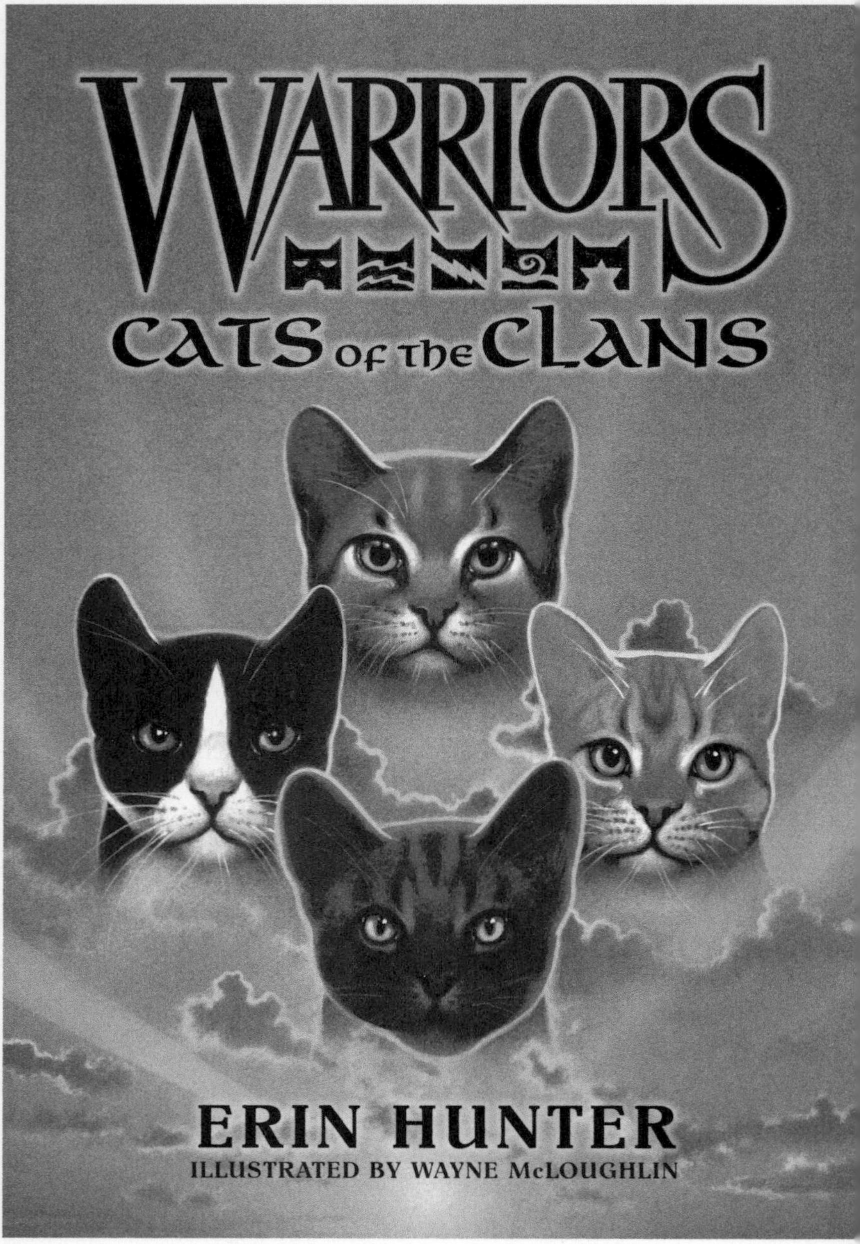
WARRIORS
CATS of the CLANS
ERIN HUNTER
ILLUSTRATED BY WAYNE McLOUGHLIN

MEET THE CLANS' HEROES IN

WARRIORS
CATS OF THE CLANS

Hear the stories of the great warriors as they've never been told before! Chock-full of visual treats and captivating details, including full-color illustrations and in-depth biographies of important cats from all four Clans, from fierce Clan leaders to wise medicine cats to the most mischievous kits.

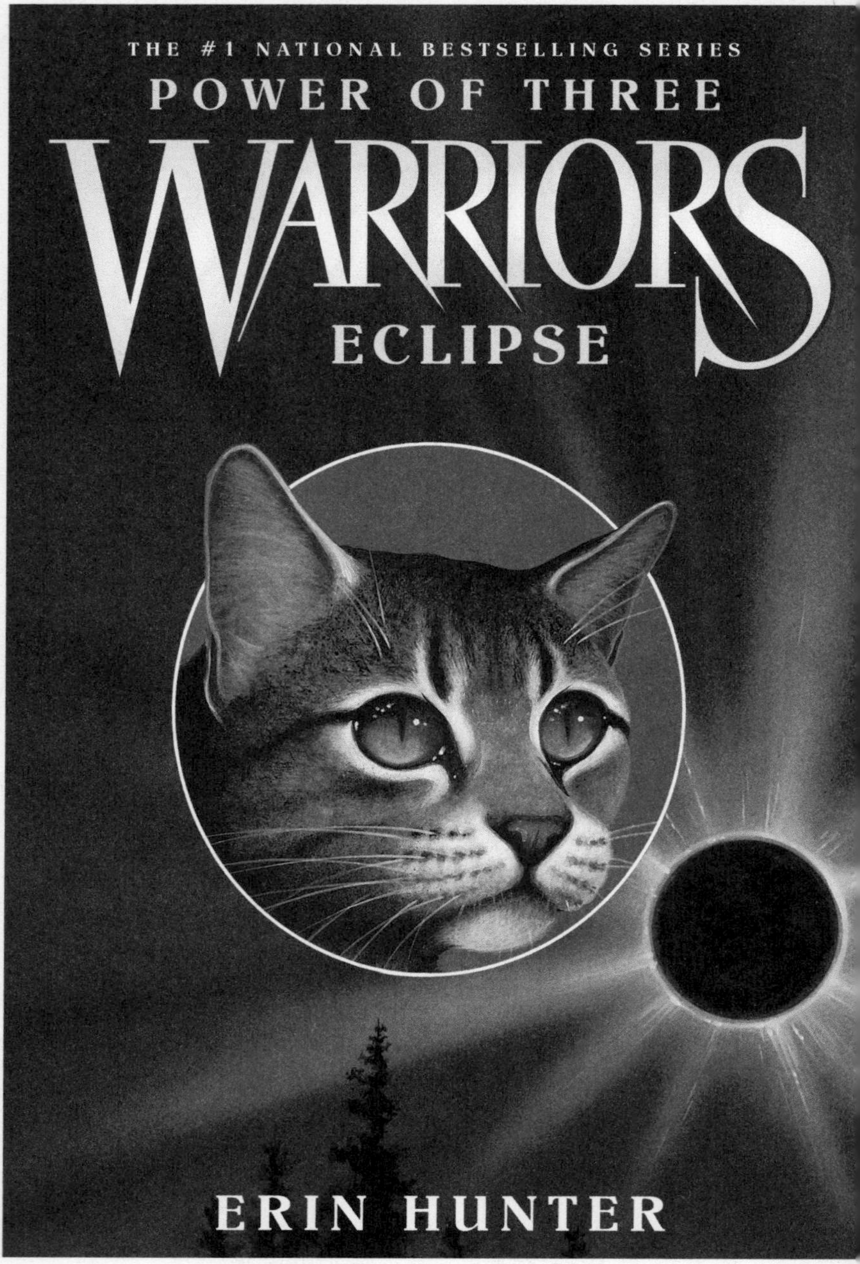
THE #1 NATIONAL BESTSELLING SERIES
POWER OF THREE
WARRIORS
ECLIPSE
ERIN HUNTER

POWER OF THREE

WARRIORS

BOOK 4:

ECLIPSE

TURN THE PAGE FOR A PEEK
AT THE NEXT WARRIORS NOVEL,
*WARRIORS: POWER OF THREE
#4: ECLIPSE.*

Firestar's grandchildren have learned of the powerful prophecy that foretells their destinies, and the responsibility of deciding the Clans' future weighs heavily on the three apprentices. Each secretly yearns for power, and their strengths are tested when ThunderClan is suddenly attacked—and all the Clans are thrown into a battle unlike any the cats have seen.

Jaypaw touched his nose to Tawnypelt's pad. It felt hot and fat. "Swollen," he pronounced. "The skin's grazed but not bleeding. But you already know that." He could hear Hollypaw and Lionpaw's faint mews as they headed away to find prey. Were they talking about the prophecy?

Tawnypelt pulled her paw from under his muzzle. "I knew I couldn't taste blood but I wasn't sure if a stone had worked its way in." She licked it. "My pads have grown so hard from the mountains, I can't tell calluses from cuts anymore."

"No stones," Jaypaw reassured her. He nodded toward the sound of water babbling over rocks nearby. "That stream doesn't sound too deep. Go stand in it. The cold water should ease the swelling."

He padded after her and heard the splash as she leaped into the water.

"It's cold!" she gasped.

"Good," he mewed. "It'll take down the swelling quicker." He pricked his ears. Hollypaw and Lionpaw's voices had faded into the distance. He had shared with them the secret he had carried with him for so long. Telling it had felt like walking through unknown territory, each word falling like a paw step on uncertain ground. Lionpaw had accepted it as though something that had been confusing him had finally been explained. Hollypaw's reaction had been more frustrating: She seemed only concerned about how they could use their powers to help ThunderClan, and kept fretting about the warrior code. Didn't she understand that the prophecy meant more than that? They had been given a power that stretched far beyond the boundaries set by ordinary cats.

Tawnypelt's mew interrupted his thoughts. "This water's *very* cold."

"It's mountain water."

"I can tell," Tawnypelt meowed urgently. "My paws have gone numb!"

"Well, get out then."

With a sigh of relief, she landed beside him and began shaking the water from her paws, scattering icy drops on his fur.

Jaypaw shivered and moved away; mountain winds and cold water were a bad mix. "Does it still hurt?"

"I can't feel it at all," Tawnypelt replied. She paused. "Actually, I can't feel any of my paws."

Squirrelflight was padding toward them. "Any better?"

"I think so," Tawnypelt meowed uncertainly.

Jaypaw felt his mother's tongue lap his ear. "Are you okay, little one?" she asked gently.

He ducked away crossly. "Why shouldn't I be?"

"It's okay to be tired." Squirrelflight sat down. "It's been a hard journey."

"I'm fine," Jaypaw snapped. His mother's tail was twitching, scraping the gritty rock. He waited for her to make some comment about how much harder the journey must have been for him, being blind and all, and then add some mouse-brained comment about how well he had coped with the unfamiliar territory.

"All three of you have been quiet since the battle," she ventured.

She's worried about all of us! Jaypaw's anger melted. He wished he could put her mind at rest but there was no way he could tell her the huge secret that was occupying their thoughts. "I guess we just want to get home," he offered.

"We all do." Squirrelflight rested her chin on top of Jaypaw's head and he pressed against her, suddenly feeling like a kit again, grateful for her warmth.

"They're back!"

At Tawnypelt's call, Squirrelflight jerked away.

Jaypaw lifted his nose and smelled Hollypaw and Lionpaw. He heard claws scrabbling over rock as Breezepaw arrived. The hunters had returned.

"Let's see what they've caught!" Tawnypelt hurried to greet the apprentices.

Jaypaw already knew what they'd caught. His belly rumbled as he padded after her, the mouthwatering smells of squirrel, rabbit, and pigeon filling his nose. If only it weren't going to be given to the Tribe.

Crowfeather and Brambleclaw were already clustered around the makeshift fresh-kill pile. Stormfur and Brook hung back as though embarrassed by the gift.

"This rabbit's so fat it'll feed all the to-bes," Squirrelflight mewed admiringly.

"Well caught, Breezepaw," Tawnypelt purred.

Jaypaw waited for the WindClan apprentice's pelt to flash with pride, but instead he sensed anxiety claw at Breezepaw. *He's waiting for his father to praise him.*

"Nice pigeon," Crowfeather mewed to Lionpaw.

Breezepaw stiffened with anger.

"And look at the squirrel I caught!" Hollypaw chipped in. "Did you ever see such a juicy one?"

"Come see!" Tawnypelt called to Stormfur and Brook.

The two warriors padded over.

"This will be very welcome," Stormfur meowed formally.

"The Tribe thanks you." Brook's mew was taut.

Jaypaw understood their unease. By accepting freshkill, they were openly admitting their weakness. Hunting was poor in the mountains now that two groups of cats were sharing the territory. And yet Jaypaw could feel fierce pride pulsing from Stormfur. *The mountain breeze stirs his heart as well as his pelt.* There was a core of strength within him, a resolve that Jaypaw had not sensed before, as though he were more rooted in the crags and ravines than he ever had been beside the lake. *He truly believes that this is his destiny.* The Tribe were Stormfur's Clan now. He had been born River-Clan, and lived with ThunderClan, but now it seemed that he had found his true home.

Jaypaw shivered. The wind had been sharpened by a late-afternoon chill.

A howl echoed from the slopes far above.

Brook bristled. "Wolves."

"We'll get this prey home safely," Stormfur reassured her. "The wolves are too clumsy to follow our mountain paths."

"But there's a lot of open territory before you reach them," Brambleclaw urged. "You should go."

"We should all head home," Crowfeather advised. "The smell of this fresh-kill will be attracting all the prey-eaters around here."

Alarm flashed from every pelt as Jaypaw detected a strange tang on the breeze. It was the first wolf scent he'd smelled. It reminded him of the dogs around the Twoleg farm, but there was a rawness to it, a scent of blood and flesh that the dogs did not carry. He was thankful it was faint. "They're a long way off," he murmured.

"But they travel fast," Brook warned. The rabbit's fur brushed the ground as she picked it up.

"We're going to miss you," Squirrelflight meowed. Her voice was thick with sadness.

Brook laid the rabbit down again, a purr rising in her

throat. Her pelt brushed Squirrelflight's. "Thank you for taking us in and showing us such kindness."

"ThunderClan is grateful for your loyalty and courage," Brambleclaw meowed.

"We'll see you again, though, won't we?" Hollypaw mewed hopefully.

Jaypaw wondered if he would ever return to the mountains. Would he meet the Tribe of Endless Hunting again? He had followed Stoneteller into his dreams and been led by the Tribe-healer's ancestor to the hollow where ranks of starry cats encircled a shimmering pool. He shivered as he recalled their words: *You have come.* They had been expecting him, and they had known about the prophecy! Yet again, Jaypaw wondered where the prophecy had come from, and how the Tribe of Endless Hunting were connected to his own ancestors.

"There's no more time for good-byes!" Crowfeather's mew was impatient.

"Take care, little one." Brook's cheek brushed Jaypaw's before she turned to say good-bye to Hollypaw.

Stormfur licked his ear. "Look after your brother and sister," he murmured.

"Bye, Stormfur." Jaypaw's throat tightened. "Good-bye, Brook." He remembered the times when Brook had comforted and encouraged him. She had always seemed to understand what it felt like to be different. And Stormfur had never patronized him, but treated him with the same warmth and strictness as he had the other apprentices. He would miss them.

Lionpaw pushed in front of him. "Good-bye, Stormfur. Show those invaders that a Clan cat is never beaten."

"Good-bye, Lionpaw," Stormfur meowed. "Remember that even though our experiences change us, we have to carry on."

A rush of warmth seemed to flood between the warrior and apprentice, and Jaypaw realized with surprise that his brother shared a special bond with Stormfur, one he had not detected before. He stood wondering about it as his Clanmates began to head off down the slope, not moving when Stormfur picked up the freshly caught prey and started uphill after his mate.

"Stop dawdling!" Crowfeather nudged Jaypaw with his nose, steering him down a smooth rocky slope onto the grassy hillside.

Jaypaw bristled. "I don't need help!"

"Please yourself," Crowfeather hissed. "But don't blame me if you get left behind." He pounded ahead, his paws thrumming on the ground.

Imagine having such a sour-tongued warrior for a father. I'm glad I'm not Breezepaw!

"Hurry up, Jaypaw!" Lionpaw was calling.

Jaypaw sniffed the air. On this exposed slope it was easy to tell where the other cats were. Brambleclaw led the way downhill, Breezepaw at his heels, while Crowfeather had already caught up and was flanking Tawnypelt, keeping to the outside of the group. Squirrelflight padded alone, while Hollypaw and Lionpaw trotted behind.

Jaypaw raced after them. The grass was smooth and soft beneath his paws. "It feels strange leaving them behind," he panted.

"They chose to stay," Crowfeather pointed out.

"Do you think we'll ever see them or the Tribe again?" Tawnypelt wondered.

"I hope not," Crowfeather answered. "I don't want to see those mountains once more as long as I live."

"They might visit the lake," Hollypaw suggested.

A howl echoed eerily around the crags far behind them.

"They have to get home safely first," Lionpaw murmured.

"They will," Brambleclaw assured him. "They know their territory as well as any other Tribe cat."

Padding beside his littermates, Jaypaw caught the musty scent of forest ahead. Before long the ground beneath his paws turned from grass to crushed leaves. The wind ceased tugging at his fur as trees shielded him on every side. Hollypaw hurried ahead as though she already scented the lake beyond, but for a moment Jaypaw wished he were back on the open slopes of the foothills. At least there, scents and sounds were not muffled by the enclosing trees, and there was no undergrowth to trip him up. He felt blinder here in this unfamiliar forest than he ever had.

"Watch out!" Lionpaw's warning came too late, and Jaypaw found his paws tangled in a bramble.

"Mouse dung!" He fought to free himself, but the bramble seemed to twist around his legs as if it meant to ensnare him.

"Stand still!" Hollypaw was racing back to help. Jaypaw froze, swallowing his frustration, and allowed Lionpaw to drag the tendrils from around his paws while Hollypaw gently guided him away from the prickly bush.

"Dumb brambles!" Jaypaw lifted his chin and padded forward, more unsure than ever of the terrain but trying desperately not to show it.

Wordlessly, Hollypaw and Lionpaw fell into step on either side of him. With the lightest touch of her whiskers Hollypaw guided him around a clump of nettles and, when a fallen tree blocked their path, Lionpaw warned him with a flick of his tail to stop and wait while he led the way up and over the trunk.

As Jaypaw scrabbled gratefully over the crumbling bark he couldn't help wondering: *Is the prophecy really meant for a cat who can't see?*

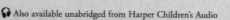
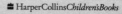

ENTER THE WORLD OF WARRIORS

Warriors: Power of Three

Join the newest generation as they begin their training as warrior cats. Prophecy foretells that they will hold more power than any cats before them.

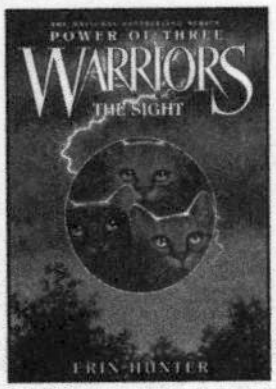
POWER OF THREE
WARRIORS
THE SIGHT
ERIN HUNTER

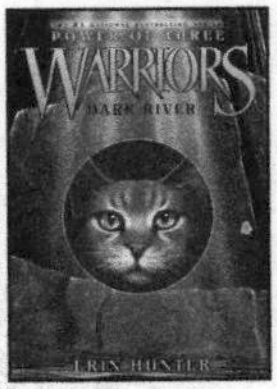
WARRIORS
DARK RIVER
ERIN HUNTER

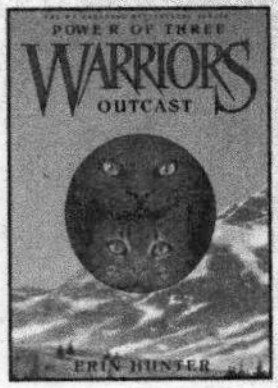
POWER OF THREE
WARRIORS
OUTCAST
ERIN HUNTER

Warriors Field Guide: Secrets of the Clans

Learn the secrets of the Clans, their histories, maps, battles, and more!

Warriors: Cats of the Clans

See the Warriors as never before in this in-depth guide.

Warriors Super Edition: Firestar's Quest

An all-new adventure for ThunderClan's hero.

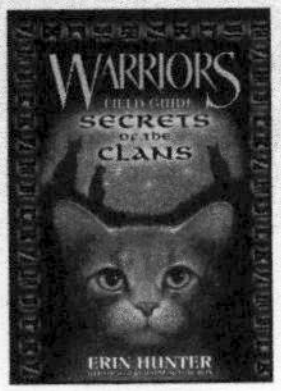
WARRIORS
FIELD GUIDE
SECRETS
OF THE
CLANS
ERIN HUNTER

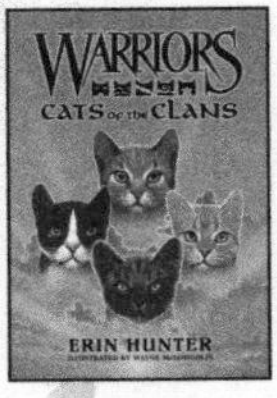
WARRIORS
CATS OF THE CLANS
ERIN HUNTER

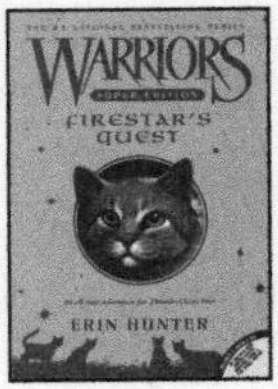
WARRIORS
FIRESTAR'S QUEST
ERIN HUNTER

Warrior cats in manga!

Warriors: The Lost Warrior

Warriors: Warrior's Refuge

Warriors: Warrior's Return

Warriors: The Rise of Scourge

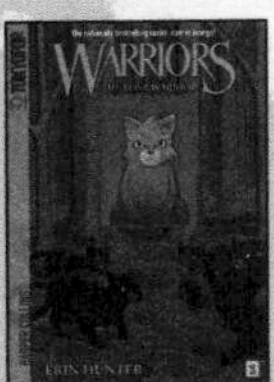
WARRIORS
ERIN HUNTER

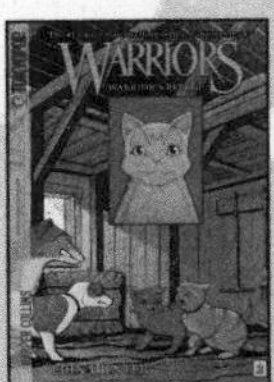
WARRIORS

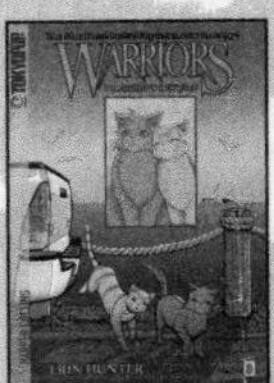
WARRIORS
ERIN HUNTER

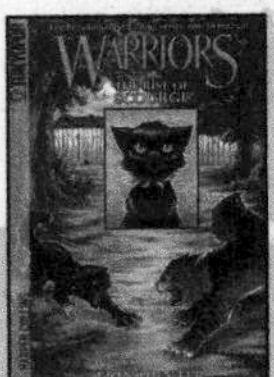
WARRIORS

Visit www.warriorcats.com for games, Clan lore, and much more!